THE SWEET TRACK

For my father

THE SWEET TRACK

Avril Joy

FlambardPress

First published in Great Britain in 2007 by Flambard Press
Stable Cottage, East Fourstones, Hexham NE47 5DX
www.flambardpress.co.uk

Typeset by BookType
Cover Design by Gainford Design Associates
Cover photograph © Corbis
Printed in Great Britain by Cromwell Press, Trowbridge, Wiltshire

A CIP catalogue record for this book
is available from the British Library.
ISBN-13: 978-1-873226-93-3

Flambard Press wishes to thank Arts Council England
for its financial support.

Flambard Press is a member of Inpress,
and of Independent Northern Publishers.

Mixed Sources
Product group from well-managed
forests and other controlled sources
www.fsc.org   Cert no. TT-COC-2082
© 1996 Forest Stewardship Council
FSC

'We are the children of our landscape . . .'
Lawrence Durrell, *Justine*

Many wooden tracks were laid across the marshes of the Somerset Levels. They took the form of raised walkways which made the wilderness accessible. The oldest of these, and the oldest known track in Britain, dating from 3800 BC, was *The Sweet Track*. It was discovered in 1970 by Ray Sweet, a peat digger.

August 1959

Lilli always knew when there was water. She could smell it. Today there was none. No sharp sting in the air. No silent salt lake, lapping the fringes of grass, but instead the iron smell of mud. Mud as far as she could see, stretching out to the mouth of the estuary to meet a cloudless sky. The mud banks were drying and cracking in the white heat of the August sun. Lilli and Rebecca jumped the wide cracks as they walked along the edge of the riverbank, swinging their parcels of sugar sandwiches and jam jars on strings.

They didn't walk far before stopping to take off their gym shoes. Their feet were still damp with the dew from the pasture and they stuck them out to dry, lying back in the coarse grass and looking up into a wide and promising childhood sky. The heat was intense. It baked their skins. Lilli held her bare arm against her mouth and nostrils and breathed in the peppery scent.

It was too hot to lie. Before long they were up and searching for sticks. They poked about in the pools on the margin where vestiges of salt water lay, sheltering bony crabs. They stirred and prodded, clouding the water and unearthing the tiny crustaceans. Dangling them by a leg they dropped them into jam jars and watched them try to climb out. When they became bored with crabs Lilli made sure they were returned to their pools. Becca looked on, humming softly to herself.

With sugar sandwiches still gritty between their teeth they set off in search of lovers. Couples often came to the banks on a Sunday afternoon to lie in the long grass, sometimes to lie on top of each other. Lilli and Rebecca hunted them out.

Once when they found the tell-tale signs of flattened green they caught the rare and dangerous glimpse of a grass snake, coiled on the makeshift bed, sleeping in the sun. But today there were no lovers or snakes and they found only winged insects and flower heads in the long grass.

They walked as far as the pillbox and entered its dark interior in silence, with a reverence reserved for holy places. Lilli shuddered and screwed up her nose at the whiff of baked urine. The pillbox was filthy but always enticing and dirty, with dirty words like *shag* and *fuck* graffitied on its brick walls, used condoms on its floor. From one of the narrow slits ranged around its walls she looked out to sea. She called to Rebecca, 'Look, out there . . . see it?'

A ship marked the horizon where the grey mud met the azure of the sky. Was this the ship, she wondered, that brought invaders creeping up channel on a high tide, calm and quiet and coming to kill you in your bed? Did ships like these bring the people her grandmother spoke of, foreigners, who would find them all with their heads in the gas oven?

Lilli left the pillbox first. Waiting for Rebecca she narrowed her eyes against the sun. Breathing in the fishy perfume of the mud flats she looked out across the elusive landscape where water appeared and disappeared, as if by magic.

As the afternoon shadows lengthened they made their way slowly back across the cowslip field to the hedge which ran along the railway line. They passed the pigpen, where the fat sow lay snoring in contentment, but did not linger. Their legs were tired, they were hot and it was effort enough to make it across the lines, through the Rec and onto the estate.

A moment of hesitation and regret, an echo of angry rooms, caught them at the dark entry, where they parted company.

Part One

Lilli
Somerset 1975

An Armlet of Shale

Lilli sat at her dressing table. Before her spread the bones of small creatures dug from the peat of the moor, black pot shards and beads of blue glass from the pools of Meare. Winged seashells lay open on their backs amongst the skeletons of tiny crabs, amid crumbs of neglected flowers from jam jars of rank brown liquid. Her grandmother's wedding ring was there; a can of Supersoft hairspray, a comb, two Lillets, a couple of kirby grips and a photograph of Charlie. Her life scattered before her in an accumulation of fragments. She looked hard at herself in the dressing-table mirror and sighed. She gathered her unruly hair in her hands, pulling it back from her face while she scanned the dressing table for an elastic band.

Lilli's hair was red and long, a mess of curls that resisted all manner of brushes and combs. Her attempts to tame it had more often than not left her frustrated and cross and for that reason she was inclined to let it go its own way. Her skin was like buttermilk, an outdoor skin that smelled of grass and last summer's sun. Her eyes were unexpectedly blue. They took people by surprise and most of the time that was fine. Lilli enjoyed surprising the world. But there were other times when the effort was burdensome, when the fun faded and the mask grew too heavy. Times when she wished she could disappear into the forest like a fawn, when she wished her hair was tame and thin and mousy and her eyes unremarkable.

Failing in her search for an elastic band, Lilli got up from the dressing table to look elsewhere. Her eye was caught by the pale glint of sun through the bedroom window. She walked over and looked out to the square church tower and beyond, imagining her journey across the flat land and out to the estuary, where the land met the sea.

At the edge of the estuary stood the small seaside town where her grandmother lived and where Maurice Hauser was waiting. She was already late but she knew that Maurice would wait. She was confident of that. And he would give her the job she needed, even though it was out of season and not the time of year to be employing hotel staff. He would not want to miss an opportunity like this; to enjoy both proximity and power. He'd been hinting at such an arrangement ever since the night she'd consented to tie him up and urinate on him, for that's what he liked. Maurice was a golden-rain freak who got off on women peeing on him. He was a weakling wife-beater who lived in secret fear of women, waiting for the confirmation of their dominance and his own degradation. Well, she could provide all of that and at no cost – whatever was required.

Lilli returned to the dressing table without an elastic band, sat down and smiled into the dusty mirror before her. She picked up the wide-toothed comb and began to pull it through her tangle of red hair. When she'd finished she raked her long fingers through, where the comb had been. Her scalp hurt. She recalled the other secret preferences that came her way, not just those of Maurice, but the others who showed themselves to her gratefully and then ran: men who could not look at her in the town, respectable men out with their wives. They had no secrets from her.

Lilli shuddered; despite the winter sun there was a damp chill in the November air.

She lifted a thick cardigan from the back of the chair and pulled her arms through its sleeves, buttoning it up over her shirt. She sighed, then moved her hands across the surface of the dressing table seeking out the treasure from the objects before her. She found it; the baby's armlet, the pale, polished band of Kimmeridge shale. She slipped it into her dress pocket where she held it. As her fingers smoothed and caressed its worn surface she saw her, the woman. A young woman like herself. A woman whose tracks she had followed. A woman with a baby, pushing the armlet gently onto her baby's arm, nuzzling it into chubby flesh, holding the baby close, smelling its smell. A woman alone with her child, walking the land, her footsteps sinking in the peat, submerged in the flood.

She ran her thumb along the smooth shale back and forth until she was no longer late for her appointment and no longer in a world of grim and disappointing men. No longer at the dressing table but walking . . .

Walking on the limewood track from Shap. The fen sucks at her grass-bound feet and the damp pulls at her hair. Beneath her, in the basin of the Brue, the soil lies heavy. In the alluvial clay marsh orchid and pennywort lodge dormant, submerged in the winter floods. Around her dunlin skim the glassy surface in a choreography of flight. Behind her the Tor. In front the track stretching across the endless expanse of water and unrelieved flatness. Clutched to her, beneath her cloak of skin, the baby and its muffled cries.

'Lilli, are you still here?' Vera's voice, frail and fearful, called from the adjoining room. Lilli heard it from afar, drawing her back. She got up and went into her mother's bedroom.

'Don't be late, Lilli, Mr Hauser will be waiting,' she said, becoming agitated. 'He's a rich man now, you know. He's got all those boarding houses and hotels and when we were younger . . .' her voice trailed, her eyes wandered, losing focus. She looked up into Lilli's face without recognition but with the bruised and disturbed eye of an animal in pain.

'I'll make you some tea before I go,' said Lilli quickly, filling the space between reason and madness, locking them in a tangible present.

When she had made tea Lilli set it down beside Vera. She knew she would not drink it, but like all rituals tea-making brought with it the comfort and safety of the familiar. She bent to lift her mother's sickly, bird-like frame from her pillows. She plumped them and lent her gently back down, careful to avoid the swelling stomach. She smoothed her thin, damp hair, which had lost its colour and, like her skin, was limpid and grey.

She'd known, of course, the minute she'd returned and saw her like a child in a hospital bed, that her mother was dying. After many years of suffering and sickness of all kinds Vera was dying and Lilli had come home to see the end of it. She was used to it – looking out for life's strays, taking care of the wounded and the underdog. It had always been that way; from childhood Lilli had collected them: the seagull with the broken wing that grew too big to keep, the lost Boxer that lived in the shed, the cat with one eye. She took them in and cared for them without thinking how it would turn out or whether they would survive or stay, and mostly one way or another they left or died, but that wasn't the point. It was the looking after that mattered and looking after Vera she was happy to do.

Bending close she said softly, 'Nell will be coming soon, any minute.' Hearing the front door open and close, she said, 'That's her now, you'll be all right won't you? It won't be long before I'm back and Nell will keep you company. I've got to see Mr Hauser about this job.' Vera's eyes widened at the mention of the name. Lilli kissed her on her forehead and whispered goodbye in her ear.

She took her bike from the shed and wheeled it through the entry and into the lane. She set out on the short cut, along the old drove, past the sluice gates and the pumping station. Water was everywhere, reflecting from the ditches and rhynes, glinting silver in the low November sun. The pasture lay like a vast mirror showing the sky its face, throwing back the sun's watery gaze. The fields were flooded and the land soaked in winter silt. All around sucked in and held the vapour, so that the air, the soil, the thatch, bedding, clothes, carpets, kindling, all were wet. Mildew and rheumatism, the dual curse of winter, had arrived with the curlew and the plover. In this uncertain and fluid place Lilli had grown. It was her home. She was bound to it, to the moors, to the water's rise and fall, and to the tides and the rhythms of the sea.

3.30 was high tide. She'd be there by then, only half an hour late, across the flatlands, feeling the sun on her face, feet off the pedals, coasting downhill to where the Levels ended at the sea. Lilli smelled the water, sharp and brackish on the wind that accompanied the tide. She bent her head and battled her way past the ice-cream parlour to The Seaview, on the corner of the esplanade. Getting off her bike, she walked across to the front where she watched the small crested waves slap at the edge of the sea wall. There was no storm, no flood, just a high tide encroaching. Not threatening, not yet. Lilli turned her back on the sea. At the entrance to The Seaview she shook her hair and dragged her fingers through to rid it of its tangles.

Maud Hauser sat at the reception desk of The Seaview, absently eating a chocolate bar and thinking of Torquay. She'd seen a framed print advertising Torquay in the railway carriage of a train once when she'd been travelling from High Bridge to Bridgewater. It was entitled *The British Riviera* and was peopled with happy, elegant bathers and dotted with palms. Since then Maud had dreamed of escaping to Torquay, preferably with her friend Dorothy, who, like Maud, longed to flee from her husband. Both men were miserable and grudging and not above a spot of wife-beating to alleviate their own petty decrepitudes.

Dorothy's husband of twenty-five years was Robert Ham, Bob to his friends. He owned the town ironmongers and a grocery store. He belonged to the Rotary and the Masons and, as a man of such standing, felt he had the right to meet out a little punishment every now and then to a wife who contributed nothing to their living or his empire and who had grown plump and recalcitrant with age. Like Dorothy, Maud bore the scars of a few *little slaps*, as Maurice called them. She remembered well the beatings suffered by her own mother and wondered if this was something women could hardly expect to avoid.

Maud was like a chameleon, mimicking her surroundings and disappearing into them. She was the mistress of insignificance. A small, mousy figure who stooped and curled in order to take up less space.

'Can I help you?' Maud asked.

'Yes. I've got an appointment with Mr Hauser at three o'clock. I'm sorry I'm late but . . .'

'He'll be in his office on the second floor.' Maud gestured at the wide blue staircase leading out of the reception hall and to the bedrooms. 'Just go up,' she said indifferently, turning down the wrapper on her chocolate bar. 'It's to the left next to number twelve. Best to knock before you go in.'

Lilli nodded and made for the stairs. As she started up she felt the carpet beginning to show its thread and saw the gathering dust in its darker creases. She paused outside number twelve and breathed deeply before she knocked on the office door.

Hauser sat sweating at his desk, his waist-coated back to the door, obscuring from view the crudely bound and typed volume of pornography (which he had received that morning courtesy of Bob Ham) through which he was thumbing. On hearing her knock he stuffed the piece into his desk drawer and turned eagerly. 'Come in.'

As she entered Lilli looked directly at him, like a big cat fixing and holding her prey. She saw at once the droplets of sweat which ran like a necklace across his nose and over his upper lip.

'Lilli,' he said with obvious pleasure, but leaving her name not quite finished, trailing away, uncertain. He tapped on the chair arm, cleared his throat and emitted a faint asthmatic wheeze.

'I'm sorry I'm late,' she said directly, 'but you know my mother's ill and so it's not always easy for me to get away. It could be a problem as far as working is concerned; there may be times when I'll have to wait for someone else coming before I leave.'

'I don't think we need worry about that. I've always liked Vera, you know, and I wouldn't want you to feel you couldn't help your mother when she needs you most.' He took a breath and paused as if to deliver a statement both gracious and profound. 'We all have our duties in life, Lilli, and I can be very understanding. I don't take my responsibilities lightly and I wouldn't expect my staff to either. When were you thinking of starting?'

'Next week,' Lilli replied, suppressing a sudden desire to laugh at his ludicrous deception and wondering how soon she would be meeting her responsibilities and duties.

'Fine,' said Hauser gratefully. His armpits were wet and his body odour had infiltrated the room. 'Let's make that Monday. Monday is Maud's day off and she usually takes a trip out or goes shopping for the day so we always need extra help on Mondays. Just light duties, Lilli, a bit of cleaning especially when Pearl's not here, sitting on reception, helping with the cooking at odd times and of course helping in the office.' He wheezed. 'We can sort out the particulars when you come in on Monday.' He got up from his chair.

Lilli looked out of the tall sash window at the turning tide and the clear sky. Hauser stood uncomfortably close to her; his cheap aftershave was powerful but still did not mask his rank smell. He brushed against Lilli. His wheeze had grown, just like the few inches he kept with difficulty in his trousers and would now very much have liked to get out.

'I'll see you on Monday morning,' said Lilli turning away quickly and making for the door. On the stairs she stopped.

She felt sick. Sick, just as she had at sixteen. Maurice Hauser's smell hung around her, filling her mouth and nose with the sweet maggoty reek of a decaying corpse. She had to get out of the hotel into the air. She needed to be rid of it. She needed to recover before going home to confront that other sickness which was slowly seeping from the bedroom into the house.

Stepping outside she was grateful for the ebb tide and the cessation of the wind. A seagull wheeled around her, diving close, flaunting the taut spread of its feet and the menace of its beak. She ducked, eased her bike from the low front wall against which it was propped and began wheeling it along the pavement until she stood outside Fiori's ice-cream parlour.

Fiori's was an exotic and tropical flower blooming in the November of a seaside town. Lilli preferred it in winter when it was nearly empty, peopled only with locals, one or two, warming their hands on fluted glasses of coffee. She felt instantly transformed and liberated in this foreign place, happy, once inside, to admire its imported cane furniture, its glamorous fittings and its dark smiling men.

The ice-cream parlour had been one of her grandmother's favourite places. Edith had often taken her there on their outings together, when they'd shopped or strolled through the town. Then, it had seemed a long walk from Oxford Street past the Baptist chapel on the one side, hurrying by the dentist on the other, even if there was no appointment, because here lingered the memory of acute, sprouting pain, which filled your head. The buzz and grind of the old drill which sought out and then dwelt on the fresh pink nerve. Even in passing, Lilli could always conjure an image of some poor soul strapped into the brown leather and at the mercy of Mr Vose.

Fiori's was paradise by comparison. Lilli had been barely able to see over the high counter then. Paolo would smile down at her, pull up his jumper sleeve and reach a long olive-skinned arm into the fridge to scoop out the Italian vanilla. Like a sculptor he would shape and flatten it on a silver dish, wafer and layer it, finishing with raspberry juice, staining and dripping pink. A North Pole had been both her and Edith's favourite, better by far than the fancier sundaes, like Knickerbockerglory and Peach Melba, lurid pictures of which now lined the wall of the parlour along the wide counter-length mirror where Lilli caught sight of her unkempt reflection. Her hair tumbled onto the shoulders of her cherry-red coat, the coat she'd bought among other items in a continuing spirit of defiance. It had started at sixteen, the wearing of red. Lilli had done it deliberately to annoy her grandmother who'd always advised against it, who'd said, 'With your hair, Lilli, you must avoid all reds, pinks and oranges, they clash and you can't get away with it, believe me.'

Lilli smoothed her hair as Paolo approached. He smiled generously.

'Hello, Lilli.'

'Hello, I'd like a North Pole please.'

'Of course.'

As Paolo bent to the task Lilli watched him in the mirror, admiring his thick, black hair, straight shoulders and slender arms. He was still beautiful, sensitive and easily wounded. It showed in his soft brown eyes. As a young man he had been a town pin-up along with his brother Vanni. Lilli had been aware of their attraction. Women had spoken of them. Women had made a point of passing by in summer in their sleeveless tops, wide skirts and high heels and glancing in.

Both Paolo and Vanni had courted a number of them although none seriously. Eventually, Vanni had succumbed to his mother Maria's protestations and settled down like a good Italian son, marrying a distant cousin brought from Italy for that purpose, and failing to make her happy. He had two sons and a daughter, now at school, unlike Paolo who had never married.

'How's your mother? I heard she was ill. I'm sorry. Is that why you've come back?' He scooped her ice cream.

'Yes, she can't really get out of bed now. She needs looking after but I don't mind. I'm pleased to be back.' Leaving the money on the counter, she took the North Pole to a seat by the window and put it down on the glass-topped table. She settled into the blue cane chair, ran her fingers across its gold-sprayed edges, then began to spoon the cool vanilla cream onto her tongue, letting it melt and linger, ridding her of the taste and smell of The Seaview. She ate intently so that she did not notice him approach. Looking up, she found him resting his arms on the chairback opposite. He inclined his body towards her.

'Is it good?' he asked, amused and pleased that, as a grown-up, she should choose a sundae over a coffee, especially in winter.

'Yes, very good. It's my favourite. It's always been my favourite since my grandmother used to bring me here.'

'I know. I remember Edith, and Vera of course, and you with your nose on the counter.' They both smiled. 'What are you doing, anyway, now you're back, apart from looking after your mother?'

'Well, I was doing some cleaning, private houses mainly but I've got a new job, starting on Monday, in The Seaview, for Maurice Hauser.'

Paolo nodded. 'Good,' he said, wondering how she could possibly want to work for a man like Hauser and whether the things he'd been hearing about Lilli since she'd come back were true. He hoped not. 'Then you'll have to come and have lunch in here sometimes.'

'I will, I could get used to ice cream for lunch,' said Lilli, smiling up at him, watching his hand lift the empty dish from in front of her. 'I better get moving now, before it gets dark.' She got up reluctantly from the cane chair.

He walked with her to the door and saw her go. Lilli turned and waved at him as she cycled off. Her spirits had lifted since her encounter with Maurice and the taste in her mouth was no longer sour.

As she cycled home a mist rose up from the rhynes and ran across the surface of the pasture. It spread across the fields hanging a foot or so above the land, rising around her and obscuring her pedals and boots. It enveloped her, wrapping itself like a winding sheet, like a shroud. By the willows cattle were gliding through the gauzy vapour, only their heads and backs visible, like targets on a fairground shooting range. The sky turned pink as the sun fell and the moon rose, as Lilli moved through the landscape travelling over the ancient pathways and vanished tracks once laid across the inland sea. She knew them by instinct; she walked them in her sleep while the land turned to water around her.

Goldfish on the Lino

The house was warm and Vera was asleep. On the kitchen table was a note from Nell: *Everything fine, Vera sleeping, had to go, Mrs Dickinson due for a fitting! Come by later – love Nell.*

Outside the light was fading. Lilli built up the fire in the small downstairs living room and sat beside it. She took off her boots and stretched out her feet in anticipation of delicious warmth. The fire was grey and smoky with wet coal. She waited for it to kindle, for its flaring in bursts, red twists escaping from black coal, waited until it caught. Then, when it held steady, she began to feel its heat and saw its flames cast long shadows about the room.

Orange ribbons appeared on the brass shell cases that stood on the mantelpiece. These had once been filled with spills cut from Cornflake boxes but were now half empty, now that Vera lay in bed. It was strange, somehow perverse, Lilli thought, how people could hate war, and yet so savour its remnants, polishing them lovingly, awarding them pride of place.

She watched the fire grow and change until its hollows opened and it became peopled with faces like gargoyles. She felt for the armlet in her pocket. She entwined it in her fingers. In the fire's soft hiss and spit, a murmur, a voice, an archaic whisper called her to another fire in a hearth, on the clay floor in the round house.

The air fills with wood smoke. The blackened weave of thatch is layered with soot. Her eyes sting and her fingers ache as she stands at the loom weaving her dyed wools into cloth and braid to trade for amber and for glass beads from the maker at Meare. Small yellow rings inlaid with spirals and zigzags. She has seen him, watched him making them in quiet concentration, moulding first, then trailing the thin rod of molten glass along the inlaid grooves. Her necklace is near completion, soon she will begin collecting bracelet beads for the baby who lies in the cradle. A bracelet for when he is older. She rubs her aching fingers and twists the bronze coil she wears on the third finger of her right hand. She is hungry. It is time to eat. She leaves her loom and looks for signs of the returning hunters in the dwindling light, beyond the woven door. They will return before dark with fowl from the reed beds, eels or fish. By the pot are chickweed and elderberry gathered from the swamps and meadows. It is time to build the fire in anticipation, time to prepare and light the candle pots . . .

Lilli returned to cracking coals, grey and orange. Above her Vera was coughing and restless. The warmth that suffused her had evaporated, gone. She pulled her cardigan to her and threw coal on the fire before making her way up the narrow stairs. She flicked the switch on the landing, throwing an arc of light into the bedroom, enough to sit by, then lowered herself carefully onto the bed beside her mother.

Vera opened her eyes. 'Where's Nell?' she asked, her voice dry and medicated like her mouth.

'She had to go, Mum, it was getting late and Mrs Dickinson was due for a fitting. You've been asleep.' After a pause Lilli said, 'You remember Mrs Dickinson, don't you?' She took Vera's hand but she did not respond. 'Nell still can't get the tape measure round her, and it's getting worse, she has to throw it and catch and she still lies about the measurements, only now it's four inches off all round and she still says, *I told you, Nell, never put an inch on, do I?*' Vera's face was unmoving. 'And her corset, she still wears it, can you

23

remember that corset?' Lilli giggled, hoping for a spark of recognition. 'Can you remember it, it was just like Grandma's?' Lilli smiled as she recalled Edith's underwear. Her grand-mother was a woman with a figure not unlike Mrs Dickinson's and many a time as a child Lilli had watched her upholstering and hooking her puddingy flesh into lobster pink.

The corset was familiar. Vera rewarded Lilli with a weak smile. 'Yes,' she said slowly and with effort, 'the corset – and the goldfish – on the floor. She gave you those goldfish, Mrs Dickinson, when we moved and you spilled them – on the lino.'

Goldfish out of water and flapping on the wet blue floor, too slippery to hold and no Charlie to rescue them. Panic and paralysis as she'd abandoned them to their dry gills and final gasps. Goldfish were no substitute for a lost father.

They'd moved not long after Charlie had left. Vera, coming out of hospital, had wanted to be near her sister Nell. So they'd moved to the village on the edge of the moors where the tall square tower of the church was a marker in the flat-lands surrounding it; where the goldfish had died on the cold lino and Lilli had watched, helpless; where she'd begun a new life without her father, without her childhood friend and with her fragile and needy mother. No Charlie to laugh and have fun with: making up stories at night, tap dancing in the kitchen, watching TV. No Rebecca to cross the fields with, go to school with, dress up with.

Nell and Ted did their best, taking her out on walks and picnics around and about the swampy land. Telling her its history. Ted sharing his secrets with her. Ted who'd lived there forever and who bought her her first bike. He knew every inch of the land. He cycled with her through the Brue valley, to Godney, to the roads green and willow bounded, which covered the moors. To Meare and Glastonbury and back down the valley to old Frog Island and the sands. They cycled and walked the land until Lilli came to know it by day and in dream; until she could feel its stirrings beneath her feet and began to absorb them like a sponge in water; until she knew its song and she could pass over and through it, in its many rhythms and times. Marooned in this great fen Lilli caught the voices of the past and began to dream with her eyes open.

Ted understood. He had worked on the moors digging peat. He too felt the connection with lives lived when the land was covered with shallow lakes and tracts of swamp, when it was overgrown with alder and willow and the hills were thick with forest.

Ted and Nell. Stalwart and kind with strength enough to help Vera whose grief lay buried like a body in the sand, smoothed over but never still, shifting and cracking until its limbs appeared. And Lilli, who feigned indifference but who felt that a light, a bright light, had gone out in her life.

The Sewing Room

The streetlights caught the first fall of an early snow. The gathering wind lifted it and threw it against the trees and telegraph poles – the verticals – so that they were highlighted as if in chalk on charcoal. Vera was sleeping after her nightly morphine dose. Lilli slipped out of the house to Nell's. As she came to the lit window of Nell's sewing room she saw her aunt bent over her machine, intently feeding the skirt of a blue satin bridesmaid's dress through its foot. Her figure was reflected in a large gilt mirror on the wall behind, like a woman in a painting by Vermeer. Lilli felt an immediate rush of warmth for Nell, a woman so different from Vera; she had been what Vera was not: comfortable, easy, fun. Nell had been there at all the difficult times of Lilli's growing up. The only one willing to keep Charlie's memory alive, recalling when they were alone together his good looks and charm and the happy times they'd shared.

Nell stopped sewing as Lilli entered the room. A length of blue silk spilled from the machine to the floor, covering her knees and legs. Lilli made for the old armchair, an item once part of a three piece, now faded and alone. From it she surveyed the room: the long cutting table strewn with layers of tissue, the ironing board and iron ready for the pressing open of seams into precise lines, the boxes of pins, the chalk and thimbles which stood on the chest beneath the gilt mirror, the floor littered with scraps of ribbon and petersham, rubbings of lace and fraying triangles of lining and net, like silk flags. The air was damp and blue with the smell of paraffin. It was silent now that Nell's feet had lifted from the treadle, and the tango – the stop-go, fast-slow advance and retreat of fabric, foot and machine – had ceased.

'Have you put the kettle on?' asked Nell.

'No,' said Lilli.

'Then shall we have a sherry?' Nell was already making her way to the bottle and glasses on the chest. 'Is she asleep?'

Lilli nodded and settled into the armchair, warm and comfortable like a chick in a nest.

'How did you get on this afternoon?' Nell's voice held a hint of disapproval.

'All right, why?' Lilli sensed Nell's mood and her body stiffened. She sat up.

Nell offered her the sherry. 'Well, why do you think?'

'It's just a job, you know, and I need something permanent now that I'm back.'

'But him, Lilli, of all people, why work for him? There must be other jobs going.'

'It's convenient. He won't bother if I'm not always on time, he knows she's sick.'

'I don't care what he knows. He's a dirty old man, ask Ted.' Nell sighed before launching into the worst. 'I'm worried about you. Ted says since you've been back there's all kinds of talk. Says you've been seen out with married men old enough to be your father. Bob Ham for one. What are you doing going out with men like that, Lilli? I can't bear to think of you with him. Why . . . is it Vera, is it help, comfort . . . you know you can come to us for that, Lilli? What is it?'

Lilli said nothing.

'I know it's not up to me, it's none of my business but it hurts to see it. It can't make you happy, surely? It can't be what you want?'

Lilli could think of nothing to say. She didn't know, hadn't got the answers for Nell. She wondered herself, why? To punish herself, to punish them, the men? To punish the women she loved – Vera and Nell? Because nothing mattered compared to her loss – Charlie, Rebecca, her child? To treat pain with pain, a defence against feeling, against any attempt at love. It parried rejection. It pre-empted hurt and it was better than risking love and romance, much better, she knew that. She wore her encounters like a cloak, like a disguise, and she retreated from them like a hermit crab crawling into its thick shell. There were no words or declarations of love, no endearments, whispers, smiles, confidences, no tenderness. Instead there were actions, brutal sometimes, often brief and sweaty, an exchange of bodily fluids, a coarse simplicity, an animal strength. It was easily put aside; afterwards best forgotten. Something in it killed the pain and the memory, and power was a satisfactory substitute when no other could be found. Without dreams, without longing or anticipation came control, and too many of Lilli's life's histories and events had not been of her own making. This way she chose and had to trust no one.

'I don't know,' she said. 'Sometimes it makes me feel better and sometimes it makes me feel bad, terrible. But I give them a tough time too, you know. Nobody's going to get the better of me . . . no, and it's my business.'

'Well you can't expect me not to care or worry,' said Nell with a certain resignation. This was not the first time they had talked about Lilli's promiscuity, not by a long way. 'Anyway, I don't know how you can,' she said, lightening the mood, 'all those shrivelled-up bits.' They giggled.

'I know,' said Lilli relieved to be sharing a joke, grateful for Nell's infinite patience. 'I'll let you into a secret. It's about Bob Ham and shrivelled-up bits. He's got one about two inches long.' She put her thumb and first finger in front of her indicating the measurement. 'It's almost impossible to know what to do with it. Poor man, it's quite a problem, really.' She dissolved into laughter.

'Lilli!' exclaimed Nell, half in outrage but more in delight at such a revelation. 'It's not funny.' She was laughing uncontrollably.

'Well, don't laugh then.'

'I'm not.' Nell composed herself. 'I want you to stop, just stop it, find yourself someone decent, young. And as far as Hauser's concerned, not him, Lilli, he goes too far, believe me.'

'What do you mean, too far?'

'Like I said, he's a dirty old man.'

'I can handle him, so don't worry I . . .' Lilli stopped. Ted put his head around the door.

'How's things?' he said, smiling. 'How is she? Is she asleep?'

'Yes, but I'll go back shortly and check,' said Lilli.

'No need. I'll go, it won't take a minute, throw me the key. You stay with Nell, it sounds as if you're enjoying yourselves. I'll have a pint while I'm out. Let you know if there's a problem.' He was gone.

Nell refilled their glasses. 'I've got something for you,' she said suddenly. 'I found it yesterday when I was raking through the cupboard on the landing. I found a few things in there.' She bent to lift a Clark's shoebox from the floor beneath the cutting table. As Nell removed the lid Lilli could see that it was full of old photographs, letters and what looked like postcards.

'Oh look at this,' said Nell as if discovering it afresh as she had the previous day. She held out a sepia print of Edith and Jack's wedding day. Lilli thought at once how handsome they had both been in their youth.

'I can't find it now,' said Nell, rummaging through the box and producing a photograph of Vera and Charlie, with Pauline and Terrence, Rebecca's mother and father, wearing their winter coats, sat together on a hillside, windswept and smiling. There was another of Lilli in a smocked dress aged two, and one of her and Rebecca holding two stray kittens they had wanted but not been allowed to keep.

'Here it is,' she said, pausing before passing it to Lilli and taking the others from her. It was a baby, cradled in anonymous arms. A baby with hair, eyes closed and fists curled, new to the world. Lilli looked up at Nell with a mixture of alarm and expectation. Nell nodded. 'Ted took it,' she said, 'before they took her. That day.'

'I didn't know,' said Lilli.

'I know,' said Nell. 'I've been keeping it for you. I should have given it to you before now. It's yours. I'm sorry, Lilli, sorry I didn't do more.'

'It wasn't your fault,' murmured Lilli, transfixed and hearing the baby's cry in her ear.

The baby was born strong. He gave a loud cry as he came into the world and the moon that fell through the thatch was full and bright enough to walk by. It was a good omen, they said. Different, they said, those who were left, different from the day of her birth, a day when the sun turned black. It had been a sign, foretelling the day to come, the day when the whole of the sky turned black. He looked up at her as she held him in her arms, washed of blood and wrapped in a deerskin, as if to say, I know, I understand, I have chosen. And she thought, he has been here before her, floating on rafts of hazel wood across flooded streams, sitting in the blossom-strewn grasses beneath the plums, standing on the beach ridge and looking out to the sea. And she knew that her life was changed and made good, that together she and her child would explore a new world, together they would walk the old tracks and help build the new. Together they would bind old wounds . . .

Nell

Nell was younger than Vera by five years, though it seemed more to Lilli. Edith's second daughter, her mother's disappointment, born at a time when Edith had longed to replace her second child, her son, who had died at just six weeks.

Nell had felt her mother's disappointment keenly and had been happy when the time had come to leave. She'd left home at twenty-four to live with Ted, quietly and without fuss. Left home when she could no longer live with Edith who was as difficult with her daughters as she was good with her granddaughter.

Nell and Vera's father, Jack, had died two years before, a quick death from a heart attack. A death which both Vera and Nell found themselves guiltily wishing on their mother, who became increasingly critical and demanding without Jack's steady and temperate influence. And Nell had struggled on until Ted had invited her to live with him.

Nell met Ted under an August moon at a harvest supper not long after her father's death. They sat beside each other to eat at a long trestle in a grand tent smelling of trampled grass and warm beer. Nell chatted easily to the large, rustic man with brown wavy hair and green eyes. Ted, normally shy and reticent, was drawn to her. They took to going out together, walking, going to the pictures, occasional trips to towns or cities about. They fitted comfortably into each other's lives, matched and dovetailed like the finest carpentry. And so, one morning in April, Ted arrived to collect her in his black Humber Hawk and Nell, her cases packed, kissed her mother, to whom she had given but a cursory warning of leaving, and felt her heart soar as she climbed into the front

31

seat and settled into the leather.

Edith had been convinced that Nell was pregnant, that Ted was married, separated, divorced . . . that they were secretly married . . . anything rather than that they would choose to live together in sin. People Edith knew did not do that, not without compelling reason. The kind of women Edith knew would avoid disgrace at all costs. They put up and shut up and insisted on respectability in everything. Living together was a disgrace and any association with such was damaging and humiliating.

Nell was happy, glad to get away from the harping disapproval of her mother. The way she looked at her, cast a glance across the top of her lowered glasses, that look of displeasure, censure, unexplained and bewildering. The silence. Silence and disdain were powerful weapons, more powerful than arguments or words. There was no clearing of the air in Edith's house, no easy reconciliation, apart from that which followed the rare glass of cherry brandy or a good thriller on the TV. It was a cold war and she was supreme commander. Her brooding presence was such that she'd invaded Nell's being as she had Vera's before her so that Nell had become increasingly unsure of the boundaries between Edith and herself. Felt her cross over and inhabit her body – stood at the sink, hands in the washing-up bowl, more Edith than herself. To resist had taken all of Nell's strength and it had been a relief to escape to a man. For men were not like that, not in her experience.

Ted wasn't like that, having to control, to own, to overpower. Ted loved her in an open, fresh way, in the way he loved his home and the land around him in which his family were rooted. Not an owner but a keeper: of the peaty soil, the black milky Friesians in lush water meadows, the cowslip fields, the willows and the moors. Digging peat in the early morning. Lining out the head and unridding to expose its black organic matter. Best black peat, laid down three thousand years ago, over the blue lias clay and the fen peats.

Benching and stooling, cutting in mumps, ready for chopping and drying. Ted knew all of this and could still see the moor lined with the beehive ruckles, three metres high.

But Ted had grown and changed with the land and new opportunity. Had gone to work at the Creamery and Nell had joined him there when she'd gone to live in Marsh. They had travelled to work together, latterly in his Mustang-inspired yellow Ford Capri. But no longer, for Nell had exchanged the frothy sheen of fresh milk for the slubbed silk of white wedding dresses, for the thing she had denied herself; the fuss, the bouquets, the soft veil and celebration of self and beauty. The 'look at me' that she couldn't do.

Nell had recurring dreams about weddings, about her wedding which was always imminent and for which she was unprepared. No flowers or dress or the wrong dress and the wrong day. She woke from her dreams with relief and regret.

But making wedding dresses, that was different. Expanding from her bits on the side for oversized ladies, Nell had started her own dress-making business. She specialised in brides and bridesmaids and mothers of the bride. She made gowns with satin-covered buttons, scalloped hems, sashes, pointed sleeves and sweetheart necks. It had turned out well. She was busy but she was at home. This meant that it was easy for her to help Lilli with Vera and watch out for Lilli too.

She'd always had a wild streak, that girl, a wildcat strength. She was like a cat stalking its prey, silent like a whisper of wind in the grass, then pouncing in surprise. You never knew with Lilli. Lilli with her eyes like blue flowers in the cornfield and her defiant hair, her strong legs and plump arms, arms that should have held a small child. Close, cheek against forehead. Gentle long-fingered hands that should have wrapped themselves beneath a baby's bottom around its legs. A head thrown back and an open-mouthed smile that would have said it all. Lilli and child defying the world, against the odds, breathing in the salty air, taking down the watery vapours that rose from the land; growing strong, belonging.

Nell wished it had been so.

Edith

They'd hushed it up as best they could. Pregnant at sixteen still a child, still collecting shells on the beach and eating ice creams. It would never have happened if Charlie hadn't gone. That's when they'd followed Nell out to Marsh. Nell and Ted, fat lot of good he was. A young girl like her growing up in that wilderness, nothing to do but roll around in the grass, boys trying to get their hands up your skirt, down your blouse, she knew. No wonder. And Lilli refusing to say who, should have been made to, she would have seen to that if it had been up to her.

They managed it best they could. Packed her off to Flo's in London, out of the way for a few months, until it was all over. The baby adopted, the slate wiped clean, that was something they'd done well. Can't have a pregnancy ruining a life. Lilli came back and there was no more said, the account was closed, closed right down. She still had her young life before her, that's what mattered, couldn't have a life ruined at sixteen, at least they got something right. Yes they'd managed it the best they could.

'House.' The call invaded her thoughts and shattered the quiet of the lounge of The Lyndor, which stood proudly on the seafront, a residential home for the elderly with 'views across the bay'.

'House.' For the third consecutive time, the cry issued from the thin-lipped, gummy mouth of George Wyatt, former saddler and part-time barber. Suddenly Edith did not want to play anymore. Hot with annoyance she pushed the crocheted blanket that covered her knees to the floor. It fell around her bunioned and plastered feet in a heap, bringing with it the

35

bingo card and a biro.

Why couldn't he shut up? Why was he always the one to call house, never giving anyone else a chance? Jiggling about in celebration, dribbling at matron. Didn't he know his place? A retired shopkeeper, that's all he was. Happy enough at one time to serve from behind the counter of his cluttered Oxford Street premises. Just across the road it was. Jack always got his hair cut there, Lilli too when she was small. To serve and be subservient was his place, hiding behind the clutter of a ceiling hung with saddles and straps, buckles and bags. Lurking in the hot leathery interior which smelt of ripe horse and dubbin. He was happy enough then to receive a modest payment and a smile from a glamorous neighbour such as herself. The kind of woman much admired in the town. Happy to repair the white stitching on her saddlebag, which was really quite a fashion item then. Then, that was when he had known his place. Now his star was in the ascendant and hers was rapidly falling to earth in the remote desert of The Lyndor.

Edith kicked the blanket from her feet and shifted her bottom around in the plastic seat of the high-backed chair. The staff were busy in attendance on George. With little possibility of relief, of making it out of the chair unaided back to the privacy of her room, she settled for lifting her gaze above the heads of the hoary residents to the window beyond. The leaden sky began to release the first spots of rain, prelude to the downpour that was to follow, obliterating all but glass and water.

Where had it started? she mused. Where had it all started going wrong? This was a question she asked herself daily now. She'd decided on the answer long ago but found it comforting to rehearse, emerging as she did blameless at the hands of others and of fate.

Probably when Charlie left. Probably then and who could blame him? Vera had simply not tried hard enough. Could have made a lot more of herself. She'd had to. Wasn't blessed with thick wavy hair like her daughters. No, had to make the best of thin and fine. But hadn't it always been admired – her hair? People would say, *I don't know why you bother to go to the hairdressers, Edith, you do it so well yourself, better than they do*, and she'd have to agree. It had been a struggle keeping herself smart, looking her best at all times. Never letting herself go, not like Vera. Vera was far too busy looking after the child and baking to keep Charlie's interest. Now she, she'd never have let a man like Charlie go. Oh, he was a ladies' man, you couldn't argue with that, but worth the effort. Handsome, and charming with it, always very complimentary to her. He appreciated a woman who looked after herself.

So that's when it had all started going wrong. Vera had never recovered, not really. She could have got him back if she'd put her mind to it. She should have done, for the child's sake, for Lilli's, for all their sakes. Jack had been no use, of course, never was, couldn't handle anything emotional, just clammed right up. Didn't even speak for a month. He played with Lilli, that was one thing, she supposed, kept an eye out for the child while she dealt with the rest. Left it all to her. Well didn't he always leave everything to her? Was he ever there when she needed him? Always disappeared, behind the newspaper or into the television.

Everyone talking about them in the town. Mind you that wasn't the first time. What about when Nell left, everyone talking? So sudden, out of the blue like that, just upped and left to go and live with that country nothing. Oh, she could have done better for herself. Told her to her face. Even Jack had agreed with her there. To this day Edith failed to understand it. What was it all about? People didn't do something like that without a reason. Maybe that's where it all started to go wrong. All those sly looks and nods. They couldn't wait to get behind their nets or into their huddles to talk about them, laughing at her. Gossip: Nell pregnant, Ted separated, a secret past? Never did get to the bottom of it. Normal girls left home when they married, normal girls did not live in sin.

She'd always considered her daughters more than normal, a cut above the rest. Had dressed them beautifully in hand-smocked, puff-sleeved frocks and camel coats. People said, *I don't know how you do it, Edith, like little princesses.* Well, she'd done her best and where had that got her? What now? It wasn't right, not in the natural course of things, your daughter dying before you and Jack gone – and where was Lilli? She could come every day now that she was back and working on the seafront – it was no distance and so far she'd been once – and she could make more of herself, always wore the wrong colours and it wasn't as if she hadn't told her. Still, people would say, *She's the spitting image of you, Edith, just like her grandmother, beautiful blue eyes.* She'd practically lived at their house. They were always in the town together, up to the ice-cream parlour, sometimes she took her friend Rebecca, funny little thing, not very pretty. But it was all wrong when you thought of those children. No wonder Lilli was next.

Of course if Martin had lived it might all have been different. No one knew what that felt like, couldn't come close to imagining. Her life, her spirit sucked out of her, her body hollow. Her only son still a helpless scrap dying in her arms like that and nothing anyone could do. She had seen a painting once of a woman screaming, of a woman opening her mouth to scream but no sound coming out – that's how it felt. And Jack, Jack saying nothing, didn't he care?

If Martin had lived, then there would have been a brother to take care of them. Another man in the house, a man to love her, different to Jack, a son of hers brought up by, shaped by – surely very different. A son like Charlie perhaps. Although her son would never have left, no, and never have messed around with his wife's sister either.

All those lives ruined and all for sex, it seemed to her. She couldn't understand what it was all about, all the fuss about sex. She'd been glad at least for that when Jack died, glad to be rid of that grunty, messy business. She could well do without it and she took some pleasure in looking around the room at its male residents, in particular George Wyatt, and reassuring herself that not one would be capable of an erection let alone the act, which seemed to preoccupy men all their lives but which had brought her nothing but trouble and inconvenience.

George began to cough. He was working up to a fit of coughing, she could tell and just before tea – so inconsiderate. She turned to the bent figure of Jean Fisher in the chair next to her and saw a tear form in her eye and make its way silently down her right cheek.

'Never mind, dear,' Edith said, 'it'll be tea soon, there's sure to be strawberry jam, your favourite. You'll like that won't you?'

The Seaview

Entering the hotel that morning Lilli had felt the usual dislocation, the sense of separation and unreality. In the hotel she was never sure who she was. Mirrors forced her to confront a self that she did not always recognise or did not expect to see. The Seaview had a life all of its own, an interior world in which people were found whispering, treading with care, taking shallow breaths so as not to give themselves away in unfamiliar territory. Captive and disabled, it was difficult to make choices or define what was their space. Guests revealed themselves. Their habits good and bad, clean and dirty, the scum left on the bath, the underwear on the floor, the neatly made bed. Go in, clean up the waste bins of other lives; remove the make-up-stained towels, strip the semen-splattered sheets, wipe the ashtrays, empty the bin of its crumpled tissue, the rubble and the wreckage of the weekends.

Passing Pearl on the stairs, weighed down with a stack of clean linen, Lilli smiled, then put her hand into her pocket to feel for the photograph now creased and worn, reminded as she was of the other woman's tragedy. She'd heard it whispered in the hotel – it had been a long time ago but Pearl had never been the same since, or so they said, not since she'd got rid of her baby. A fate delivered at her own hands but one determined by men.

Whichever way you looked at it, Lilli thought, it was women who took the blame, who shouldered the responsibility. Women blamed for their fertility, blamed for getting rid, blamed for having and giving away, blamed for keeping and not coping well enough. And worst of all blamed themselves. She paused at the stairhead; the bracelet was damp in her hand. From the long window she saw a grey sky, darkening and heavy with rain . . .

*It came just as she was growing from youth into womanhood
– the sudden darkness that led her to lift her gaze from her
lap, from combing wool. A passing cloud? An approaching
storm? She had been greeted by an unfathomable sight: water
in a great wave that filled the sky, spreading across the land,
rushing towards her, carrying all in its wake, tossing boats
and palisades in its sparkling crests, swallowing deer and
alder in its troughs. She had dropped the wool, the comb, and
run – others with her, someone calling to her, a hand held out
from the spread of the ancient tree. She'd survived clinging to
its branches watching while the sea boiled beneath them.*

*Many died that day – her father and mother among them
– washed away. When the water subsided they climbed down
and walked on a bed of silt and seaweed, crushing white
shells underfoot. Black cormorants watched from the beech
on the ridge.*

*Their kin, their camps; wool, claypots, looms, dried fish,
grasses, antler, baskets; all were gone. But the following year
the land was the greenest, and the harvesting the best, that
could be remembered.*

*Still now as the clouds pass overhead or a momentary
shadow is cast she remembers and lifts her head in apprehension, fear biting at her heels and fingertips, pulsing through
her body ready for flight. She has never seen a wave like it
since, a giant thing with sparks flying as if from fire. She is
ready, in case, she will keep him strapped to her, safe from the
invading sea . . .*

Lilli breathed in hard, pushing away the crackling wave and
swallowing the cries of drowning creatures. She inhaled the
familiar smells of polish, biscuits and soap, hot paint on

radiators and boiled vegetable. She listened for the mostly unheard noises around her, the hum of the generator, water bubbling in copper pipes, the distant drone of the Hoover.

At the door to the office she selected a key from those she wore on her belt and let herself in. Lilli had the petty cash to attend to and the takings from the bar to bank. Maud had entrusted her with the job, although it was not Maud's day off. It was, in fact, Tuesday and Maud was presently enjoying morning coffee and sugary shortbread with Dorothy in the Bluebird Tearooms in the high street.

Life for Maud had improved since Lilli had come to work for them. Over the last few weeks she had begun to see Lilli as something of an ally. She believed she was the sort of person she could trust with important tasks, practical things; Maurice obviously thought so. She couldn't quite put her finger on what it was but Lilli somehow seemed to soak up the pressure. Maurice was definitely better tempered now that he had someone to help in the office, something, she had to admit, she'd never been good at. It was a relief to her. She got out more. She was even thinking of broaching the subject of a weekend away with Dorothy, out of season, of course; Torquay would be nice. That's why she couldn't understand him ending up in hospital like that; still she wasn't wasting time worrying on his account.

'You're not anxious about Maurice then?' Dorothy had asked when she telephoned that morning.

'No it's just the usual,' Maud said disinterestedly, impatient.

'But he doesn't usually go to hospital does he?'

'Well he doesn't usually have such a bad attack.'

'What brought it on then?' persisted Dorothy, who took delight in picking over the entrails of the sick and unfortunate, like a bald-necked vulture sat proudly on a pile of bones.

'I don't know. He's been overdoing it, they said, maybe he needs a stronger inhaler. I don't know, but he'll be out in a day or two,' Maud said, attempting to put an end to it.

'Well, we'd better make the most of it,' said Dorothy, finally waking up to the opportunity.

Lilli had been unaware of Maurice Hauser's fate until her arrival at work. His hospitalisation, reported to her by Duncan the cook, had followed a very nasty asthma attack at teatime the previous day. Far from dampening the mood of the hotel staff, the news appeared to enliven them, imparting an almost celebratory air to the day.

Maurice for his part had little to celebrate and a lot to ponder and rue from his hard and high hospital bed. Over the weeks Lilli had been working for him, Maurice had become increasingly demanding but had suffered a growing frustration when Lilli had evaded him. Only once had he reached the peak of excitement he had experienced on their first night together. Lilli seemed less than keen to indulge in his favourite water sports, and on the one occasion when she had relented, she had flatly refused to urinate in his mouth. Her evident distaste had angered him; that's when he'd pushed her hard into the side of the heavy oak desk, bruising her hip and letting her feel his fist in her face. She was a teasing bitch – weren't they all? – but he shouldn't lose control like that. He'd gone too far but he was stretched taut, something had to give and as usual it had been his temper.

They hadn't got nearly as far as he'd hoped, anticipated; so much still to explore: domination, submission. Maurice couldn't make up his mind; he got confused when he thought about it. He craved humiliation at her hands and would not be averse to taking it a step further but then there were times, black times, when the tables had to be turned, when suddenly he saw she needed pushing about a bit; when she needed showing, when she was asking for it.

Maurice fantasised about it. He was plagued by elaborate fantasies yet to come to fruition, the greatest of these being his desire to submit as a baby, to be a baby once again, a baby in a nappy and rubber pants. He imagined Lilli taking his clothes off, laying him down, bottom on nappy, bringing it up between his legs, pinning it at the sides. Pulling on the rubbers tight. Talking baby talk, while he wet himself. A tight wet nappy around a hard cock . . . but they hadn't got that far, nowhere near. Although he'd surprised himself with the way yesterday lunchtime he'd bent her over the desk and taken her from behind. Perhaps this heralded a new departure in their relationship, another rich seam of fantasy to mine. He'd achieved quite an erection, one to be proud of, quite an erection but it had been an exertion – he really would have to be careful not to overdo things. His chest let him down, wasn't up to it, tightened up with all the excitement so that he couldn't breathe.

Lilli went over to the desk drawer. As she bent to open it and remove the petty cash box, she was reminded of Maurice's sweaty performance the previous day. It had been over in a matter of seconds, thankfully. How pathetically pleased he'd been with himself. How puce in the face. Well it had done for him, seen him off for a few days. Maud was out on the town, the chambermaids were free from his fevered gropings, and Lilli was feeling quite pleased with herself. There was a knock at the office door.

'Come in,' said Lilli.

Pearl appeared in the doorway. 'I was just making coffee,' she said tentatively. 'I wondered if you fancied one. I gather Mr Hauser's not around.' She winked conspiratorially.

'Why not,' said Lilli. 'In fact I could fancy something a little stronger. I think a celebration is in order, don't you?'

Pearl stepped into the office. 'Now you're talking,' she said as she closed the door behind her.

'And it just so happens that I know where mucky Maurice keeps the booze,' said Lilli. She walked over to a tall oak cabinet that stood by the window. She unlocked it and revealed an array of spirit bottles. 'This'll do, I think,' she said lifting one, 'there's no smell with vodka.'

'I'll fetch the orange,' said Pearl.

'And a couple of glasses and make them big ones.' Within

a couple of minutes Pearl was back with a bottle of orange and two tumblers. Lilli was sat behind Maurice's desk. She'd pulled back her hair and stuffed a cushion up under her overall. She leant back in the chair and said in a voice not her own, 'Come in my dear, do sit down . . . or bend down more like.' They dissolved into laughter and spluttered into their hastily poured drinks.

Pearl put her hand over her mouth to suppress the noise. 'Poor Maurice,' she said, her voice thick with irony, 'it couldn't have happened to a nicer chap.'

'Definitely not. I vote we drink to it. Let's drink to Maurice.' Lilli poured another.

Pearl added the orange. 'It's just like drinking fruit juice.'

'Exactly. To Maurice, long may he rest in hospital and long may he call for the bed pan and the bottle.' Lilli raised her glass.

'Till he wets himself and till that crabby old matron – what do you call her? – gives him a good telling off.

'I know who you mean,' said Lilli, 'don't know her name but I bet she's no Florence Nightingale.'

'I wonder if he'll have to have an enema. I hope he does.'

'That's no good. We don't want him enjoying himself, might bring his asthma on again.' They howled and drank another vodka on the strength of Maurice's misfortune.

'I hope nobody finds us,' said Pearl, suddenly aware of all the noise they'd been making.

'There's no one to find us. Maud's out with Dorothy, not that she'd care. She'd probably join us if she had half a chance. I'm in charge of the office, keys and all.' Lilli jangled the bunch of keys that hung from her waist.

'Well then,' said Pearl on her third large vodka and feeling a certain, if slight, movement of the normally solid furniture around her, 'perhaps we better have another.'

'Why not,' said Lilli, feeling decidedly warm and very happy. She smiled at Pearl. 'Yes, one more for the road and then I think it's a half day for you.'

'But there's . . .' Pearl slurred.

'There's what? There's nothing, nothing for you to do but go home and put your feet up. You deserve a rest.' Pearl was too tipsy to argue. While they drank their last vodka Lilli delighted in the thought that Pearl would go home, fall asleep on the bed maybe, rest, instead of her daily grind of stripping beds and polishing furniture. 'It looks like rain,' said Lilli, who had swivelled round in her chair and was looking at the sky through the window. 'You better get a move on.'

'But . . .'

'But nothing, I say so. You've got no choice.'

Pearl looked across the table at Lilli, at this woman young enough to be her daughter. They'd none of them been too sure when she'd first come. They weren't sure what she got up to, especially with Maurice. But over the weeks they'd realised that far from doing them harm she'd done them all a favour, getting Maurice off their backs. Besides there was something about her that was hard to resist. It was her smile, Pearl thought. The way she always smiled and the way she didn't complain. How many girls her age would have come home to look after their mothers and never whine about it? Pearl couldn't think of one. And it was great the way she poked fun at Maurice. It was a pity there weren't more women like her. Lilli wasn't frightened of men.

'All right,' said Pearl feeling the room begin to swim around her.

'We could have another, there might just be time.'

'No, definitely not, I might fall off my bike,' said Pearl, growing alarmed at the prospect of cycling home.

'I thought you caught the bus?'

'I did, but David – that's my son, works out at the Creamery – got me a new bike. He just turned up out of the blue a week back with it and I thought why not. I always used to go everywhere on my old bike. I loved it, but then, well, it got rusty and I didn't bother.'

'Maybe you should get the bus home,' said Lilli trying to look serious but giggling despite her concern. 'No seriously, I don't want you to fall off your bike.' She didn't. The last thing she wanted was for Pearl to have an accident. On the contrary she wanted Pearl to have a good time for a change, to have a treat for a few hours. 'We don't want you ending up in a hospital bed next to Maurice now do we?'

'Oh, God no, please no,' screamed Pearl. 'Look I'm going before I get plastered. If you're sure . . .'

'Of course I'm sure.'

'I'll get the bus.'

'Very sensible,' said Lilli in a fit of giggles.

Lilli sat for some time with her feet up on the desk, a rueful smile on her face. When she got up she walked, somewhat unsteadily, to the window. She looked out at the rain now falling heavily, painting out the grey seascape. She would have to go to the bank, she decided, or it would be closed.

She would enjoy it, a trip out. What did she care about the rain? While others sheltered, stayed out of the wet, preserving lacquered hair and mascara, saving new shoes and shopping from a soaking, she would venture out. But which way? She really should go and see her grandmother but she knew she could not be witness to Edith's litany of complaint today, nor taste the bitterness that had tainted all their lives. She must avoid the stranger with hair like bleached sorrel and skin like withered lemons. She could not feel her grandmother's anger or hear her lecture on how life might have been, should have been, if people, if they, had lived their lives properly, decently. Not today, not when she was enjoying herself. Instead she would go through the town, but when she passed the ice-cream parlour she would have to hurry and hope he wouldn't see her.

She was beginning to regret her arrangement with Paolo to meet after work that day. She was unsure of herself, unsure of him; thinking about it made her feel foolish and she wished she hadn't told Nell about him.

Nell had, of course, been convinced that she should go. Had straight away volunteered to sit with Vera. She'd begun work on a winter wedding, red and green, the colours of Christmas. There was plenty of hand stitching to be done and she would do this at the bedside.

'You must go,' Nell had insisted.

Now when it was only hours away Lilli was beginning to wish it wasn't happening. Why had she considered it at all? Because she wanted to see him, she had to admit, she looked forward to it. Each day she got out of bed wondering if she would see him. And *no* had not been an option. Not when he'd stood in front of her, palpable, smiling good naturedly, handsome and direct. She wished he wouldn't do that, wouldn't look at her the way he did, wouldn't find her out. No one had looked at her like that, at least not since Charlie, not since her doting father. When Paolo looked at her there was a connection and an understanding. She felt it, felt as if this was not the first time of their meeting or the only place.

The town gave her shelter. The air cleared her head. The windows of Fiori's were steamed over. It was easy to pass by and through the flat-faced terraces. A baby cried from beneath a pram hood but Lilli resisted the temptation to feel for the armlet, to smell the wood smoke, and feel the rough planks of the track beneath her feet. She concentrated instead on the shops, small and neat: the Co-op outfitters, Stanton's Shoes, The Record Shop, The Candy Box, jewellers, grocers, bakers, all kept her from the rain; she made her way there and back to the bank unseen. Arriving back at the hotel she went straight to the kitchen where she sat with a glass of water and a large pot of tea, after which she took herself off to number forty-six, a small double in the attic, where she lay down on the floral bedspread, which she pulled round her, and slept like a cat curled in the sun, for the best part of the afternoon.

The Land Under Water

At 6.30 Paolo was waiting in reception. Lilli, who'd come to regret her lunchtime drinking session with Pearl, had done her best to make herself look presentable; taming her hair by tying it back, scrubbing her face and applying fresh make-up and smoothing out the creases left in her pink jumper from her afternoon nap. It was the best she could do and after all she didn't want to look too good, not as if she'd made some special effort. She didn't want to give the wrong impression. Really she wished she hadn't agreed to them meeting like this.

Paolo helped Lilli on with her coat. She searched awkwardly for the arms, unused to such attention and preferring to deal with her own clothes. They left the hotel together and made for The Queens further along the front where Lilli settled into cold, mock leather and kept her coat around her shoulders for warmth and protection. Paolo fetched port and lemonade and beer and sat closer than she'd expected. They'd grown used to each other's company at lunchtimes, safe in idle conversation; Lilli watching while Paolo played his father at chess, he bringing her coffee and food, checking on her, asking after Vera. But this was different and they'd never been as close as they were now – sat so that his arm pushed against hers through the layers of their coats, through the armour of winter. Lilli found it difficult to concentrate . . .

'What will you do when Vera . . .?' He hesitated.

'When she dies?' Lilli finished the question for him.

'Yes, will you go again?'

'I don't know,' she replied as if she'd not thought of it. 'I don't know, except that I never really was gone, well not that far. Here seems far enough at times. Besides most of my friends are scattered. My two best friends who I shared the flat with have gone travelling. I was thinking of going with them but . . . well Mum was ill and . . . anyway I belong here. I like it here. What about you, are you going to stay forever?' Alone in this small seaside town, playing chess, eating salami and Dolcelatte, watching your brother's children . . . she thought but did not say.

'I want to go back to Italy again sometime, and see where it all began. It's years now. I went when I was a boy, when I was ten. I loved it, felt instantly at home there. It's greener than you'd expect with mountain oaks and pine, south from Rome. My grandfather Emilio talked about it all the time, about how the valleys flooded in spring and covered the fields in silt. *The land under water* he called it, not so different from here really. His house was right in the centre of the village square with green shutters and a red tiled roof and a kitchen garden. I liked the garden best, chasing the lizards and climbing the fig tree. I think he liked it best too. Would have stayed there, forever, if he could. Never would've been homesick, if it hadn't been for the bandits riding out of the mountains and capturing his father. The family had to sell everything it possessed to find the ransom. Jewellery, sheep, horses, even land. The bandits threatened to cut off his ear. In the end they sent him back but my grandfather couldn't stay. The family was ruined and one by one all the young men had to leave and seek their fortunes. Emilio walked across Italy and France, then sailed from Calais to Scotland. That's where he opened his first ice-cream shop. Then he sent home for a decent coffee machine and for the family and we've been here ever since. It calls to me though in a strange way – *the land under water.*'

'Me too,' said Lilli.

'Times I feel I am almost there. I can smell the thyme and rosemary, feel the heat or the cool stone behind the shutters, as if I am there in that time.'

'I know what you mean. The Greeks have a word for it, it's *chora*, it means place, only different from the way we normally think of it. *Chora*. It's the experience, the trigger to memory, we can only understand if we learn to listen to the land. You can do that anywhere if you concentrate hard enough, and look, and smell and breathe it in. The land never changes, not really. It holds our secrets. People come and go but the land remains.'

'Well this is my place too. I like my life here, it's just that sometimes I feel I live a kind of exile as if I'm breathing in another time.'

She could see that. It was true. In the town, in the ice-cream parlour, he was warmly acknowledged and comfortable. Lilli felt he was the kind of man people might share their secrets with, and their sorrows. He was the kind of man who helped. But there was an air of detachment around him. At times he was dispassionate and remote. It was something she liked in him. It made things easy.

'But anyway, where else could I see such sunsets?' he asked

'In the bay of Naples. Over a sparkling sea instead of a dirty brown tide?'

'Well maybe, but it's all the more beautiful here when the brown turns to red.'

'We should walk along the estuary together sometime at sunset,' Lilli said, surprising herself.

'Yes, soon in the spring, if you're still here.'

'Let's go down to the beach.'

'What now? It's dark?'

'Yes now. I like the beach in the dark. You can hear the sea better at night and smell it and the sky will be full of stars, it's perfectly clear.'

'And cold . . .'

'Come on,' she said, already out of her seat and putting on her coat.

'All right, if you want to. Why not?'

Outside the night air was cold. Lilli blew into it, a long stream of steamy breath like a geyser. She was warm and light-headed from the port. She was happy. He was beside her. He was like her. She felt it. He had the same longings.

They crossed the empty front and came to the gritty steps where the sand gathered in the corners. He ran down before her and waited hand outstretched at the bottom. For an instant she imagined them together in the land under water, sat outside his grandfather's house, then she set off, flying past him, ignoring his outstretched hand and running into the darkness across the beach.

'I'll race you,' she shouted, her words lifting and swirling in the wind off the sea. She ran through the soft sand to the hard, where it was still damp from the tide and where she could run faster. She heard him behind her. She ran until her chest was fit to burst, until he caught her by the arm and she fell. They both fell and had to pick themselves up breathless and laughing. Paolo brushed at his coat and legs in an attempt to shake off the sand that clung like wet cement. Lilli bent down and began untying the laces of her boots. The luminous white skeleton of a small bird lay next to her boot, stuck with a few remaining blood-spattered feathers. She put it in her coat pocket, then took off her socks, tucked them too in her pocket, rolled up her trousers and made for the barely discernible white lace at the edge of the quiet, black sea.

'What are you doing?'

'Paddling, come on.'

'You'll get frostbite, it's far too cold.'

'No it's not, the sea's always warmer when it's cold like this.'

Lilli ran into the flat waves and screamed as they broke over her feet.

'I told you.'

She laughed into the night and ran in again and screamed again. 'Come on, it's not that bad really.'

'No, really? It doesn't sound it. You're crazy, mad.'

'I know.' She walked back to him. He was holding her boots. 'My feet are too wet for those,' she said looking up into the shadows of his face.

'Here,' he said, bending and arching his back, 'I'll give you a piggyback, only don't get sand everywhere.'

She climbed onto his back, trying to keep her feet away from his coat, put her arms around his neck and rested her chin on his shoulder. She heard the frail skeleton crack and him breathing and the sea shushing like a lullaby.

'Gee up, come on. Can't you go faster than that?' she teased as they crossed the beach to the steps.

On the front Lilli put her socks and boots on before walking uncomfortably back to the bus stop outside the Co-op. Paolo waited with her until her bus arrived. He touched her lightly on the arm as they parted.

'Goodnight. Will I see you tomorrow?'

'Yes, tomorrow, all being well. As long as I can get this sand out from between my toes.' She would need a bath, she thought, and she would have to wash the bird's bones in a sink of warm water. The bus home swayed through dark streets and country lanes, and she settled into its hypnotic rhythm. Pulling her coat around her, she reached for the armlet in the pocket and pushed her finger into the groove of its oval patterning. It was cold . . .

She shivers and crouches before the fire, sheltering behind the hurdles of woven willow. Around her other fires and the tents of travellers who have come to meet and trade and feast before the winter floods. The night air is filled with carnival voices, rising smoke and roasting meat. She sits with others half seen in the drama of the firelight; whittling, cooking in iron pots, eating, talking. In her bundle she carries goods to exchange; the cloth she has woven and dyed with sloe berry, bunches of dried herbs and long-handled weaving combs of antler. There is fresh moss to wrap her feet and the tools of her trade, clay loom weights and spindle whorls, bobbins and bone needles for the making of braid and coarse lace. Wrapped in her cloak, lulled by the voices and the fire's warmth, the baby sleeps swaddled, gently rocking in her arms. Rocking in the fire's glow.

He looks across at her from the other side of the fire, the maker of glass beads from Meare. He smiles, and when the flames of the fire subside into blue ash he steps over to sit beside her. Whilst others drift away to lie on rush beds, he smooths the baby's head and talks to her in his low, sweet voice, of his work, of blowing patterned glass using the sand and the fire. They are the last to settle, lying together, he at her back, the baby at her side. All night she can hear the filling and emptying of his lungs, breathing with the land.

The Parlour

Lilli looked up at the chandelier of blue and white glass which hung from the centre of the ceiling. Crystal snakes curled out from the stem turning upwards into leaf and bulb. Its underbelly was draped with silver chains and pear drops of lemon and raspberry.

The flat was above the parlour, its interior ornate but cool, furnished in *eau-de-nil*, in subdued and elegant greens. It smelled of lemons. Chinese medallions of blue and white hung in its alcoves. The tall Georgian sashes were curtained in coral damask. White porcelain figurines of Our Lady and a dancing horse, gold scalloped ashtrays and family photographs adorned the mantelpiece and the inlaid coffee table.

To this English seaside town, unremarkable and small, Maria had brought her great sense of style and with it a rich and crowded palette; echoes of the distant blue of Tuscan hills, white almond orchards and the scarlet and purple of bougainvillea. They were her lifeline and her cause, and it pleased Maria to note the recent appearance of colour washes on the shop and seafront facades. It reminded her of the colour of Italian streets and she was confident that she'd set the trend by always insisting that the exterior of the parlour be painted terracotta. Her home was her refuge and her only regret was her lack of a garden. In idle moments she'd furnished her garden many times; with water and fountain, with gushing mouths, writhing fish, sea monsters, horses, lions and palms. All in lustrous veined marble and glittering bronze, frothing and fizzing in the sun.

Angelo indulged her, his Northern girl. She'd been brought up amid the elegance of Padua and it did not surprise him that she was reluctant to relinquish her culture and refinement; he was rather proud of it. He enjoyed the landscape she created for him and the traditions she upheld. She had shown great forbearing, did not ask to go back. It would have been impossible, she knew, so she made the very best of it she could, but left her husband and her sons in no doubt that she lived in exile.

At times Paolo found this hard to bear for he was the son on whom the mantle of displacement fell. As the youngest and the longest alone with her, he had inherited her stories and her dreams. No matter how hard he tried, Paolo never felt he quite belonged here, where there were no hills, where the landscape was reduced and small, and where the women were foreign, lacking in her chic, failing in the main to fascinate or draw him.

But in Lilli he sensed an affinity, a meeting of souls. Like him Lilli had the air of one in transit, of a life that was never stationary despite remaining close to home. He wondered what she thought of him and he surprised himself by considering his future with a woman, something he hadn't done for seven years. Not since his heart was broken by a French au pair who had spent the summer with him before returning, much to Maria's relief, to Poitiers.

Lilli was glad she had chosen her navy dress. Glad that for once she'd heeded the advice of her grandmother. It had been a long and difficult choice. She'd spent more time than usual on her hair too, which she'd finally twisted into a bun that nestled in the back of her neck and flattened with the contents of a can of hairspray. Despite these attempts to tame and subdue, Lilli felt decidedly scruffy compared with Maria, particularly when it came to the hair. Maria's was worn in a well-cut bob that swished like a velvet curtain on a track as she moved. Lilli wished she had not been invited. She was clearly a stranger in the salon. Maria was watching her, waiting for her to show herself. She didn't like her, she could tell. She'd probably heard the rumours about the town and considered her entirely unsuitable for her son. The conversation was perfunctory and loaded: 'You're working next door at The Seaview, cleaning . . . I see . . . You grew up . . . Your mother . . . I'm sorry really, a very respectable woman . . . Your grandmother, in a home, really? Carrots? Angelo, the Chianti. Parmesan?'

The men were mostly silent. Lilli spoke when spoken to in between mouthfuls of food. Paolo tried to catch her eye when Maria wasn't looking. He squeezed her hand underneath the table between courses. Finally signalling enough, Angelo began to talk chess and football with his son. Maria retreated to the kitchen. Lilli was relieved. The ordeal was drawing to a close.

Paolo led her down the back stairs into the empty ice-cream parlour. 'I'm sorry,' he said as soon as they were out of earshot. He touched her on the shoulder, stopping her as he bent down to kiss her softly on the cheek and then more urgently on her lips.

'It was fine,' she lied, looking up at him, 'but I don't think she liked me or approved '

'She liked you very much.' It was his turn to lie. 'I can tell. Besides it's not important,' he said, his thoughts turning to fantasies of fucking her, there on the cold marble floor, on the sands in the dunes, underneath the overhang of the sea wall up against a pillar, in the back of a car he didn't have. Anywhere.

Lilli shivered. The parlour was unheated, cold like ice cream. The light was dim and shadows from the streetlights played in the long mirror and across the walls. Lilli saw it filled with ghosts, shades, the colour of ice cream, lounging in its cane chairs, lying across its wide counter, dipping long fingers into silver cylinders of ice. Spectres melting at the arrival of the day.

Floating Cradles

Lilli drew the curtains against the dying light. She switched on the parchment-shaded lamp beside the bed. Her vigil had lasted several days. Vera had deteriorated, slipping in and out of consciousness. But she was not yet ready for death. In fact she seemed better, her eyes more focused. Vera lay awake, propped up on the pillows watching. Lilli, pleased that her mother had rallied, suddenly felt hungry.

'I think I'll get some tea,' she said. 'Are you hungry? What about soup or an egg? A soft boiled egg with soldiers?'

'Maybe an egg . . . I could try.' She spoke as much to please as anything. 'Yes.'

Lilli went down to the kitchen and made boiled eggs and soldiers and brought them upstairs on trays. She ate quickly both hers and Vera's who only managed a mouthful. Vera was not hungry, at least not for food. She was hungry for conversation. She was awake and lucid and wanting to talk.

'I wish spring was here,' she said. She was restless, discontented, fearing it would not come for her, that she would not see out the long winter. 'We always went to Locksley Woods in the spring, do you remember? Usually twice. First for the primroses, banks of them. We brought bunches and bunches home. We always took your grandmother and she always wore those silly shoes with the heels. On a Sunday, we went.'

'I remember.' The soft, honeyed scent flooded back to Lilli, filling the room, and she saw the pale yellow and green primroses hugging the ground, not wanting to yield their fragile stems to a child's hot hands.

'And then back for the bluebells,' said Vera, 'the woods

were blue with them, the ground was covered in a mist, like a carpet we said . . .'

'Bunches and bunches . . . bluebells everywhere, all over the house in vases and jam jars. We used to have Edith's too, said she didn't like the smell, sweet and sickly, she said, didn't she?' She would pick some, she thought, to put beside her mother's bed with their succulent milky stems and pervasive perfume. Or maybe pussy willow with its soft yellow paws, harbinger of spring, they would be out soon. It would please her, cheer her, Lilli thought, allowing her mind to run through the year, a year of posies, making a list: narcissi, wallflowers, old-fashioned roses, pansies and poppies, sweet peas, ox-eye, love in the mist . . . A meaningless list, a forgotten and wasted list, never to be put to use.

'What about the picnics,' exclaimed Lilli, discarding her inventory. 'Holford Glen. I loved it there.'

'We all did but that road was impossible, your father praying we wouldn't meet another car coming up. Such a steep bank and so narrow and overgrown, then suddenly you were down, it was the perfect place for a picnic, grassy hollows, hills all round . . .' Vera was breathing hard. As she fell back into the pillows Lilli took up the story.

'And the stream running through, we spent hours in it, in and out, our hands and feet numb with the cold, building a dam, forcing the water into a pool. It was so clear that water, not like the sea that always stained my blue and white swimming costume. It was fast, cracking the stones as it ran over them. We used to stand the squash and beer bottles in it to cool, stack them up against the bank sides by the yellow flags and the dragonflies and wasps. I got stung there.' She could feel it still, the sharp sting, the shock, could still see Ted running over and picking her up in his sunburned arms. Ted who'd rescued her, Ted who'd been there when Charlie had not. In time, Charlie had faded. He'd become like a distant star whose light still travelled to the earth but who had long since ceased to exist. In time, Ted's star shone undimmed.

Ted had been brought up in the summer country and winter flood. Lilli knew all about his life, about his father Samuel – 'You'd have liked him,' Ted told her. Samuel. She'd seen a photo of him once with a pipe and moustache. He'd worked at Meare digging in the peat, unearthing animal bones, barrow loads of grain, boxes of pottery, tools, combs and beads. It was hard work but men like Samuel were used to it. They were the peat diggers, they had the skills, didn't they? They took care, were careful and precise, uncovering and wrapping all the finds. Everything written down, logged in a great ledger. Samuel coming home at night to his children with tales of treasure and occasionally – very rarely, mind – one or two of these found their way home with him: pottery shards, beads of bone and glass, an ammonite spindle whorl, a patterned weaving comb with six teeth, a spiral fastener of bronze and a baby's armlet of grey shale, the one which rested on Lilli's dressing table.

Ted and his father, and his father before him, roamed the swamp, foraging, gathering its harvest of elver and salmon, wildfowl and willow. They steered its flooded rivers, walked its tracks and travelled its rails on the old Slow and Dirty. It was through Ted and the stories of his forefathers that Lilli came to realise the duality of life on the Levels; the contrast of nature with artifice – the farmer embracing the land, putting out his cattle to summer pasture, his geese to graze, moving upstairs in the winter to avoid the floods; the monks, the engineers, the men who dug and drained and pumped, restraining it.

For centuries those living on the land had both acquiesced and wrestled with its vagaries. The struggle to resist the constant shift of water and silt seeping into and spilling from the low-lying plain filled boots with water and buried spades in slime. Elsewhere farmers welcomed the *thick water* of the flood to replenish their fields and guarantee the harvest. Questions posed were often without solution; sluices and weirs, sea walls and pumping stations were partial. Still the

60

rivers flooded and the sea broke through the defences. A wild land of flooded marshes with myriad islands, secret places where kings might hide, was not easily tamed. A great basin spilling at its rim not easily discharged when its rivers were sluggish and their estuaries silted by the tides.

History records the flooding of the land by the sea – on 20 January 1607 a sea wall gives way: *huges and mighty hilles of water, tomboling over one another, in such sort, as if the greatest mountains in the world had overwhelmed the lowe valeyes or marshy grounds.* The sea poured in to a depth of ten or twelve feet, the flood extended for twenty miles inland and thirty villages were submerged.

A century later after the great storms of 1703 when boats were driven ashore and grounded in meadows, the lowland women designed a floating cradle to ensure that no baby's life was ever lost in the flood. Men and women living with the threat of deluge. Ted's family – boats moored to bedroom windowsills, barges steered across moors and butter made on rooftops – gave witness to their tenacity and tolerance.

Ted had shown Lilli. Everywhere the mark of intense activity to drain and resist, keeping the sea out, helping the rivers to carry their upland load, rhynes and cuts, canals and embankments, pumping station and clyse, diverting, draining, defying gravity, reversing the flow of rivers and all the while a constant seeping, a resurgence of water in the hollows, rising up through the soft peat to fill the pits and ditches. The land inundated. Poisoned with salt at the equinox when the high winds whipped the sea and there was no time to empty the sluice.

A wetland, once busy with navigation, with shipping and barges up river on the tide, ports and wharves. Goods set ashore to be plied upstream, food, livestock, building mate-rials, church seats for the abbey masons. A great seafaring centre which had left barely a trace. Had left only the ghost of a reflection in the pool of history that is the land. Ted had seen it. He'd shown her.

Vera twisted restlessly in the bed. Her sleep was fitful. Lilli got up and stood at the window. She looked out over the droves and ditches, over fields where water lay in low metallic pockets reflecting the black willow crowns of winter. Overhead a skein of geese rippled seaward in the sky . . .

Geese gather in the meadow, their long necks rising above the myrtle and the purple flowering heads of teasel. Mist lies at the edges of the stream and fingers the hem of her skirt. She watches him go, now when the fire is cold and the pit is filled with ash. He ventures out into the uninterrupted stillness along a line of willow, beside the track, beyond the first elm and across the wide expanse of the moor, southwards to Meare. He carries with him her gift of woven cloth, the finest she has. She watches him go, feeling still the warmth of his body as he drew her to him, his soft breath as he kissed the baby's head, his whisper like a seashell at her ear . . .

The Lighthouse

Paolo could not settle. He had closed the parlour early in the growing gloom of the winter's afternoon. The sky and all about was featureless. The wind was chill. Only the hardy were inclined to take the sea air; most avoided the front. The town was colourless, drained of life. Its inhabitants were closed in on themselves, clutching their arms about them. They conserved their energy and warmth, wrapped their bodies from the cold damp and waited for the fire and the steamy kitchen at the end of the day.

He was cold. Despite the thickness of his navy wool sweater he could not get warm. He felt no benefit from the lounge gas fire. The *eau-de-nil* interior, the precision about him, the lack of clutter, the soulless perfection of polish and placement were icy. He paced the floor, switched on the radio only to switch it off immediately, in irritation. Why did they broadcast such dull plays mid-afternoon? The radio could do nothing to alleviate his mood.

He stared from the long sash windows out towards the lighthouse which stood at the throat of the estuary. It was just discernible. Nearby was the churchyard whose north side had been reserved for the internment of dead sailors. The lighthouse had been built on the site of a fisherman's cottage where a wife had once placed a candle in the window to warn of the treacherous Gore Sands. Lilli had told him.

Lilli, where was she? It was the thought of Lilli that was bothering him, making him restless and agitated. She was the reason he was unable to settle. She was most probably at home with Vera. He knew that. At least that's what Maud had told him when he had gone to inquire. She had not been at work for several days. Maud was missing her. Vera was apparently worse and Lilli wanted to spend more time with her. Maurice had agreed. So Paolo had not seen her. She'd not had lunch with him or called by on her way to and from work. He'd seen less and less of her these last few weeks. Going out had no longer seemed possible, what with Lilli rushing off home or busy at work for that creep. Was she avoiding him? That's how it felt.

There were times when they'd been close, when they'd shared their feelings and hopes. Surely he hadn't imagined it? They'd begun to reveal themselves to each other little by little. He'd ended up telling her more than he'd expected and he was left with the feeling that he had revealed too much.

What was it about Lilli? Why was she so evasive with him? She seemed to live in a different space and a time without a past or a future. From what he could tell she had her friends, one or two, but no one who seemed to matter much. They'd lived in a series of dingy flats and worked in dead-end jobs; they were saving to go travelling and she'd wanted to go with them. But then her mother's illness had put pay to all that. She never complained, though, and he admired the way she looked after Vera and seemed happy doing it; everyone admired that, no matter what else they said about Lilli, even his mother.

He liked the way she enjoyed simple things, liked the way she ate her ice cream. There were times too when it was really fun to be with Lilli. He felt comfortable with her, talking about Italy, about going back maybe. He hadn't felt like that for a long time. He had to admit she brought something out in him, changed things. When she was around he laughed more. When she wasn't there or he didn't see her it was disappointing. The day was ordinary and he was less inclined to smile.

He'd been watching out for her, hoping to catch sight of her passing the parlour window, wanting the passion stirred by just a glimpse. It was enough. But then again it was a kind of torture, this wanting. He wanted her now, physically. It had become impossible to ignore. She was his first waking thought. He would think of her in the morning lying in a half sleep, aroused by dream, lying naked and wanting her body naked next to his, wanting to lie on top of her, to look down on her face from above. He had to have her; others had, he knew. That was sex of course, sex without love or desire, wasn't it?

What lay between them was different, surely? He needed to believe it was. Maybe that was why she evaded him, why she kept her distance. She didn't dare to get too close. Did not or could not trust. Was that it? He could tell she didn't trust him. He'd caught her watching, standing off, but then he knew he could draw her back. He was not powerless. He knew about trust. It wasn't easy for him. It had grown harder not easier. He felt he risked more the older he got. But he wanted to trust Lilli and wanted her close, he wanted to prise her away from that hotel and from her mother's deathbed.

He went into the kitchen and made himself toast and tea. Perhaps the food would warm him up. He took it into the lounge and sat in the armchair nearest the fire. It was peaceful at least. Angelo and Maria were at Vanni's, spoiling the grandchildren and testing the patience of their daughter-in-law. Maria had not helped. She didn't like Lilli, she'd made that clear. She discouraged him from mentioning her in conversation and insisted on viewing her as a passing fancy for a bored son who was worthy of so much more, but he saw through it all. Maria could please herself, he would do as he wished. She would accept eventually. In the meantime he was frustrated and depressed by the persistent desire which dogged him, but which he had, so far, failed to realise beyond an embrace or kiss.

He wanted her, but not just that. He wanted to help her too. Share with her. He didn't want her out there alone with Vera to care for. He imagined them living together, setting up home in a new place, going home to each other, laughing together, fucking in bed, on the floor, in the shower, up against the kitchen wall, by the fire – everywhere, anywhere.

It was growing dark. The beacon of the lighthouse pulsed out on the estuary. It was impossible to stay in the flat. Paolo put on his coat and went downstairs, through the parlour and out. He turned his collar up against the wind.

Shifting Sands

Vera woke with a low moan; her back ached as her stomach swelled. Pain came and went like sleep and she moved from one to another, from sleep to waking, pain to comfort, without understanding or control. Lilli wondered, how long? How long could Vera maintain her struggle, her uncertain grip on life? How soon before she would slip back into the muddy soup of her origins? How long before she was sucked through the treacherous sands to the heavy clay that lay beneath? Lilli offered the morphine. Vera's lips were cracked and dry. She fetched the Vaseline to moisten them for her.

An unexpected knock at the door below startled her; no doctors or nurses were due and Nell never knocked, just came right in. Lilli went downstairs to answer it Opening the door she found Paolo stood there. She was surprised to see him. It caught her off guard. She felt her cheeks flush and her heart move in her chest as she smoothed her hair with her hands.

'Hello,' he said.

She paused. 'Come in,' she said cautiously, stepping to one side to allow him into the narrow hallway. He sensed her reservation, her hesitancy.

'I've come to see if you're OK,' he said, quickly offering her an explanation for the visit. 'I haven't seen you for a few days now. I was worried. I asked at the hotel and they said they didn't know when you'd be in and that Vera was worse.' He whispered this last with inflexion, questioning gently, glancing upwards as he spoke.

'Yes, she's worse.' Saying it made her feel weary, feeling the truth of what she said . . . yes, her mother was worse, was going to die and she did not know how she would be or feel when the time came. Alone she supposed, alone and tired. 'They say it won't be long.'

'Can I do anything?' he said, wanting to help, desperate to please her. 'Do you need anything?' She didn't answer. 'You shouldn't be alone here like this.'

'I'm not alone. Nell and Ted are just across the street, you know that.'

'I know, but it still seems like you're on your own, no sisters, no brothers, no . . .'

'Family. No gathering around the death bed, you mean, no grand finale.' She was angry. 'It's always been like this anyway, me and her on our own, looking after each other, without men. We managed.' She spoke with none of her usual grace or kindness. He'd unnerved her, arriving at the door like that, looking the way he did.

Sometimes being together was easy and other times not. It was better when she could plan for it. It was fine when they were friends, good friends having lunch, drinking coffee, while he played chess with Angelo. Fine too, or almost, sitting next to each other in a pub or in the dark of a cinema or out on the beach. But there was more, more that she would like to deny, which she tried to deny but which percolated beneath. Disappointment and denial erupted in anger. Sparks flew between them, skewing off in all directions like a Catherine wheel with its pin loose, landing on the wet grass, smouldering. There was no smoke without fire, her grandmother always said, but the fire only smoked, neither igniting nor going out. Lilli had been tempted to extinguish it. Better a coal-black, dead-black fire with no warmth than a teasing curl of smoke never quite finding the oxygen of life.

He was showing his concern, she knew, but his kindness unsettled her. For a long time she'd wanted kindness above all and yet still she did not dare meet its face. Instead she fended it off. It frightened her the way weddings frightened Nell.

'I'm sorry,' he said sensing her mood. 'I'll go.'

'No don't,' she said quickly, knowing at once that she did not want him to leave. 'Do you want a drink or something?'

'Not really.' He looked at her directly, his eyes demanding that she look at him. Lilli looked down. Paolo reached out, putting his hand behind her head and into the back of her neck. He drew her towards him so that she was buried in his coat and his arms were around her. She could hear his heart beating in his chest. Her ear was pressed against it through the thick layers. She lifted her head and mouth to his and in their long kiss she tasted the weeks of wanting and half touching, of lips brushing cheeks, of holding back. She allowed the desire, which had lived stifled without expression or voice, to wash over her.

She was alarmed when he took her hand and made to lead her upstairs. She held back, he hesitated. She glanced above her, wondering about Vera. He began to climb the stairs treading softly, noiselessly, still with her hand in his. He stopped at the top, waiting for her to show him where. She looked in on Vera first, while he stood. Her head lay turned towards the window, she breathed with effort, her jaw lay slack.

Lilli took him into her bedroom, lit only by the late afternoon glow of a street lamp through the net. The square tower of the village church cast its shadow across the floor where they stood, cold. They undressed each other, allowing their clothes to fall around their feet. The shadow draped itself around their naked bodies like a mourner's ribbon, wide and black. It moved with them, encircling them as they kissed and touched, as they felt each other, as they fucked. First on the floor and later in the bed. Until they were wet and warmed by each other's sweat.

When he was asleep Lilli got out of bed and wrapped the faded bed cover around her. She would not sleep. The night would be too precious. She would watch him and listen for Vera. She sighed contentedly as she crossed to the window and looked out over the darkening fields to the sea. She pictured the mud flats out in the bay, the fisherman pushing the mud-horse homeward through the sucking silt, unable to stand upright in his alluvial domain, leaning as it cradled him, prone, across the estuary, a place in which there was no foothold, no steady step, where the balance was fragile and dubious, in a landscape of shifting sands and tides, rising and falling with the moon.

Part Two

Becca
London 1975

Seaside Girls

In her bed, in the flats, by the Creek, Becca dreamed of Pearl. In her dream Pearl comes riding by on her old black bicycle, along the wide seafront. Sailing effortlessly past she calls to Becca but her voice is lost, lifted high on the salty air like a gull and Becca can only watch the fish's mouth open and close silently. As she turns seawards Becca finds the tide rising about her, lapping the sea wall until it begins to flow over.

Drifting from dream to waking, Becca recalled Pearl and her fierce, black-haired beauty. Pearl, always working hard – worn out, the women said – to keep her three sons – handsome like their father who was dead or long gone, Becca could not remember. What she did remember, what everyone remembered, was that day. The day the ambulance came to West Avenue; the children, Becca amongst them crowding round, the women calling them back in. The day Pearl, on finding herself pregnant for a fourth time, had taken a knitting needle to her cervix and nearly died.

The ambulance had come and taken her to the safety of the place that had failed to keep her and the other women about her safe, and she had recovered. But when she returned Pearl was changed. She didn't smile in the same way. She didn't wave or call out to Becca and her bike remained unridden – laid down to rust in the backyard shed.

There were other casualties: the bright young hairdresser, who cut Becca's hair, haemorrhaging in a London hotel room; seaside girls looking for anonymous solutions. Why had they not known about Widow Welch pills and the benefits of a little quinine and castor oil? The round, white, papery box and the tumbler that stood on the kitchen draining board until a foetus made its slippery exit in a gin bath. She knew, young as she was, when her mother Pauline left. Becca knew that babies could be got rid of. She knew just like she knew the corners of the wide, flat fields she roamed with Lilli, the hairs on the back of the snout of the sow in the pig pen, the way the women always huddled by the lupins when there were secrets to be told. Becca grew up knowing. As it turned out, Becca grew up knowing a lot of things that might have been best kept from a child. But knowing was one thing and deciding was another. It was confusing. Stainless steel and white gowns could not seduce her but nor would she take matters into her own hands. This getting rid of was more complicated than she'd realised.

Shaking off the remains of her dream and remembering, pushing all thoughts of deciding to the back of her mind, Becca forced herself awake and out of bed. She dressed carelessly in yesterday's clothes: a pair of black trousers, a creased T-shirt and a navy-blue jumper. In the bathroom she closed her eyes and washed her swollen face in the basin. With a cursory glance in the mirror she pulled back her thick, wiry hair and twisted it into submission. Her reflection was filled with sleep still and her eyes, which changed colour like the sea, were pale, more green than blue. Her face already looked different; she was surprised no one had noticed. It was drawn in, hollowed out. She couldn't be bothered with make-up; instead she abandoned the mirror, went out into the hallway, put on her coat and left the flat. Out on the landing she looked across the Creek, registering the distant hum of the power station and the grey November sky. The Thames was briny with flood tide. She held her breath to stifle her nausea and went out into the winter air.

Becca hugged the line of the wire, the fence crowded with the detritus of days, as she made her way to the Broadway. She shouldered the used plastic and the crumpled can of the fast-food fix that crackled and shifted in the wind, caught like scaly, lifeless fish in a thick diamond net. She closed her coat about her and bent her small frame against the cold. She had to find Joe. She needed to buy bread and cigarettes, chocolate, a Crunchie maybe, a bunch of flowers and then a cup of coffee at Rosa's.

Rosa's was warm and steamy. It smelt of fried bacon and bitter coffee. Joe was not there. He was most likely still in bed or in the bookie's. The monster Gaggia sucked and hissed, filling the air with a hoarse, throaty roar. Rosa stood at its pipes banging out its grounds, for only she with her devotion could coax the machine into life, squeezing from it the thin trickle of dark liquid. Becca had watched her perform such rituals with the intricate, knowing care of a musician tuning her instrument. Rosa was the Paganini of espresso and Becca her apprentice.

For the perfect espresso, Rosa said, you needed only three ingredients: good fresh coffee, the best equipment and know-how. Rosa knew how. She told Becca about it the day they first met. Becca had been sitting there eking out her coffee, waiting for Joe who'd failed to turn up. The café had emptied and Rosa had come to sit next to her with more coffee. They'd chatted easily and before long Becca had become acquainted with Naples and Gambrino's, the golden *sala*, where Rosa had learned her trade. Becca understood Rosa's longing for the blue skies of her childhood, for southern warmth and certain comfort. And not for the first time Becca had found herself drawn to a woman older than her, a woman with daughters, a woman who might have been her mother. Rosa was real. She was plump and always there, telling her it was time to stop biting her fingernails, bringing her the dark chocolate she adored, scolding her for smoking too much. Rosa was always there. She did not run away.

Rosa turned from the Gaggia. 'Becca, how are you? You want coffee and bacon? I'll bring it over – yes?'

'Just coffee,' shouted Becca, sitting at one of the tables by the window and settling into the delicious warmth. She rubbed a hole in the steam where she could watch for Joe. There were three or four others scattered about, heads in newspapers, but no one she knew. Rosa arrived with coffee in a wide white cup and saucer. She sat opposite Becca and spread her hands on the marble top of the table.

'How are you?' she asked. 'You look tired and pale; you're working too hard. That's why I don't see you?'

'I'm not working anymore. I've given up, told them I was ill.' Becca grinned, hoping Rosa would not disapprove, and then lit a cigarette. 'These are for you,' she said, pushing across the table in Rosa's direction the small bunch of violets she'd bought in the market on her way.

'Becca, you shouldn't, there's no need, thank you, but what about the job?' Rosa pouted and raised an eyebrow. Becca decided to hold back on the full story.

She'd not been the one to tell them. Joe had done that. He had gone down to the tax office and told them. A sudden affliction, very debilitating, personal difficulties, that sort of thing. Becca liked the way Joe had not minded doing that. He was good at it; it was a kind of speciality with him. He delivered such apologias with intelligence and wit. His graceful charm was evasive and not easily refuted, and he had no conscience when it came to lying. He was quite honest about it, had got her out of a tight spot, out of a dreary and depressing corner of schedule D. Out of an office full of dry old men and dusty files where the fear of a lifetime spent thus had grown around her until she felt paralysed. Joe understood for he was equally afraid.

'I'm OK. I'll feel much better now I don't have to work and I can still sing and rest and think about what I'm going to do – maybe take up the piano, study music, who knows – and I'll see more of Joe,' she added, drawing deeply on another Piccadilly, the last from her packet of ten. With the in-breath came a moment of nausea before the nicotine rush.

'You'll ruin your voice with those cigarettes. Anyway, singing is no living and singing in pubs – what would your mother think?' said Rosa, without thinking, for she knew all about Pauline, or all there was to know. 'It is dangerous when men are drunk and fighting around you. I don't think it's good. Maybe you should work here? You're good with the Gaggia, the only one who can make it really work, apart from me. I don't know, something else if you like but not in the pub.' Becca nodded a kind of agreement but the pub was fine by her. Rosa left to find a jug and water for the violets which were beginning to wilt.

The first meeting of the day was at Haydock Park. The bookie's was quiet. A couple of slack, inconsequential figures studied the form – grey men wreathed in smoke, prematurely aged and paupered by life and Ladbrokes. The floor was a no-man's-land of discarded betting slips and fag ends. This was a male habitat. Women entered it briefly to find their men or place a bet with money they didn't have in the hope of defying loss. Becca tasted the stale tobacco and fermented alcohol on the air. She felt like throwing up. She could see at a glance that Joe was not there, closed the door and set off back across the Broadway to the flats. She bought bread, a Fry's Chocolate Cream bar and ten cigarettes on her way.

Becca let herself into the flat. It was light. He was up. She put her head round the door of the front room. Joe was stretched out full length on the brown shag pile rolling the first joint of the day. It needed Hoovering, the shag pile. Tobacco, grains of cannabis, fine shreds of Rizla and stale biscuit crumbs lived in its twists.

'I've been looking for you,' she said, 'Rosa's first and then the bookie's. Aren't you betting today?'

'Dunno,' said Joe, 'haven't looked yet.' He got up and stood next to her. 'Do you want some of this?' He handed her the long unlit joint, his fingers brushing hers. She wondered, should she? Would it quell or worsen the sickness? Would it gnaw away at her, creating an edgy paranoia, a fear of what grew inside? Maybe it would flush out her anxiety, carry it away. But there was no real decision. She drew on it as he held the match up. She sat down and leaned back against the old doubled mattress that served as a settee. The room was empty apart from a TV in the corner and a stereo on a low table to one side of the fireplace. Unlike Becca, Joe did not believe in keeping things. On the floor beside the rolling gear sat a hefty ashtray full of cigarette ends and torn corn-flakes boxes. In the corner a solitary spider plant ailed, pale and sickly.

Joe brought coffee. 'Are you alright?' he asked. The colour had drained from Becca's face.

'I'm fine,' she said too quickly, then hesitated. She thought of telling Joe about her dream that morning but decided against it. 'I need a rest then I'll be fine. I told Rosa about work this morning but . . .' She stopped, she needed to get to the bathroom. Once there she vomited thinly and instantly into the pan. Her head spun and she embraced the cool porcelain, putting her forehead to it, steadying herself. The smell of egg frying in cheap oil enveloped her as it drifted in from the kitchen. She stood up and breathed deeply as if preparing to hit a high note.

'Do you want a fried-egg sandwich?' shouted Joe from the kitchen. Becca imagined a loose, undercooked egg settled between two insipid slices of white bread.

'No thanks, just a coffee.' By the time she had wiped the traces of sick from her chin with the pink toilet paper and gone back into the living room, Joe had eaten his egg and her coffee was waiting. After a few sips she reached in her pocket and brought out the Fry's Chocolate Cream and began to unwrap it until she reached the thin layer of foil. This had a tendency to stick to the chocolate so she peeled it with care, then held it out to Joe. He shook his head. She broke off a piece and put it in her mouth.

'So what did Rosa say?'

'Oh she's worried but what else would you expect?' said Becca through a mouthful of chocolate. 'Doesn't think I should sing in the pubs, wants me to work with her in the café, somewhere safe. Worried about what my mother would think.'

Joe smiled, 'Well she's not to know, she doesn't know how you feel.'

'But she does, of course she knows, I've told her,' protested Becca. 'Why don't people listen?'

'It's hard when it's not what they want to hear, you know that, Becca. They think they've listened but they wrap it up in their own experience and it comes out different or with bits missing — like us I suppose. Anyway you know Rosa means no harm, she's just fussing.'

Becca couldn't argue with that. It wasn't Rosa's fault, and besides, her life felt like an incomplete jigsaw with strangely shaped holes in the sky and crucial straight edges missing, so that it could never be complete or contained – her self, leaking and invaded. She was different from the others she'd grown up with, the families on the estate with their neat gardens and cosy front rooms. If only she were more like them. Perhaps one day she would live in a house where the cushions matched and the dinner was on time, she thought about it sometimes, children and washing on the line, but she couldn't imagine herself living like that or growing old. Becca imagined she would have to die young.

The only time it was different was when she sang. Then the veil lifted, the edges were clearly defined, and she was complete. A little coke could have a similar effect. With a little coke inside her she sparkled with confidence, felt beautiful and sang like Billie or Ella, depending on her mood.

'Can you get some coke for Saturday? I can give you some towards it.' Becca reached immediately for her purse. 'What about the painting? Will he take that? It's not far off finished, is it? And you know how much he likes it.' She gestured towards the canvas. The painting was in oils and based on a

Matthew Smith nude. Joe had been to see it in the Tate: *'Fitzroy Street Nude No 1'*. Becca had gone with him and while he'd made sketches and notes she'd sat before a Turner sunrise allowing the colours to wash over her, reminding her of those early mornings out on the estuary with Lilli, when the sky was like a lemon rose blushed with pink and when for an hour or two she could forget the anger and recrimination that lurked at home. Joe liked the Matthew Smith for its raw clash of red and green. He liked to think of himself as a *fauve*, seeking the excitement of contrast and exaggeration. When Joe talked about his painting, Becca thought it was pretentious shit – not that she said so – but she liked the picture. It was unmistakably a painting of her. John would definitely want the picture, Becca thought, just as he wanted her.

'Why don't you get started?' she said. 'I'll make us more coffee and tidy up a bit while you paint.' The morning stretched before her, Joe absorbed in his painting, she moving quietly around the flat, watering the plants, washing up. She smiled inwardly and began to hum a song about morning and blackbirds to herself. She disappeared into the kitchen.

Joe stood back and considered the canvas. It was good, worth a lot more than a gram or two of coke. But he could do a good deal with this picture, keep them in gear for a while, and maybe help Becca relax. She wasn't looking good. She was thin in the face suddenly and her skin had taken on tones of grey and green. He looked closely at the painting. It was nearly finished although the left-hand corner needed more work. It lacked balance but he could fix that. Immediately drawn to it, he picked up his wooden palette and began to squeeze burnt umber from its twisted tube. Taking up his brush he mixed and moved the paint until it was ready to apply.

Becca, returning from the kitchen with mugs of coffee, stood silently watching Joe, his wide shoulders bent to his work. She felt a surge of warmth and unexpressed tenderness for him. It burnt a hole in her. She wanted to reach out and touch him, feel his comfort, if only momentarily. But she couldn't afford to make any more mistakes so she resigned herself instead to watching. She moved around the room quietly then lit a cigarette. She sat smoking, content in the realisation that she was where she wanted to be and that was enough.

Songs and Wishes

'Want some of this?' Joe asked. 'Here,' he said, without waiting for a reply and offering her the mirror on which he had shaped six neat lines of cocaine. Becca snorted three through a rolled-up note. She was starting to feel nervous. She was always like this before she sang. Living in a permanent state of nausea she found it difficult to tell whether her stomach was contracting with the usual nerves or whether the desire to vomit accompanied the tingling in her breasts. Her stomach was empty, which probably didn't help, but she couldn't eat before she sang and she never drank. The bottle of cheap wine in her fridge remained unopened. Drinking and singing did not mix and singing was too precious to spoil.

For Becca, song was existence. Providing she knew the song she could find her way. In her songs she could retrace her steps, evoking fragments of her past, but she could make new journeys too. When she sang she was weightless, moon walking, taking great leaps, leaving footprints in the dust. She swam in lunar seas: The Lake of Dreams, The Ocean of Storms. Her songs were wishes, like bubbles blown and floating in the atmosphere, growing and expanding, heavy with their own weight. When she sang she felt the power of her voice as it cut through her audience, then came back to her, breaking down their defences, shoring up her own.

So no food, no alcohol, but coke was perfect. It kept her sharp and confident and only called up the souls of the good.

* * *

Becca started singing the day Billie Holliday died. She remembered it, her mother Pauline playing 'Good Morning Heartache' on the radiogram with the arm back for repeat play, even though her father was in the house. Pauline with tears running down her cheeks, her record collection stacked on the sideboard behind her. Billie Holliday had been Pauline's favourite and it was she who taught Becca to sing.

When Pauline left shortly afterwards she took nothing with her but her clothes. Becca found it hard to understand. She was sure Pauline would come back, if not for her then at least for Billie. Her father Terrence had wanted to throw the records away but Becca had shouted and screamed, 'No,' taking him by surprise, and she'd won out in the end. The records and the Dansette record player were removed to her room, out of the way of his anger. Becca played them over and over, copied and sang and sang and copied, calling her mother back. But Pauline did not come back and it was more than a year before a postcard arrived with a postmark she could not make out.

Becca never stopped singing. Songs lived in her head, playing through the day, and at night she sang to her toy animals and dolls. It kept the demons at bay and reminded her of happier times. The radiogram on, Pauline singing while cooking the dinner, slow jiving with Terrence in the back kitchen. Pauline and Lilli's mother Vera getting ready for a night out with the girls from the factory, hair rollered beneath their scarves, feet up, drinking gin and singing 'Ain't Nobody's Business'.

The gas fire whispered in the small room. Becca's flat was round the corner from Joe's on the second floor. Unlike Joe's, it was homely, warm and overcrowded. Becca had crammed it with her junk-shop foragings and bits from home. She threw nothing away if she could help it. The back wall was papered with pages she'd torn from magazines. They'd been a great find, a soggy box full of *Woman and Home* and *Wilson's Woman's Journal*. From them she'd constructed a collage of lives firmly anchored in home and family, where pink blancmange and Fairex, embroidery transfers and knitting patterns, Californian Syrup of Figs and Bovril cried out to Becca as a reminder of what Pauline had escaped and what she had missed.

Pauline's record collection was stacked high in a corner of the room and on top sat Lilli's doll, Marianne, with her stiff nylon hair and purple crocheted dress. Becca had wanted to return it but the chance had never come and she'd kept it as a way of not saying goodbye and as an omen for the future. Patterned boxes, diamante shoes and chiffon hats cluttered the remaining three corners. In the hallway stood a full-size mannequin in a Frank Usher dress. Becca, who wore trousers and mostly black, and who didn't go in for frocks, thought the blue-and-white-printed nylon beautiful. It reminded her of the seersucker skirt Pauline had given her on her seventh birthday.

In the whole flat the only clear space was the surface of the long oak table that stood in front of the double windows. Becca sometimes put a vase of flowers on it, but nothing else. She liked to eat and sit there in the light, like now when a faint glow from the streetlights suffused the room.

Becca sniffed, rubbed her nose, then pinched it. The coke hit the back of her throat. 'Shall I put some music on?' she asked Joe, who lay stretched out on the eiderdown that covered the old high-backed bed.

'I'll do it,' he said, jumping up. 'You finish getting ready, we need to go soon and get the sound check done. You know what Derek's like.'

From the red gloss bathroom Becca could hear Joe in the other room tapping out rhythms on the chair leg. She looked into the mirror above the basin. Her small oval face was drained of colour and her eyes, more blue than green, wore heavy, dark circles. She took a bottle of cheap, liquid foundation from the glass shelf and unscrewed the white top, tipping it gently into the palm of her left hand and releasing a small puddle, which she began to work with her fingertips. Her left hand shook and the mirror moved. She leaned against the basin and closed her eyes. She breathed in, then opened her eyes. Her reflection held steady and she returned to the task of applying the crème, starting with streaks down her nose and across her cheeks. As she moved around the contours of her face she heard the voice of Dylan, 'on the heels of Rimbaud', hot and raw. The track filled the air, it came clear and bouncing with light like crystal. She smiled at herself in the mirror, for once she liked what she saw; the wide-necked shirt and the wiry hair, unloosed and full. Becca blacked up her eyes and began to sing along, loosening up her throat and letting her voice explore the air.

The Dartmouth Arms was in darkness when they got there. Joe knocked on the side door and they waited for Derek, who hit the light switch, slid the bolts and let them in. The normally shabby interior, ground in with the stale smells of tobacco and alcohol, sparkled. Derek poured a couple of brandies while Joe went over to the gear, which stood at the back of the main bar.

'How's it going then, B?' drawled Derek, pushing a brandy towards her across the bar. Usually his use of this diminutive annoyed Becca, as did the patronising tone he used with her, with all women. Tonight it didn't matter.

'Got to go down your place myself, you know, sort out my tax.' He shook his head. 'Christ, I wish they'd get off my back. I've got enough to worry about just now. I mean Christ knows. They ought to leave blokes like me alone – only trying to earn an honest crust and they hammer us – the bastards.'

'I've finished there,' said Becca. She played with the brandy glass in front of her, tipping and swirling the liquid, drinking nothing. 'I couldn't stand it any longer.' She felt a sudden rush of pleasure at the release, enjoying over again how good it felt to be rid of the place and the people in it.

'You're well out of there, girl.'

Becca smiled. 'I know,' she said, taking off her coat. She was warming up. 'How's Jenny?' It was out before thinking and she felt a knot of anxiety catch her breath.

'OK, but she's knackered. She's on the couch with her feet up now. It's only six weeks to go. Well, I'll be glad when it comes, can't come soon enough, she looks like a bloated cow and she's scared stiff. First and bloody last I say. Any more and we'd have to move out, there's not enough room here now as it is. Always complaining, she is. Says it's no life for a kid, growing up in a pub? I say why get pregnant then, why bloody bother?'

Becca nodded although she was no longer listening. She was thinking of Jenny and her inflated body and her own fear. Next week she would go down to the market, buy something for the baby, something for Jenny too.

Joe called her over for a sound check. Mick and Dave had arrived and the first few customers were drifting in. It was always jazz night in The Dartmouth on a Friday. Derek was an enthusiast. He liked the big bands best, Artie Shaw, Count Basie and The Duke, and he liked playing the saxophone; gave him a hard-on, he always said. He liked Becca, well more than most women. He admired her because she could sing. She was some singer. She had all the technical ability, great timing and pitch, but there was more. It was the way she could make you feel the song, the words and the feeling, almost as good as playing the sax. That was her success. That's why she sang in his pub – that and the fancying bit.

Becca watched the bar fill with people out to forget the week and have a good time, happy that it was Friday. Becca liked Fridays too, times when Terrence would come home with fish and chips, even play a couple of rounds of gin rummy before he made off for The Top House. Friday, a day to pin your hopes on, better by far than most days.

By the time the band kicked off with 'Love is Here to Stay' the bar was packed and full of noise. As the early, relaxed rhythms gave way to swing, Becca felt her voice come thick and sweet, improvising across a canvas of cigarette haze. Scatting from melodic highs to gritty lows she watched the smoke drift by. She saw the room as if through a faint veil, like dusk in the city. She could just pick Rosa out, sitting at the back. She was surprised to see her. She'd not really expected her to come. Pubs were not Rosa's sort of places, she disapproved of them. Becca had heard her say more than once that only women looking for men went into pubs.

Other familiar faces caught her passing eye but did not distract. Becca swung her voice into the last number of the first set. The pub was hot. Her hair lay damp on her face. The tempo and volume rose and the music that had gently washed through the place threatened to drown. Joe closed it down on the drums and the crowd whistled and applauded.

Becca made her way through the bar towards Rosa, stopping first for a lemonade. 'I'm going to sit with Rosa,' she told Joe, who had squeezed in next to her and was starting on his first pint. Turning towards Rosa, Becca threaded her way through the now overcrowded pub, saying hellos here and there, smiling at the generous responses to her singing. As she approached the corner table she realised that Rosa was not alone. Rosa was sat next to a man, a man wearing a dog collar.

'Becca, that was so good, so good,' cried Rosa, taking her arm and drawing her in. 'I didn't know you could sing like that.' Then shyly, like a young girl introducing her first love, she said, 'This is Patrick, Father Patrick, from St John's, you know.'

'Hello,' said the priest, extending his hand. Becca looked at Father Patrick, a child's painting of a man with a round face and ears at right angles. She guessed him to be about thirty-five, the generation between hers and Rosa's. She was immediately suspicious. What was he doing in a pub, and with Rosa? What was she doing? Surely women of her age in pubs were only looking for one thing and why was he smoking? He put his cigarette out, offered her one from his packet and took another for himself. Was he a chain smoker, a chain-smoking priest?

'I enjoyed the band,' he said with assurance, as if he were a man who knew about music.

'Did you?' said Becca. 'It seemed to go OK. It's pretty full.'

'Do you sing here every Friday?'

'Most.'

'Anywhere else?'

'Wherever I get the chance.'

'Do you make a living?'

'We don't make much but that's not really the point.' The question seemed impertinent.

'What about the church? Have you ever sung there?'

'No,' replied Becca, laughing at the suggestion and looking at Rosa who was looking at Patrick.

Well that could change . . . that could change, most definitely. What about the crypt, that would be a fine place to play surely?'

'I don't know. I think you'd have to ask Joe about that.' Becca looked in Joe's direction and saw him making his way to the backroom behind the bar. 'I'm off, I'll catch you when we finish,' she said; already on her way. She glanced back at them. There was something about him. Rosa definitely thought so.

A few more lines and they were ready for the second set. The music took off as they ran through a few standards and into 'Summertime'. Becca knew she made it look easy, careless almost, but while she was calling up a memory, a face, a feeling, she never let go of the strings which made it work. She tapped a gentle beat with one hand on her thigh, closed her eyes and let her head tilt. Then she was lost and weightless, her being centred in her gut and chest – breathing, smelling lilac on the air, tasting strawberries, walking the shoreline with Lilli, watching a skylark above the meadow. In her song, in the orange, nicotine interior of the dark pub,

Becca conjured the happiness and the heartache of a summer's day. The ardent heat of summer love, the black eclipse, when what you felt did not match the blue of the sky or the white of the sands.

The set finished with a dramatic and bluesy 'Come Rain Come Shine'. Becca let her voice shimmer and spiral to a close. She moved across to Rosa and Patrick, as the pub slowly began to empty, and waited for Joe. When he joined them it was Rosa who introduced him to Patrick and they fell straight away to talking jazz and blues. Rosa, flushed and attentive, listened in. Becca remained lost in the music. The sound reverberated in her ears like the amplified whoosh of the baby's heartbeat she'd heard on the radio earlier that week. She worried why Jenny hadn't come down and wondered if a speck of a baby could hear a voice. She shook her head as if to dismiss her thoughts.

It was past midnight when they left. Derek was still dealing with the night's debris in the stark silence. The Dartmouth, like Cinderella at twelve, had returned from glittering palace to grey hearth. Outside the long-necked streetlights hissed, like orange-headed cobras poised to strike, casting arcs of yellow and catching the first soft flakes of snow. It fell haphazardly, dissolving in wet patches on their shoulders, settling like spots on a fawn, on the back of Joe's coat. Becca imagined the same snow falling on the flat fields and moors, settling and marking the skeleton of the land and the outline of its clothing. But this was the city. It was warm, and snow would not settle here, not such quiet, benevolent snow as this. Becca took Rosa's arm. Joe and Patrick walked ahead.

'I like your priest,' she said, drawing herself into Rosa's side. It was true, despite herself, despite the already growing fear that he might take Rosa away, she liked him.

'Yes, he's a good man. I didn't expect him to come to the pub though. Not many priests would, I think. I don't know what they'll think of him?'

'Who?'

'The others from the church, who go to mass, the women. What will they think?'

'Well who cares?' said Becca. 'It doesn't matter. At least he's human. So he drinks and smokes and likes music. It's not a crime, is it? Better than sitting around praying all day or getting a hard-on listening to all that lust and self-abuse in the confession box, wallowing in all that sin.'

'Ssh, stop, you're wicked, Becca,' Rosa said, smiling. She knew she should be shocked, should express it, but secretly she enjoyed the way Becca just came out with things. 'You shouldn't talk like that. You should try going to mass, it might do you some good, eh? You ought to.'

Becca let it go without reply. There was no way she was going to mass. Her brief relationship with the Catholic church had come to an abrupt end when Pauline left. Despite the dogged efforts of Father John, who visited regularly in the hope of finding Terrence sober enough to discuss his return to the faith, Becca stayed away. She kept well hidden on his visits, usually out in the back shed, amongst the bicycles. Becca could think of no good reason to go to church and praise the Mother of God when she had no mother of her own and when God had seen fit to do fuck all about it. Nothing had changed. But Becca kept her angry thoughts to herself, for love of Rosa, not wanting to upset her.

'They say he will forgive any sin, whatever you confess, birth control as well. He understands.'

'Who?'

'Patrick, at confession. The women are pouring in.'

'Then they won't give a monkey's what he does,' said Becca, remembering only too well how her own mother and others like her had wrestled with fertility and conscience. 'They won't mind if he drinks or smokes or whatever else he does, will they?' She grinned.

As they reached the railway arches Patrick turned to say goodbye. 'Are you coming this way, Rosa? It's quicker and I can see you home safely.'

It was true. The shortcut led alongside the arches to the high-walled lane that ran between Patrick's house and the church and then led into the high street. Rosa smiled in agreement, hoping he had not heard any of their conversation.

'Don't forget to come and see me about the crypt,' he said to Joe. 'Goodnight, Becca.'

Rosa kissed Becca on the cheek, said goodnight to Joe, then disappeared into the shadows of the arches with Patrick.

Becca and Joe walked on and up to her flat. Once inside they were suddenly ravenous and they set about making cheese and tomato sandwiches. They drank tea and smoked a joint before they got into the high-backed bed where Becca curled into Joe's back with her thumb in her mouth.

Rock Pools

Toast. Joe was bringing her toast. Making it in her kitchen. Becca lay with the sheets pulled over her head, obliterating the world and creating her own camp, pink and embryonic, beneath the soft flannelette.

He'd been up and out early, bringing back chocolate, milk and *The Racing Post*. When Becca woke up he was sat at the table studying the form, drinking tea and rolling the first joint of the day. Becca had made straight for the bathroom and thrown up. Crawling back into bed she'd lain half awake, listening to Joe coming and going. His presence was comforting, as was the quiet drone of the radio and the lunchtime news and football round-up. Something about the BBC voice, she thought. The immutable male voice that inspired confidence in his news, his facts, his world – while you lay small in yours with the smell of frying bacon drifting up steep stairs on the radio waves. On rare Sundays with her grandparents it had been like that. Her grandmother cooking breakfast, then out with grandfather and Chang, his white-haired dog, his love, along Berrow Sands. The dunes on one side, the incoming tide on the other and the lighthouse on legs ahead. That world, where all you had to fear was the quicksand out on the tidal flats, onto which you never ventured in case it sucked you in to your neck and you couldn't be pulled out.

'Shit,' cried Joe as he bumped into the mannequin in the tiny hallway, spilling tea on the Frank Usher dress. Becca smiled. He did it frequently, each time imploring her to get rid of it, pointing out its size in relation to the space. Becca knew it annoyed him but liked to keep it and was always careful never to bump into it herself.

'That fucking thing,' protested Joe, 'I don't know why you don't get rid of it.' He handed her half a cup of tea and toast.

'Thanks,' she said, eyebrows raised. They laughed. Becca tried to eat and this time it was Joe's turn to raise an eyebrow. 'It's the coke,' she said as she struggled to ingest. 'Always gets me like this the next day – that and the adrenalin.' It was true; to a degree. Her body, her joints and limbs, ached. Her head felt like a walnut trapped inside a pair of nutcrackers slowly breaking open.

'We should go and see Patrick,' suggested Joe. 'I like him. He's all right, and he's serious about us playing in the crypt. He wants us to go and have a look and see what we think, maybe take Mick and Dave later, try out the sound. He said to come today, Saturday, in the afternoon, not his busy day.'

'I don't know,' said Becca, now propped up and feeling less sick. 'It's the church, all that religious crap. I don't know if I want to get involved.'

'So what? I don't see what difference it makes who or where. It's playing and money. Anyway what's your problem with religion? You're always talking about forgiveness. I would have thought it suited you to play there. Besides he wants to pay us, we need money. He even asked me if I'd paint something for the church or his house. He talked about a commission.'

'That's ridiculous. He doesn't even know if you can paint.'

'Rosa told him.'

'Well what does she know? I mean, really, has she ever seen anything you've painted?' Becca was angry and suspicious. She didn't like Patrick today. Who was he, this priest, this holy smoke man, to come barging in on their lives the minute he met them?

Becca and Joe. Joe and Becca. Always together, always. Never talking about the things that mattered, just in case, just being. Safe with each other so that others were not necessary, did not really stand a chance. Men and women, transient lovers, drifted in and out of their lives changing nothing.

   She'd first realised her feelings for Joe the day of her sixteenth birthday. It was after a visit to the local Co-op when they had returned home hungry, with bread, milk, a box of Sugar Puffs, a celebratory chocolate cake and a pomegranate. They'd devoured the chocolate cake, then halved the fruit, picking at its translucent seeds with pins. Impatient, they had sunk their teeth into the red cups, ignoring the sour skin to rake out the flesh. Juice had run down their chins and they'd wiped the bittersweet liquid from each other's faces. It was then, then, she'd wanted to run her fingers down the face of this beautiful green-eyed boy, down into the hollow below his cheekbone to his jaw. She hadn't of course, had taken her hand away, but ever since, uneasy feelings had trailed her. She felt like an inky mollusc, fearful of its shell prised open to reveal a secret silver interior, a soft, fleshy pouch.

   It was risky, very risky, the way she felt about Joe because you weren't supposed to have these feelings. They weren't normal. She loved him and knew that any man she wanted resembled him in some way; the shape of his face, his profile, his smile, all part of herself so that she felt like the figure at the pool, in love, gazing in at her own reflection. This incestuous spirit hung on her shoulder, never daring wholly to manifest itself. It stalked her, insistent, until she longed to close up, retreat, to nestle by the other in threads of green algae, in rock pools safe from the wind. It would have been enough to co-exist undisturbed. To be safe with him as she had kept him safe, when there was no one else, when they were children in the guise of women and men, playing house and parentless.

   Joe had been her child, her brother and her child. The one she got up for in the morning, made tea for at night, played with to drown the angry voices. Told stories to, told not to worry, told what they would do and how they would make a life, but never told, especially now, never told it all.

Joe and Becca. Becca and Joe. Always together since child-hood. He admired her, felt she was the one who knew about life and people. She was the best person he knew to talk late into the night with. She calmed his unspoken fears. She reminded him of the beach in summer, paddling in the sea, its foamy edges running across his feet and the wet sand sucking at his toes. Walking back barefoot from the front down to the bus stop outside the Co-op and waiting for the bus home. On the top deck, in the front seat, driving all the way – home to ketchup sandwiches and Bonanza.

Becca and her music, which at first he couldn't bear because it reminded him too much of his mother but in time grew around him like a second skin. Like the taut skin of his father's drums that he learned to play. Happy times when the caul of music protected them both.

But Becca was strange now and becoming stranger. She was pale and anxious; he'd noticed her sicking up in the bog quite often and now their dependency seemed reversed. Although she asked for nothing he found her needy and he found himself looking after her. He wasn't sleeping right; things were bothering him. He was finding it hard to paint and he was having nightmares. A recurring dream where he crouched shaking behind the war memorial at the bottom of Seaview Road, while a tidal wave like sheaves of corn formed on the horizon. No, Joe was not feeling right and he wondered increasingly if it was time for them to stop sleeping in the same bed, the bed that so closely resembled the beds of his grandmother's house, the high beds of innocence.

'It's about time you got out of bed, Becca,' said Joe edgily.

'What's wrong with you? You look like shit and you're getting too thin again. Anyway, I've got a bet on in the 2.30 at Newmarket. Are you coming with me or not?'

'Fuck off.'

'I will,' said Joe making ready to go.

Becca got out of bed. 'I'm coming,' she said anxiously, 'just wait.'

'I'll go to the flat then and pick up a few things. I'll come for you on the way back, about twenty minutes.' On the way out he deliberately pushed the mannequin hard, so that she wobbled and her handbag slipped.

Miracles and Madonnas

When Joe failed to return, Becca wasn't surprised. She wasn't angry, she made a point of always saying that anger was a waste of time. Instead she went looking. She pushed her way through the Saturday market and its gaudy offerings of pink salt fish, cheap party clothes and tacky cosmetics. Becca felt at home here. It reminded her of their uncle Percy and the October fair; walking together up the long stretch of stalls hung with crinoline dolls, teddies and goldfish to the fairground, to the Wall of Death and the Freak Show, where the Siamese twins lay curled and pickled in a bottle. He had taken them every year without fail after the apples were harvested and pulped.

She searched for a present for Jenny and the baby but found nothing suitable that she could afford. A lace shawl caught her eye but she guessed it would be too much. She thought about taking it whilst the stallholder was busy with a customer but decided against it. It didn't seem right, a stolen shawl for a newborn baby. She would look again when her giro came through.

Passing an empty bookie's, she arrived at the iron gates of St John's, incongruous in the over-decorated high street, standing tall and black, framing the classical facade of the white church within. They were padlocked. Entry was through a smaller side gate that delivered Becca up to the sanctuary of the churchyard. The grass was long and ragged with winter. The trees were bare, apart from the yew. Several large plane trees stood to the back behind the church. In front stood apples, which would blossom in spring, and beneath them a solitary bench.

Becca slowed down. She was glad to be out of the street with its demands and risks, its push and shove and people, people you might have to talk to, the women from the campaign for instance, Simone and Mags. She was surprised not to have seen them but relieved. She sat on the bench and lit a Piccadilly. She was starting to feel guilty now each time she lit up but what was she to do? She depended on cigarettes. They punctuated her day, ordered her chaos. They were hers and without them she was diminished and withdrawn, her rebellion quelled. Without them her nails were bitten to the quick and she had to fight the sometimes overwhelming urge to put her thumb in her mouth.

Becca skirted the side of the church along the high stonewall stacked with slender headstones from old graves. Finding the gate in the wall she was through and into the narrow lane between church and house, which was square and double fronted; solid, despite its flaking paint and powdery woodwork. She rang the crudely fitted electric doorbell and rubbed at a blister of blue paint while she waited. Patrick opened the door and greeted her warmly.

'Becca, come in, come in,' he said, turning sideways and gesturing with outstretched arm. Becca entered the dark interior, catching momentary sight of her pale reflection in the mirror on the hallstand. Patrick led her along the shadowy passage to the kitchen. It was surprisingly light and warm with a window onto the long back garden, dense and full of sprawling lilac. In the centre stood a small table covered with a gingham cloth on which Becca detected the remains of a fry up: a greasy plate with spots of ketchup, cold curled bacon fat and egg yolk dribbling onto the tea-stained cloth.

'I thought Joe might be here,' she said, feeling awkward. 'Has he called? He said he was coming to see you.'

'No, he's not been here,' said Patrick gently. 'Why don't I put the kettle on? What would you like, tea or coffee?'

'Tea please,' said Becca, wondering what she was doing here and what she would say and where Joe was. 'Joe said he was coming to see you about the music and the crypt. I thought he'd be here.'

'Well, he must have been delayed or found something better to do – maybe?'

The Dartmouth, thought Becca – a winner in the 2.30 and a session in the pub. 'Yes he must,' she said.

'Well not to worry. I'm glad you're here. I don't get many visitors, not yet anyway. Not unless it's to arrange christenings, weddings, that sort of thing. I don't know what they think we do in between . . .'

'Visit the sick?' suggested Becca.

'Oh, I forgot visit the sick and the elderly and the dying.' They both smiled. 'It's enough to turn a man to whisky and cigarettes and that's just for starters.'

Becca was warm in his kitchen. She felt comfortable, and as Patrick poured the tea she shrugged off her coat, pulling at her jumper sleeves, draping it over the chair back and settling into the table. Patrick removed the greasy plate and replaced it with a packet of Rich Tea and two mugs. Becca drank and joined the priest in dipping biscuits into the hot liquid, holding on until they were soft enough to suck tea from. He was an expert; she lost one or two along the way and had to retrieve them with a spoon. The tea was topped up and Patrick offered Becca a cigarette. He shared her passion.

'Don't people object to you smoking and drinking?' she asked.

'Like who?'

'I don't know, the Pope maybe. He seems to object to everything.' Then before he could answer: 'I forgot, you're a man, so you're allowed. It's only women and what they do that the Pope objects to isn't it?'

'Not only women, but I grant you women don't have an easy time . . .'

'No, they have a bloody awful time. I'd hate to be a Catholic,' she said vehemently. 'All those thermometers and babies and no choice in it. No choice whatsoever.'

'Well they have the choice, make the choice of faith, Becca, and they know what that means.'

'No they don't, they don't make a choice at all. Did your mother make a choice? Most women are born into it, seduced by Mary and Sunday gloves,' she said, remembering the girls around her and their descriptions of that mysterious and cryptic world. A world of painted idols and incense glimpsed and smelled through the delicate white veil of the virgin. Boxes for confession and limbo for torture. Miracles and Madonnas, and no room for whores.

'You seem angry?'

'You're right, I do, I'm sorry. It's stupid. Anger is a waste of time and it's not fair of me to take it out on you. I don't mean to offend. I'm not angry – just.'

'There's no offence. I know what you mean. I understand.'

'I doubt if you do,' said Becca. 'I've seen it, you know, desperate women, desperate for some control over their fertility and their life, over their own body, finding desperate solutions. No birth control, no abortion, poverty, hard lives, unrelenting bloody misery.'

'Yes, I agree.'

'You agree?'

'Yes.'

'How can you? You're a priest, you represent the church, you preach it.'

'Do I?' he stopped her. 'Have you been to my church? How do you know what I think or do?'

'Well, why else would you be here? Why else would you be wearing that collar and living in this house if you didn't agree, if you didn't want to be called father and hear everyone's confession?'

'I have to admit confession's the interesting bit, the rest . . .' He lit another cigarette and exhaled loudly. 'I'm no different from thousands of others, Becca. Brought up to be a Catholic priest, eldest, brightest son. It was what my mother wanted, prayed for, saved for. It made sense of her hardship, when everyone stopped her in the street to ask, *How's Patrick doing? Where's his first parish to be? You must be so proud* . . . Not much of a choice, Becca, a question of desperate women, you understand.'

'I do,' she said after a pause, 'I guess there aren't really that many choices we can make.'

You could make a choice all right, thought Becca, and then be stuck with it, strapped into its straitjacket. This was the illusion of choice. With choice, fate was cheated, cast aside, leaving no room for the pre-determined. But once made, choice sealed fate and decided paths and these were not predictable and no one could say what would have happened if . . . if you'd chosen otherwise. If you'd taken a different track. In the end only one way lay ahead. Choosing could be as simple as opening a box of Black Magic chocolates and deciding which to have. But Becca had never been able to decide on a soft centre over a nut, or a caramel over a fudge. Maybe she wanted them all too much, maybe not enough, an orange cream versus a hazelnut cluster, a baby or an abortion? Some things were harder to choose than others. Some we'd rather choose might lead to less choice, those we'd not, to more. For or against, yes or no, will or won't, stay or go, the temptations of choice. Get me behind thee. Becca felt like jumping on a trans-continental train, the kind Joe was always talking about, and running away across Europe to the East.

'Have you ever been to Europe?' she asked.

'I've been to France, near Arles, a monastery to the west by a beautiful green river, where they made red southern wine. I was pretty pissed most of the time. Not really cut out for the contemplative life, all far too reclusive and celibate.'

Becca was transported to the yellow cornfields and black crows of Van Gogh. She saw Patrick staggering drunk through them.

'Nowhere's perfect,' she said. 'Nobody either.'

'No point in trying,' he said, wondering what it was she wanted to escape. 'Just stick to the singing.'

'And you stick to the forgiving of sins, as many as possible. That's a good thing. I'd better go. Joe's obviously not coming. It'll be dark soon.'

She pulled on her coat and stood up. Patrick showed her to the door. 'Come again,' he said, 'come anytime, Becca.'

'Thank you.' She turned and went back to the gate that swung in the gathering wind and into the churchyard. Emerging from the dusk into the neon night of the high street she was met with a morass of litter from the market, flapping at her ankles, catching on her coat. A little way off she saw another figure fighting with the wreckage of the day. It looked like Rosa.

Across the Flooded Moor

A moon like a fat blue-veined cheese broods jealously over the land, waiting for the sun to rise. Becca and Joe crouch in Percy Upham's flat-bottomed boat while Terrence stands at the back with a long pole pushing through the water and down into the earth, across the flooded moor. The front of the boat is festooned with willow. As the wind catches its slender, green leaf it blows through like a sail, so that it is no longer necessary to push, so that they drift, all three crouching, holding to the shallow sides, gaining speed until they are skimming a vast moonlit lake. In their wake a trail of silver eels undulate. On the bank Percy stands next to his old carthorse, calling out to them and they turn to see them both disappear, sinking slowly as water sucks and gurgles through the peat, dragging them down, down through the layers; sphagnum, cotton grass and ling, down to the deepest, oldest from the reeds and sedges. Down to the basin of blue limestone, the saucer of the great fen above which they fly.

Becca woke exhilarated, no high tide, no threatening wave, no dream of Pearl – instead memories of Percy. Percy, their uncle, whose remote moor cottage flooded unfailingly every winter, and Arthur, his shiny, black horse, whom she had once helped pull from the ditch. It took about six men to pull a cow from a ditch but a fully-grown carthorse like Arthur was a much bigger problem. At least a dozen were required. That morning in May, after a dry spell, Arthur, in need of a drink but finding his trough empty, had lumbered over to the ditch, stepped into it and stuck fast in the mud at its bottom. Once word got around, chiefly thanks to her and Joe's running between the scattering of farms, the job of roping up and digging began but not until twelve men had been gathered. Stopping whatever they were doing, the men had grabbed ropes and spades and the cider jar to make for Percy's.

Becca had helped dig the slipway up which Arthur was eventually dragged, roped by front and back legs, and rolled onto his side. The black horse had stayed like that for some time, in the recovery position, while the men drank their cider and he regained his strength. When Arthur was finally able to stand, it was Becca who led him back, patting and singing softly in his ear, to be hosed off, watered and fed.

Percy it was who had shown them how to catch eels, the dark delicacy, retrieved from swamps and murky brown rivers. Eels sliding over meadows after seven long years, curling and convulsing their way to the ocean, caught in Percy's nets, by rayballs and spears. Better still the elvers; thin transparent bodies with ghostly black eyes moving up river on the night tide. This was the prize, taken to clandestine rendezvous in Percy's van; cash changing hands, the catch handed over, just enough kept back for a breakfast of scrambled egg and elvers fried in butter.

Percy knew everything there was to know about the wild moor out on the Levels and the people round about. If you went anywhere with Percy you could spend a lot of time hanging around while he stopped to speak to this one or that one. Or a lot of time hanging about outside the local cider house while he and Terrence drank away the night. Percy had drunk whole orchards, crushed and pulped, pips and all, in his time. He'd grown and pressed Yarlington Mills, Lambrook Pippins and Porter's Perfection. But Slackma-Girdle, they were the best and Percy made great play of the variety. Whenever the name was mentioned he enjoyed their childish giggles. He shared their sense of fun. He encouraged their laughter.

She and Joe gathered apples with him from the wet grass

in baskets, lagoons of yellow and red piled high in the cider shed. Washed and crushed to a pulp by men in fat aprons and wellingtons. Becca could see the shed and smell it still; the slanting light of autumn that fell from the small, high window, illuminating the red brick of the interior, her nose full of tannin and acid, snuffing up the bittersweet perfume, pushing and spreading the pomace on the cloth, wrapping it in great wedges. She heard the cranking of the press and tasted the cheese dripping like honey from a comb. She saw herself standing in pools of cider juice, drunken wasps crawling at her feet.

Cider, now there was a drink, said Percy, it made your hair curl. A gallon of cider in the hayfield was every man's friend, for cider quenched the thirst and shifted the body into a happy rhythm of work. Cider sustained. It was after a night of cider drinking at The Ring O' Bells, not wanting to return old and alone again to a damp and empty house, that Percy had taken his gun, the one he used to shoot wild duck, and shot first Arthur and then himself dead.

Becca was sometimes surprised that her father had not gone the same way, a brain poisoned with apple pips. Although Terrence was still drunk most of the time, he was in one piece and working now and again in the timber yard, on the wharf, stacking wood. Becca wondered about going back to see him, at Christmas maybe. But Terrence did not encourage them to visit. The last time they had been home had been about a year and a half ago. A brief visit in a weekend in July when the weather and the seaside had provided sufficient distraction; when they had been mere tourists on a pub-crawl, day-trippers on a Bakers Mystery Tour. It was a risky business. Thankfully they had arrived on a sunny seafront but there were other destinations less favourable. Becca's recollection of the Mystery Tour, embarked on particularly on Sundays by those of her grandparents' generation, had been coloured by her discovery that a popular destination was Hinkley Point.

Hinkley Point nuclear power station loomed on the horizon of her childhood out on the curve of the bay, its crane like a great gallows. It sat, a brooding monster, drawing in, chewing up, spewing out the sea's creatures wasted on the land. She once went there and daren't look. It haunted her like the mushroom cloud she grew up under.

'Do you remember the mushroom cloud?' She asked Joe. 'It was always there every time we switched on the TV. You used to dream about it and tidal waves, you used to wake up crying in your sleep and I had to sing to you or tell you a story to make it better.'

'Hmmn,' said Joe, feeling edgy and still hungover from his session the night before. He sat at the table and helped himself to a square of Caramac from a half-eaten bar, then rolled a cigarette while Becca went to the bathroom. Joe felt as if the cloud still hung above him. He needed to get out from under it, further away into the future and not the past. He'd been thinking increasingly of leaving the city, moving out into the open to paint the landscape. But it was difficult to think of leaving Becca. Becca who relied on him more than ever and for whom he was becoming more and more unreliable.

Joe felt dislocated, alone. He had nothing to give, didn't want to give, the effort of it, the investment. What he wanted was to smoke, drink, play music and paint – if he could. Painting was the hardest. Half trained at a London college, he had drifted away from its scant demands into his own interior world. That's where he painted best but his painting was growing dull and polluted by the city. He needed a change of place, he told himself, a change in light like Monet. He needed to go south to paint the vibrant canvases of Antibes. He needed a room overlooking the sea away from the choking, wheezing city where it wasn't getting any easier to get his breath, what with the cigarettes and the smog. Perhaps it was the spring that called and unsettled him. The prospect of plane trees unfolding their fresh lime leaves and magnolias blossoming in the sheltered avenues warmed by the walls of brick.

He was reading *The Dice Man*. Maybe that's what he would do, let the roll of the die decide, weight the options in favour of leaving – but not forgetting Becca, it was no contest without her.

The baby fluttered and moved inside Becca, like the pickled Siamese twins must once have moved in their mother's belly. She tried to put it out of her mind. Instead she retreated to her dream and conjured the happy times; summer days at Percy's while Terrence helped him mend his boat and she and Joe played on the thick-runged ladders of the hayloft, jumping off into hay so that their arms and legs smelled of grass and clover. Days of eating cottage loaf and cheese from cracked willow patterned plates and pickled onions from bottles, taking their first forbidden taste of cider. She and Joe lying on their backs in the evening sun with the cider jar tipped to their mouths, until Percy had found them and scolded them, then taken them indoors for supper.

What About the Fish?

They'd talked of playing in the crypt for months. Now at last it was happening. Joe had to get out and meet Mick at Patrick's to set it up. He'd imagined the Crypt dark and dank with peeling paint and cold stone. It was cool, yes, but the kind of cool that would soon become hot with bodies and noise. It was dry and surprisingly airy. Becca liked it, although she'd seen straight away that she would have to play with these strange shapes and the ceiling to get it right.

Joe called at Mick's and after several cups of coffee, persuaded him to get up and into his van. They went to The Dartmouth to collect the gear. Derek was not there; instead his brother Mort opened up. Derek was at the hospital with Jen, he said. He was still waiting for news, might even be an uncle now for all he knew – 'God help me.'

Setting up in the crypt was OK once they had negotiated its narrow, twisted staircase. Patrick was there to help and Rosa arrived with coffee shortly after they began – Rosa looking more girlish every time Joe saw her. Happier and younger, he thought.

'Where's Becca?' Rosa inquired as they sat at a slatted folding table and similar chairs, cleaned up in anticipation of the evening.

'I don't know,' said Joe in an offhand way that masked his guilt. He knew that until recently he would have known exactly where she was, would have called on her, checked on her, would have woken with her. But slowly, insidiously, he was letting go. He saw that it hurt her, although it remained unspoken, this withdrawal. He took some comfort in the fact that she was, at least, looking better. She'd put on weight, not much, granted, but enough to lose that gaunt and neglected look she had worn through the winter. And she'd stopped being sick all the time, she was eating chocolate again, so surely she was feeling better. Surely she needed him less now.

'Will she be in the flat still, do you think?' asked Patrick.

'Maybe.'

'I'll go look,' said Rosa.

'No, I'll go,' said Patrick.

Joe was left with Mick. Rosa busied herself with the tables and cleaning. Over the years she had grown increasingly resentful of domesticity, so that the chores and sacrifices, which had once given pleasure, ending satisfactorily with everything in its place, had become burdensome. She no longer cherished the arrangement of oranges in a blue china bowl, plants skimmed of their dusty layers, leaves polished, cushions positioned, tomato and basil waiting in the kitchen. Her favourite smells – basil, olive oil, garlic – no longer gave such pleasure for they were dampened by familiarity and use. She sometimes felt her skin exhaled them as a marker of what lay within, of women who breathed their lives in home and food, whose creativity was captive, whose tears dripped in pasta pans, whose desires stirred in cream sauces, whose love lay on plates warming in the oven. But cleaning at least had become tolerable in the new climate of her life for it was an activity she could perform without design or thought and which left the space she craved in which to invent, fantasise and make an improbable arrangement of the future.

Rosa had begun to daydream. It surprised her to find she could spend so much of her day in this way. She felt she'd given her life over to wishes and imaginings. Her dreams ran amok and had nothing to do with dusters or Hoovers or saucepans. They were, as she was becoming, unpredictable and perturbing. She dreamed of running away, of lying in the sun with Patrick next to her, the warm sand on their skin. She dreamed of passion and romance, of unhindered love and beguiling tenderness. While she ironed, while she polished, while she cleaned, she imagined herself a different woman, in a different place and with a different man.

'I'm out of here in the summer,' said Mick. He was sat next to Joe at one of the small tables. Mick generally said little, remaining withdrawn behind a dense helmet of thick hair. He appeared to have little use for others; a friend or two, not women, not work – he drew his dole at Norman Road – signing on weekly, earning what he needed from dealing, just a small business, mainly dope and occasionally tropical fish.

'I'm thinking of taking the van down through France maybe for the grape harvest in the south, or possibly Italy.'

'Are you?' Joe was immediately interested. This was preferable to the lonely and slightly sinister trans-European train he had been contemplating whenever he lay down and closed his eyes.

'Why not? Nothing to stop me. I can rent out the flat, just the fish to worry about really. Fancy a fish tank? You could keep an eye on them for me, couldn't you? I'll only be gone about six months, less maybe, set off end of May, June, back before winter.'

'What about the petrol, that'll cost a bit?'

'I've got money from the business. Besides I'm not planning on going on my own, might put up a postcard down in the union, see if anyone wants a lift to share the petrol.'

'I'll come,' said Joe, surprising Mick so that he turned quickly to look more directly at him.

'Great. Great, shit, I didn't know you were thinking of going away.'

'I am, I have been for a while. I want to go south,' Joe said, feeling suddenly like a bird about to flee a changing northern climate and its harsh terrain. 'Only don't say anything, not yet anyway. I haven't, you see, said anything, not to Becca or anyone.'

'OK, man, that's fine. I won't,' said Mick and Joe knew he wouldn't.

So that was it, his escape route charted unexpectedly, arrived at by chance, simple, requiring a minimum of effort, rolled out before him.

'What about the fish? I'm going to have to find someone else to look after the fish now.'

'How about Rosa? She's good at looking after things, she could put them in the café . . . or Derek.'

'Derek, you must be joking. They'd be bloody poisoned in no time, all those dregs and fag ash and God knows what.'

'Piss more like,' Joe said. 'Dave might.'

'Yeah, Dave's not such a bad idea, maybe.' Mick drifted away. He took to thinking of his guppies and his catfish.

Joe thought of white canvases and wine. He would tell Becca, of course he would, especially with her having been ill and all. He wouldn't just up and leave without saying anything, leaving her on her own. Not that she'd mind, he reasoned, she wasn't heavy like that. Not that she'd be on her own because there was Rosa, and Patrick now as well. Becca liked him. He could tell. And then there was the campaign and Mags and Simone. She was involved in all of that. She wouldn't miss him and it was a good thing for her to be involved in a cause, she had that kind of energy. And she could still sing, any band would be glad to have Becca sing with them, any band.

Joe and Becca, Becca and Joe, always together in their myopic world, living in symbiosis, like honeypot ants and their aphids. Well, surely it was time for that all to change, for them to move away from each other. After all it couldn't continue. If he didn't get away from her there would never be anyone else. He already feared that no one else would do. Unspoken fear wracked him nightly, fear of leaving her and losing love, fear of remaining and drowning in a sea of high-crested waves like those which inhabited his dreams.

He felt as if he were in some dark, subterranean hole, one

from which he would crawl, only to be blinded by the daylight. He knew he would have to learn to see again. He was thinking of Becca again, thinking of her. Why was it always Becca? He didn't want to think about her. He would stop, he told himself. He began to tap out a rhythm on the table in front of him. He moved over to the drums.

Platform Shoes

Patrick knocked on the door of Becca's flat. Becca heard it but chose to ignore it. She was making tea in the kitchen. It would be Joe, she thought, calling for her to go down to the crypt. She would go later, alone. There was no need for Joe to feel responsible for her. She didn't want it, didn't want him there if it was a chore or a duty. She wanted him there by choice. It was a rule she set herself. It was a kind of a cheat, a way of having without owning up. If it was his choice, then there was no payment or payback, no lingering purgatory of arms and legs akimbo, falling into fires and landing on pitch-forks, mouths open, screaming, eyes wide, worm-like bodies accumulating in pyres. None of that, it was safe. Still, she dreaded the thought of Joe needing her less. It was like the stab of jealousy she felt when he met a new woman, the fear of losing him, of him no longer needing her.

She'd got used to looking after Joe, and others too. The children in the avenue had gathered around her, especially when Terrence was out. And she earned herself pocket money that way. The women came to her when they needed some-one reliable – *She was good with young ones*, they said, *comes of being left like that.*

They played elaborate games. Becca and Joe and the others went on great journeys; travelling on cushions across lino seas to distant lands, dancing on stages, becoming film stars, princes and princesses. They sang. They made a lot of noise. Becca encouraged them for the noise filled the void, the pit of sadness that surrounded her. There were always comings and goings, kids trooping in whenever Terrence was out and sometimes when he was in if the cider or the

113

beer had put him in a holiday mood. Children welcomed in, called in, all except Diane Liversage.

She was the same age as Becca, maybe older by a few months. She was solid and tall against Becca and she made her feel very small for her age. She told Becca what to do, ordered her around and that's when the fun stopped. She made the little ones cry and Becca was powerless. If she saw her approaching the gate, or just through it and walking like a giant up the thin path, Becca would shout, 'Livers. Get down. Quick.' And they would run for it and hide out of sight of the window or the letterbox, behind the three-piece suite or in the cupboard under the stairs, Joe latching onto her, next to her. And Livers would bend and shout through the letterbox, 'I know you're in there,' and they would freeze and remain silent until she'd gone. Then they came out from hiding one-by-one, once they were sure, and Becca would shout, 'Bugger off back to your own house.'

After a visit from Livers they always needed something to eat. Becca made squash if there was any, occasionally there was limeade, then cream crackers and jam, and they ate it under the table in the kitchen with the curtains closed just in case she came back.

Becca did not always let the children in. Sometimes it was bad enough having to look after Joe. Sometimes she would send them away afraid that they might come to harm, or get lost, afraid that something would go wrong and the laughter and singing would change suddenly to tears and regret. She felt the weight of her responsibility. It was a big word. 'You're responsible,' her father would say and she was never sure whether it was something to be pleased about, grateful for, or something to avoid, something that left a knot of unease in your stomach, something that could lead to trouble and blame. It was confusing. It wasn't always easy to work out who was responsible for what. Mostly it seemed to be her, she couldn't get away from it. But then what about when someone did something bad to you? And you felt sad and hurt, whose responsibility was that? 'You make yourself miserable,' Terrence would say, 'It's in your nature, like your mother, never satisfied.' She believed him. But the older she got the less sure she became. Was he right? Probably he was. When she left, when she and Joe left for London, it was one of the things she was glad to leave behind, or so she thought. For it wasn't that easy to get rid of your responsibilities and in the end she was fairly sure if something wasn't right then she was in some way to blame. Joe disagreed. He got angry with her. He said, 'What the fuck has it got to do with you, Becca!'

It didn't help. And she didn't want to see him now. Becca ignored the second knock on the front door of her flat and went back into the sitting room.

Mags sat in the armchair heating tarry oil in a blackened apostle spoon. Simone sat at the table picking and twisting at a matchbox. Becca handed them both a mug of tea. A bitter scent filled the room and sent a shiver through Becca. Mags licked the paper, rolled and turned it, then curled a torn strip from a cornflake box and poked it at the end of the white tube. She lit it and inhaled, shuddering as she did so. Within minutes all three were rooted, felled by the black liquid. Becca stretched out on the bed and looked at Mags.

Mags voiced her opinions loudly and with authority. She belonged to the Communist Party and was sleeping with a prominent local party member, which somehow made her difficult to disagree with. Becca did, from time to time, disagree with her, particularly when she was at her most dogmatic and stupid. 'All men are rapists' was a favourite, unequivocal theme. Becca considered it to be bollocks and told her so. They often argued.

Simone was not like Mags; she was sleeping with no one. She was smaller and thinner, prettier than Mags, with curly red hair. Unlike Mags she was not powerful. Becca felt glad of their female company and their desire to sit and talk. They talked about everything when they were stoned but especially about sex and men and food. It was odd really how women so preoccupied with establishing their feminist credentials were so desperate to talk about men. Becca wondered at times what kind of relationships they made and whether they were ever able to see through their own carefully constructed façades to their dependency on male attention. She wondered what they would say if they knew about her and Joe.

'It's a bowl of soup in the morning,' Mags was explaining, one at lunch and one at night. 'You can mix in any vegetables you like.' Was this a recommendation, Becca wondered; was Mags seriously trying to make this sound attractive or even reasonable? 'I have the odd piece of fruit of course, it's definitely working.'

'Good,' Becca found herself saying. She knew how Mags struggled with her weight and she felt sorry for that. Inwardly she thought it a fucking ridiculous way to eat and that's what she would have liked to say. Instead she added, 'I couldn't do it, for a start I need chocolate too much.' She waved her hand in the direction the half-eaten bar of Bourneville by her bedside.

'You don't need to, although I think you've put some weight on recently?'

The conversation was fractured with cannabis-induced pauses and loss of connection. After a few minutes Simone said, 'I might try it next week. I don't want to put on any weight, especially on my legs.'

Christ, they were obsessed with their weight, thought Becca. How did that happen? Surely feminists weren't supposed to worry about all that? Of course not, but then to be fair there was still a long way to go on that score, still a lot of women with their hands in the sink and the razor at their armpits, herself for one – well certainly the razor bit. That was what the campaign was for.

The campaign group met above the Halal butchers in the high street. Becca went to the meetings, sometimes just to socialise, at other times to support the cause, but she never felt quite a part of it. She was an onlooker, a misfit, and the reason why she did not fit was a puzzle which she edged closer to unravelling but had yet to solve. They were the same age, had the same concerns, shared the same politics, same pop music, same experience – or maybe not. Becca had a sneaking suspicion that this was where the difference lay. Her experience was different. Her growing up, her life on the estate, was different, was not like theirs in suburbia. They'd been privy to a different world of privilege, at school, at home, a different class. It gave them an ease and confidence she lacked. They could always go home to the family, the piano in the dining room and clean linen in the cupboard.

She wondered what they knew about the lives of ordinary women, the kind she had grown up with, the Pearls and Paulines, with their struggles. Becca believed: believed in the Abortion Campaign and equal pay and equal rights for women but couldn't see how anything would change without the involvement of ordinary women, real women. And how was that going to happen when these women were out there hassling to feed and clothe, to pay the rent and gas, when they were battered and bruised by life and husbands?

'She was wearing heels, you know, did you see, and make-up?' Mags and Simone were talking about someone Becca didn't know but for whom she felt immediate sympathy.

'She's got a fur coat, it's disgusting,' said Simone, shaking her head. There was a long silence made of scattered thoughts. Becca looked down at Simone's platform-soled boots. She'd like to see her run to catch a bus in those. She'd been there – hadn't she? – that evening in the room above the butcher's when they'd crammed together on the hard chairs, lights dimmed for the slide show; when the carrier had clicked in the dark throwing its images onto the screen: a peep show of wasp-waisted women in tight metal belts, mistresses of fifteenth-century Venice in their nine-inch chopines, the Gibson girl, corsets of whalebone, a woman and her stays. For what was a woman without her stays? Out of control, loose all over the place, and what was a teenager without her roll-on or panty girdle? Let it all hang out and you got a bad name for yourself. Harness the flesh, keep it in; redistribute and reshape were the name of the game.

This dark, erotic celebration had reached its horrible climax in the slide of the bound foot. An image of mutilation and pain inflicted at the hands of a mother. A foot mimicking a shoe, a white hoof. Its profile was not unlike that of Simone's platforms.

Becca said, 'I don't know how you can walk in those. Don't they kill your feet?'

'They're OK, I'm used to them.'

Mags had gone in the kitchen to make more tea; it wasn't time yet for her soup. She came back and, handing Becca a cup asked, 'Are you coming on the third?'

'Of course.'

'Anyone else?'

'I don't know, maybe Joe and a few of his friends,' she said, knowing she would not ask them. 'I'm not sure.'

'I'll let you know more about the arrangements. We're finishing in Trafalgar Square. We're meeting up tonight to make some banners. DOCTORS DON'T WASH NAPPIES. That kind of thing. What do you think?'

'Good. We're playing in the crypt tonight, come later if you like.' Becca's head began to fill with the words and melodies of songs, the songs she would sing tonight, the songs she'd learned as a child. She sang without opening her mouth while the other two talked. She pictured herself at a piano in a small school hall, playing for the children sat cross-legged on the shiny floor, while the sun filtered in at the high windows. *'All Things Bright and Beautiful . . .'*

Rosa

Rosa was making pasta in her kitchen. She wasn't sure why
or for whom, but pushing and folding served as a kind of
therapy, an involuntary activity, like the dusting and cleaning
which leant itself to daydream, leaving her free to wander
over the past and walk into a future, in a kitchen, at a sink,
where a man stood behind you and wrapped his arms
around you. There was something about being caught from
behind and pulled in spoon-like, as if you were about to
embark on a great feat of daring, a leap from an aeroplane.
She felt she should pull herself together, as they said, and
stop these girlish hankerings. That night in the crypt she
hadn't imagined it, but what to think, she wasn't sure. His
hand on her back, in the dark, the way he drew his chair in
close to hers, the way he looked at her. But no, it was impossible. She must have imagined it. These days she found she
no longer knew what she thought or felt even; she found she
did not look at things in the same way, so that her sense of
the world was altered. She see-sawed from resolutions to
escape to the south coast to her daughter and her grandchildren where a dose of reality would await her, to knocking
on his door and demanding to see him, coming straight out
with her feelings and asking him what it was he felt. These
great shifts from hot to cold, manic to maudlin, sane to mad,
plagued her – was she mad? It was a kind of madness, this
longing for a man fifteen years younger than she was, a man
with whom she had shared nothing, not children, not work
or home, family, sickness, none of it, none of the ordinary
things or events which bound people. Wasn't it all too late
for sharing to be starting again? It was disturbing the way she

felt like a young woman, like an adolescent quick to blush, unsure, hot and hoping, reading – or was it misreading? – the signs. Could it be that she was still learning to read, had never learned properly? The wisdom and security she'd expected with age had fled. The composure that resulted from no longer being desirable or desiring, which she had once looked forward to, eluded her.

She wished her hormones, every last one of them, would shrivel up and die and with them her feelings. No she didn't. She said it out loud sometimes when talking to herself, said it, thought it, but didn't wish it. She couldn't wish it away for it was too intoxicating. It was too heady like a head full of soft red wine and a tongue rolling in pesto and olives.

She wiped her floury hands. There was flour everywhere, on the table, on the floor, on her forehead, over her shirt. Rosa moved away from the table and stood beside the tall open cupboard in which she kept her china. She stretched her hand out to one of its shelves and picked up a bottle of cheaply coloured liquid, holy water from Lourdes. She tipped it and watched the bubble move from neck to base. There was little point in making pasta. There was no one else in and she had no desire to eat alone. There was little point either in looking for miracles in bottles of water. He probably pitied her, she thought. Liked her well enough, yes, well enough to have noticed the wrinkles at the corner of her eyes. When was it people started to notice? When did people say, 'She's showing her age, she's not looking as young as she did.' Would he utter such banalities? Did he think them? Did he say to himself how once she must have been a good-looking woman?

He can't have missed the sagging at the jaw-line and on her neck. She hadn't, she saw it every day in her mirror, well in the worst mirror, the one in the bathroom where the light was cruel. Vanity caught her just as she had hoped to escape, shamed her, stared her in the face. He liked her well enough, she knew that, but *like* was not the territory in which she dwelt; *lust* more like. Tongue-hanging, panting, knicker-wetting lust, she was ashamed to admit. She returned to the floury board. She had known all along, and could no longer pretend, just who she was making pasta for.

Above the Halal Butchers

'We have to align ourselves to the left. There's no other choice. It's the only way we'll ever get anywhere, make any lasting impact. Just you see, on Monday in *The Morning Star*, they'll have something to say.'

Becca had heard it all before. It grated on her and for once she was unable to distract herself with the songs in her head.

'I saw her there, Jenny Morris, that reporter, works on *The Star*. She was there. You can rely on the CP when it comes to these issues, there with us, right behind us, in the struggle.'

'Who reads *The Star*, though?' Becca looked over her wine glass and directed the question at Mags, who was stood in the midst of a group of women and a few token men, all of whom had been on the march that day and were gathered in the meeting room above the halal butchers. 'We want it in *The People*, *The News of the Screws*, fuck *The Morning Star*.' Becca knew she was on dangerous ground but felt herself inexorably drawn towards a showdown; they all looked so damn smug. 'There are a quarter of a million people out of work.' She was warming up. 'They're mostly men of course, men whose women are grubbing about trying to make ends meet. They're the ones who are struggling, not us. What's it like for them?' Her voice grew louder. She was forced to admit to herself that despite her insistence on anger being a waste of time, there were times when it just spilled out, needed out.

'It's them were fighting for, Becca,' said Mags, with a hint of condescension and an exaggerated calm. She looked about her to catch the eye of others, seeking a tacit approval.

'But you don't even know them. You can't speak for them

or fight for them – patronise maybe. All this ideology, this middle-class crap. They wouldn't come within a mile of here, not to something like this, and you wouldn't want them here with their snotty-nosed kids and their short skirts. You can't fight for women you wouldn't even give the time of day to. You haven't got a clue about their lives.' Becca felt the baby turn inside her, twisting in her abdomen. 'It's not that simple anyway, is it? Having an abortion, I mean. You make it sound like catching a bus or clearing out your wardrobe, it's not, it's getting rid of a baby.'

Becca believed in it desperately, in this right to choose, in a woman's freedom to control her own fertility, to decide no more or not at all, to take charge of her body. She didn't want women knocking at the doors of priests and doctors who were waiting forearmed with their sermons and their Hippocratic oaths. She didn't want to hear that it was time a healthy young girl like herself was starting a family. She didn't want women to defer and agree, as she had found herself doing; that the best form of contraception was to say no. Begging for the pill, the magic pill, dished out by men OK if you could find a decent one, even then what then, how did you feel when you took it, what was it doing to you? Well, no matter, there were worse things to worry about than babies in your womb.

There was a man at the Town Hall once who understood; he spoke to them from the platform and said the right things. He knew better than Mags, better than all of them. He said all the things she'd wanted to say, although she hadn't known it until then, about how hard it was, about how giving people choice was not about giving in. That it was only laying another great burden at the feet of women and wasn't that punishment enough? Wasn't it heartbreaking to choose like that? How could there be any rights or wrongs? There was only the agony of decision or its postponement. Becca had wanted to cheer, to shout out loud. He understood.

Becca poured herself another drink and lit a cigarette. 'You don't understand,' she accused.

'Haven't you had enough to drink?' Simone said.

'No, not nearly enough.'

'Well, we try to understand,' said Mags, 'as much as you do, we all know it's not easy. All we're doing is trying to help. Focusing on what needs changing to make it easier for women; to get abortions, equal pay, equality all round . . .'

'Well hurray, bloody great, free sanitary towels all round and vibrators while we're at it.'

The crowded room fell silent. Ignoring the growing look of alarm in the faces around, in what seemed like a sea of bodies without heads, Becca continued, 'You've spent too bloody long looking up each others fannies and criticising men while all the time you're dying to get in their trousers, sleeping with one anothers' men, or trying to.' She looked at Simone who she knew to be sleeping with Mags's man. 'Sisters don't do that – do they? – unless they're hypocrites. That's what you are – hypocrites, you're all fucking hypocrites,' she shouted. Then she turned away quickly and left.

She was hot, burning inside and afraid she might cry as she rushed down the stairs and out into the high street. She hurried towards the iron gates and into the sanctuary of the churchyard. She sat on the bench beneath the blossoming apple, amidst the curled cups of its petals. Shed in the wind they lay sticky on the wooden bench and scattered in the grass at her feet. She lit a cigarette and hoped they wouldn't come looking for her. She realised that it was unlikely, that just now they would be talking over her emotional outburst. Strange girl, they would be saying, odd, not normal, unbalanced, confused. They would use this as proof of their own stability, of the depth of their political understanding.

Becca decided she didn't care. She'd spoken from the heart, like she sang. It was fine to do that when it was what people wanted to hear, when they listened, when they couldn't sing. It was different when they had the song sheet.

She never followed the music. It followed her. She'd never been good at following or at any kind of conformity; it didn't fit with her. Besides, what she'd said had been true. It needed saying. They needed shaking out of their middle-class complacency, from their smug self-satisfaction and their cosy cliques, which made her, and others like her (there must be others like her), feel inferior. It was like taking part in a drama with no script, trying to pick up on the lines, not sure when to come in or where, not sure of what part you were expected to play or if you had been cast at all.

The baby was fluttering about still. She lit another cigarette to calm it. She would smoke it and then she would go and find Joe or Rosa or maybe even Patrick. Perhaps she would tell him what was happening to her, make a confessional: forgive me, Father, for I have sinned. But it was not absolution she sought, it was more like old-fashioned courage, the courage to persist. She'd found enough of it in the past. She'd had to. So why should this be any different? It was the fear that did it, the nagging doubts, the turmoil that grew inside her until it threatened to paralyse. She'd be a crap mother, she'd leave like Pauline, she'd drop the baby, she didn't have a pram, a cot, she wouldn't love it, Joe wouldn't understand, she wouldn't stand the pain, she'd die. She didn't even have her father to help. He was drinking more heavily since they left and she blamed herself. None of this would have happened if they'd stayed at home. She thought about going back, about finding Pauline one day, of searching her out. She dreamed of reconciliation, of ending the separation and hurt. She hadn't planned anything, nothing with any definite shape, but for a long time now she'd begun to consider that this might be the only way. Best not to think about it, she told herself, and she began to sing quietly, a song Pauline had sung to her: 'Hush little baby, don't say a word, Mama gonna buy you a mocking bird . . .'

* * *

'Don't be stupid.'

'I'm not.'

'Yes you are, you're always blaming yourself.'

'It's not that, I'm not . . .'

'Becca, shut up, you're always doing it, always the bloody same. If the world was blown up tomorrow, if a nuclear bomb landed on London, it would be your fault. I mean it, don't look at me like that. It's true. Well how can it be your fault? How can Dad's drinking be your fault?'

'I didn't say it was. I just said if we went down more or if we'd stayed, not left home, we could think about going back for a while.'

'Becca, it's got nothing to do with us, whether we go down or don't, or where we live. He was drinking long before we left. The day she left that's when he started big style.'

'You were too young to remember.'

'Maybe, but I know – I'm right, aren't I?'

'I suppose so.'

'See. So don't go blaming yourself then. I don't get it with you. You can't solve everyone's problems you know, you're not that important.'

'I know. I'm not saying I can, it's just that . . .'

'What?'

'Never mind.'

'What? Come on.'

'I don't know, I get confused and sometimes I wish I could just talk to her and sort things out.'

'Like what? I don't want to talk to her. I don't ever want anything to do with her. Ever.'

'Don't say that, Joe.'

'Why not, I just have. I hate her. No, I don't even hate her. Nothing. I feel nothing for her. It's all her bloody fault. If anyone's to blame for anything it's her.'

'But you can't say that.'

'I can.'

'But she must have had her reasons. I feel sorry for her in a way.'

'You feel sorry for her. You must be fucking mad then. Sorry for her – you're mad, Becca, fucking mad . . . don't start crying, Becca.'

'I'm not.'

'Well don't. Ssh. Come on, Becca. Let's have a cup of tea. Come on, I'll put the kettle on, roll us a number, put some sounds on.'

'No, not music. Put the telly on. I'll make the tea. The sun's come out, we can sit by the window.'

Olive Oil and Coffee

Patrick looked out at the garden. After a day of cloud the late evening sun gave rise to an intensity of colour, catching the sharp green of newly opened leaves and lighting on the budding lilac. In the sky above, an aeroplane stretched a milky trail across the blue. Still he felt grey all around. His celibacy hung over him like a black-hooded cloak, blotting out the light, making him less than human. He was restless and angry with his church.

There were others like him, he knew, who'd wrestled and succumbed. He'd absolved them in the confessional. It could be confessed. There was no sin that could not be confessed and absolved. But the church demanded too much. He'd once had hopes. He'd shared with others the excitement of Rome's awakening when the windows of the Vatican had been thrown open, only to see his hopes dashed against the hard rock of *Humana Vitae* and the shutters screwed back down. Still he listened to the same weary confessions and felt the same heavy chains of priesthood around him, which from the beginning he'd feared.

Patrick moved away from the window and over to his desk where he began a search for a packet of cigarettes that wasn't empty. The room was a mess; haphazard and muddled with piles of clothes, clean and dirty. His desk was strewn with crumpled paper, broken biros, books and papers and a half-empty packet of custard creams. He would have liked it tidier but found it impossible. Inertia grew around him, choking like bindweed. The city closed in on him, providing no escape. He wished for Rosa, a ridiculous wish he told himself. Rosa who smelt of olive oil and coffee, who wore flesh on her bones and the promise of warmth and softness in her smile. He was already sick of the parish, tired of its demands, of its catechisms and collections. He belonged to them. He was tied to their need for forgiveness.

And how could he forgive? Did they not realise? He was sick of the poor and the ill and the needy. He was needy, damn it; couldn't they see that? And damn Rosa, couldn't she see what it was he needed? Patrick looked down at the cat, brushing at his ankles. Damn it, damn the cat. He pushed it a good way across the room with his outstretched foot. Where was she, damn her? She said she'd be there, after she'd finished the altar flowers, and she said she had something for him.

The pasta burned in the oven to a hard-edged and curling brown. Above, the bed creaked to the rhythm of an unsuccessful coupling that had none of the beauty of the prelude but all the passion and release of a final movement. She hadn't known if he would be in or if he would want her there. The wine had helped. They'd drunk enough to approach each other, enough for him to touch her arm, take her glass and put it down before he kissed her. On the way to bed she'd hesitated, a voice inside telling her *No*; she stifled it. This was for her, after all the years of *No*.

Later he had come too soon and she not at all and it mattered nothing. It was their being together, skin on skin, their closeness, his smell, the sky through the window and the trees which filled the frame brushing their leaves against the glass. Now looking out from his bed, now that it was over, they could begin.

'Are you hungry?' he asked. 'Shall we eat the pasta?'

'Yes, but I think it's burning. Can you smell?'

'It still smells good to me,' he said, burying his head into her neck, 'like you. I'll get it.' He banged about in the kitchen and returned with the half burnt pasta and another bottle of red wine. They ate in bed. Rosa felt elated, as if she were twenty-one. Patrick stroked the cat, which had joined them and was sniffing around their plates.

'It's terrible,' she said.

'It's great. I could live with you and eat pasta every day.'

This troubled her. 'What are we doing?' she asked, looking up at him.

'Nothing, there's no harm. There's no harm in loving.'

'But it's mortal sin.'

'I can get absolution. We can be absolved.'

'But not if we keep on. It mustn't happen again.'

'No,' he agreed, remaining unconvinced.

'Have you done this kind of thing before?'

'No, but I've thought about it. I'd be lying if I said I'd never been tempted, but never actually before. Have you?'

'What, with a priest?'

He laughed. 'No, with anyone?'

'Never. I've been faithful for twenty-five years, although I'm not sure why. I don't think he could care anymore as long as I'm there to run the place – you know cook, wash. That was fine for a lot of years when the children were small and we were younger, when there was a struggle. I'm not so sure anymore if it's what I really want. Did you always want to be a priest?'

'Not really. I don't know what I wanted except . . . I think I was always looking for an adventure. When I was young I wanted to be a fireman or a soldier. Then the missionaries came to school, when I was about twelve, it fired me up, seduced me really. I joined up, went to the retreat centre and that was it. That was my adventure, I suppose, my excitement.'

'What about your family, your mother, was it what she wanted?'

'It wasn't like the usual mother's vocation, it wasn't like exactly that, but she was happy enough. A daughter a nun, a son a priest, it was what they hoped for, all of them, because then you were someone in the community, someone to be looked up to, you know – *How's your Patrick, you must be so proud?*

'And your father?'

'Well once it was decided, there was no going back, as far as he was concerned, and when I wanted to, when I thought about going back, he couldn't understand it. You made up your mind what it was you wanted and what you were going to do and you stuck to it. That was my father for you.'

'My mother didn't want me to leave,' said Rosa wistfully. 'I think she knew that sooner or later I would miss it all, the sun and the family and her. She was right. Not straight away of course, then it was love and it was my adventure, I suppose. It seemed daring to leave with a man and start a new life in a new country. A few years later, a few cold grey winters on, it started to feel different.'

'Do you go back often?'

'Not so often, not for a few years. My mother's getting old now. She lives with my sister. I keep thinking I must go back and see her before something happens and it's too late.'

Rosa pictured herself in the tiny courtyard at the front of her sister's house, escaping the heat, in the cool. She would water the peppery geraniums in their window boxes, startling red and pink. She would talk with the women, shop at the market and walk down to the harbour to see the catch.

It was growing dark outside. Patrick was acutely aware that she would soon be thinking it was time to go home, but that he wanted her to stay. He pulled her down next to him under the white sheets. Putting both his hands to her face he pushed back her hair and looked at her.

Rosa wondered how she would look up into his face the next morning at Communion and then remembered that she would not be there. For she was no longer in a state of grace.

Shadows

Becca stands small by the figure of her father, their shadows cast against the mauve of the dawn. The land stretches around them delineated by the long drains lined with the pollarded willow. Water ebbs and flows beneath, sucking and gurgling, rising above the peat in small pools about their feet. A water snake skims the surface of the rhyne causing barely a ripple. Her father digs, down into the moor, into the rich black seam, uncovering with each turn of the spade a pile of fine white bones, the skeletal remains of small mammals, birds and eels. As he digs and exhumes so she collects all, every delicate piece, filling the woven basket at her side until it is brimming with bone; vertebrae and sternum, skull and sacrum. Quickly, he says, don't miss one. Quickly before the sun is up, before they disappear. They work hard as the light grows in the sky, quickly before all is lost again, before the bones are drawn back down into the black morass.

She woke breathless with effort and filled with a fearful urgency. Her head ached and her mouth was dry. Joe was still asleep with his back to her. He stirred as she trailed a finger across his shoulder. She wanted to wake him and tell him that she had dreamed about Terrence but instead she got up and went into the kitchen to make tea.

The filling of the kettle, the reaching down of the mugs woke him – Christ, his head. Christ, he'd slept at her place again, in her bed. He'd promised himself he would stop that. Not that they did anything but sleep, lie close mostly, in between the dolls and teddies. Except that one night, when awash with drink they'd fallen into bed – that night. Nothing had been said, the next day, nothing was ever said. For a while he'd stayed out of her bed but they had soon resumed the old habit, needing the comfort it brought them both. Sometimes it was the only place he could find sleep, and when she'd looked so ill how could he not? But he'd have to tell her now, it was no use putting it off any longer. She'd understand, she always did. He had the money now; a good win, a cert. at fifteen to one, had come in. He'd celebrated with a bottle but given Mick the rest to keep for him. It was about time his luck changed. He wouldn't fritter it away either, this time, and he would leave her some just to help out.

Becca thought it odd that Joe had not gone for his paper. He was up and dressed now but showed no signs of going out. He sat in a shaft of sunlight, drinking tea at the table by the window, motes of dust spinning around him. Becca sat in the armchair and wondered when he was going to roll a joint.

'I'm going away in June,' he announced, 'to France, with Mick in the van. I thought I might as well, he's going any-way . . . just for six months or so, down through France to the south. We can pick grapes or something, earn a bit and then maybe into Italy if the money lasts. Share the petrol, it's cheaper for Mick that way.' Becca sat immobile, saying nothing. 'I can paint when I'm down there. I need a change. I need to get out of the city into the light. You know, like the impressionists, like Monet.'

'You said Monet was shit,' Becca said, her coolness belying her rapid heartbeat.

'I know I did. It's all the calendars and cards, all that pretty chocolate-box stuff that's shit, but he was a great painter, and Cézanne, he worked down there too. Now there's a fucking brilliant painter for you.'

'Apples falling off tables, you mean?' She said it coldly not ready to acknowledge him or sanction his going.

'What do you think then?'

'Why not?' she shrugged. She was shocked. She hadn't seen it coming. But when she thought about it, there had been a change. Lately Joe had stopped looking at her as if she was his. Lately he looked at her as if they were separate. And how did she look at him? Through a changing eye, from a distance. It would be easier – wouldn't it? – if he left. When the time came. There would be less covering up to do, easier to get away with. But she was screaming inside. They'd always been together, always, and now when she needed him he was leaving and she'd lose him just like she had Pauline, just like she'd lost Lilli, suddenly gone and never replaced.

'Can you look after Mick's fish while we're gone?'

'No, I bloody well can't,' she said, fighting back the first tears, biting at her nails. 'They'd die. Anyway, I'm no good at looking after things.' She got up abruptly and went to the bathroom; she didn't want him to see her cry or throw up. She sat on the edge of the bath and closed her eyes to the red gloss walls around her. She pushed her damp hair away from her face and lifted it from the back of her neck. She waited for her heart to slow and her nausea to subside. She would not cry. When she came out he was rolling a joint.

He looked at her anxiously. 'You OK?'

'I'm fine, great. I was thinking of taking a holiday myself, later on, maybe going home for a bit.' She reached for the chocolate by her bedside and pulled at the gold foil and red wrapper. She broke off two squares and put them on her tongue.

'Home? What for?'

'See Dad,' she said, her voice thick with the chocolate. 'Look for her. I thought I might find out where she lives, go and see her. Dad'll know where she is. I want to see her, Joe, don't you?'

'No, I don't and I don't see why you want to. We've already had this. I've told you. Christ, Becca, she pissed off, she left her own kids and not a word, just a poxy postcard a year later. She doesn't exist as far as I'm concerned. I'd rather she was dead. Why keep going on about it?'

'I don't know, but she's my mother. I want to know what she's like. I can hardly remember. I try to, to see her face, but I can't.'

'I think you're bloody crazy. It's asking for trouble. Don't do it, Becca, let it lie. We've come this far without her.'

And no further, Becca thought, but held back. Not wanting to argue, she said, 'I'll see. Are you going to smoke that whole joint yourself?' He passed it to her. He was relieved to have got off lightly, as he saw it, no scenes, no recriminations.

'I'm off down the high street. Do you want anything?'

'No, I'm going out to see Rosa later. I'll get what I want on the way. I need to go and look for a present for Jenny and the baby.'

She watched him go, his thin frame and straight shoulders, the back of his neck bony and pale, like someone she no longer knew.

In a street not far away, coming in from the bright sunlight, Rebecca hears her father's voice raised above her brother's sobs: 'Shut up, shut up.'

They are sitting in the back room, at the ugly brown utilitarian table with its four hard chairs. Terrence sits with his elbows on the table-top, head cradled in his hands. The sobbing quietens.

'What is it, what's the matter, Dad?' she asks. 'What is it?' She catches his arm and shakes it when he fails to reply. 'Don't cry, Dad. What's happened? Dad?' Her brother begins to whimper.

'She's gone, your mother's gone,' he screams, 'fucked off, gone. Pauline's gone and not coming back. She's gone for good.'

'Where, Dad, gone where?'

'Gone with another bloody man, that's where, bloody Charlie Porter. She's cleared off with him, hasn't she? She's left us and he's left Vera and Lilli. Off to have a fine time together, no doubt, never mind the kids. Selfish bastards. Bitch. Bloody bitch. Whore.' He thumps the table. Joe cries louder.

Terrence rises from the table and wipes the tears from his eyes with a sweep of his arm. He goes to the hallway and lifts his jacket from the banister end. From his pocket he takes what money he can find. 'Look after him,' he says, nodding towards Joe, and then leaves for The Top House to begin a lifetime of drinking.

Rebecca goes over and puts an arm around Joe's shoulders. 'Don't cry. Don't cry, she'll come back. She'll be back. Let's see what's on TV. Come on.' She leads him into the front room. She switches on the television and they sit close together on the sofa of the grey three-piece, only moving when it grows dark. That night Terrence comes home drunk and goes upstairs without a word. Rebecca and Joe curl up together in a bed full of teddies and dolls. She hums softly to him until he falls asleep.

Becca let herself back into the flat. She emptied a carrier bag of its contents, spilling them onto the bed; a loaf of bread, a packet of chocolate gingers, ten cigarettes and a baby's cardigan wrapped in tissue paper. She lit a cigarette, unwrapped the cardigan and lay it on her lap, smoothing it with the palm of her hand. It was delicate, lacy, it was the best she could do. The shawl had been too expensive, the cardigan had cost enough, more than she could really afford, but never mind, she was happy that she'd bought something for Jen and the baby.

The flat seemed empty now that she knew Joe was going. Becca felt tired, her legs were heavy, her thin ankles were swelling. She made room on the bed and lay down thinking she would sleep. The baby kicked at her stomach and sleep would not come. Questions swarmed like bees in her head. Did she really want to find Pauline like she said to Joe? Maybe. Perhaps if she went back she would stay, make a life for herself, meet up with old friends. Would Lilli still be there? Perhaps there was no going back. Had it all been an excuse to draw him in and keep him from going? Had she wanted to make it more difficult for him? It was true that she'd been thinking of searching Pauline out. But when? When and how, with or without a baby? And why? It wasn't as if Pauline could really change anything. There was no reason, Becca felt, no excuse enough for her mother's abandonment. But there was remorse. Did Pauline feel remorse? If so, it would be a place for them to begin, somewhere to start again.

She wasn't as angry as Joe. She'd felt the anger, of course, after the long-held grief, after a childhood in shock. Then she'd felt anger so brutal and cold that she'd come to wonder herself what she might be capable of, what she might do to a child of her own. Betrayal and rage were dangerous play-mates. Could she forgive, did the rage lurk still?

Becca got up off the bed, crossed the room and reached for the remains of a box of Dairy Milk Joe had bought her, from the floor beside the armchair. He'd eaten most of them. Milk chocolates were not her favourite. She rummaged through the box and discovered a square caramel. She put it in her mouth and began to suck the chocolate from its hard centre, looking for somewhere other than the floor to put the box. On top of the record pile she noticed Marianne, picked her up and put the box down in the doll's place. She blew the dust from her nylon hair, then sat at the table with Marianne on her lap, straightened out the doll's arms and legs, and hugged it to her like a baby. She thought of her bed filled with teddies and dolls. How she'd kept them there, laid them out scrupulously every night, barely room for her but still she was never without them. Dolls and teddies were constant. They looked at you and didn't take their gaze away, had wry smiles barely detectable but you could see if you knew them, if you looked closely enough. They smelt woolly when you wet them with your tears, and tears hung about on their surface, not easily absorbed. They stayed where you put them, never moving out of your sight and they were easy, so easy to look after. They got grubby sometimes so you had to wash their arms and legs with flannels and scrub away the dirt but they didn't mind. They still smiled and the thing was they knew how you felt. You didn't have to tell them, they knew everything. Dolls and teddies were on your side, there through those dark watchful nights of childhood, when you lay next to them, when sleep wouldn't come and every sound was a returning footstep on the stair.

She hugged Marianne to her and thought of Lilli; the doll reminded her of their summer days in the open, on the wide riverbank. Becca smelled the pill-box, the fishy mud flats and the white crabs and she wondered where Lilli was.

Part Three

Lilli

The Heron

A heron, lean at the dark of the moon, scratched the surface of the frozen rhyne. Blonde reeds pierced the ice like sentinels, stood through winter, frayed and rattling in the wind. The grey bird fractured the water with its beak, pinning its prey, gulping it down, turning an eye to the lovers escaping the house.

Frost lay like crystallised sugar on the edge of a glass bowl. The sky was clear and blue and the land white as they set out. Vera had not yet fallen into the final part of her dying, but it was close and Lilli was not at all sure that she should be out for the day. Uneasiness dogged her as she called goodbye and closed the door. What ifs . . . what if she needed her . . . what if she became worse . . . what if she died too soon, that very day? She should be with her.

Eventually, all her *what ifs* had been fended off by Nell and Ted, by Paolo's insistence; she needed a break if only for the fresh air. She wanted to believe them. She knew she needed to escape the waiting and the sweet, cloying smell of the sick room. An escape, a walk by the sea, she relished the thought, but a deep sense of unease accompanied it. She knew that Nell and Ted could look after Vera, of course they could, but it wasn't the same. At the end it could only be the two of them alone, no one else. She comforted herself with the knowledge that Vera would wait for her, that she would know when.

'The tide's in,' she said, exhilarated, smelling the water as she stepped out of their borrowed car. They walked over to the seafront, leaned on the sea wall and watched the brown rollers break on the beach, lacing the wet sands. 'Let's go down,' she said eagerly, taking his hand and pulling him down the worn steps, her hand sliding on the cold polished slate of the wall top. The sand was gritty with melting frost. They walked in the direction of the dunes and the brave church that stood on the promontory, with the sleeping whale of the down behind.

They followed the tracks of seabirds woven across the shoreline. Lilli picked up an amber pebble that caught her eye, brushing the sand from it and secreting it in her coat pocket. She found a stick of bleached wood from amongst the tangle of seaweed and trailed it behind her, marking the way, just as she and Rebecca had done many times. The wind was in their faces, battling them, lending a sudden air of elation to Lilli's day, to the guilty escape she had made. Let free she wanted to celebrate, feel the keenness of life and her warm breath clouding the cold air, run, call out to the gulls above, make great footprints across the sand, pop the seaweed underfoot.

They turned back when they got to the grey beast jutting out into the bay, clinging to the land by its thin neck, fortified at its tail, looking out for the invader. They turned and ran laughing with the wind behind them. They were easy with each other after their lovemaking. There were fewer misunderstandings and they found they made each other happy. A simple enough thing, but one that brought with it disturbing complications, for along with happiness and affection came what Lilli most feared. The fear that she disguised behind her wide smile and her red coat and her caring for others; the fear of loss and separation. For who could say who would leave and who would stay, or who would find another love? Who was to be believed? People said all kinds of things and meant them at the time, but later changed their minds, maybe changed them back again, fluctuating, back and forward along a sliding scale of love, a spectrum of feeling.

People loved their children and left. Was that possible, she wondered, to love and to leave? Were the two mutually exclusive? 'Love you and leave you,' they said but only if they were coming back.

Maybe it was possible to put love away for a while, if you had to. Rest it on a velvet cushion, like a trinket in a musical box. Open it and see the ballerina dance, see the ballerina dance, the glittering lady as she pirouettes. Open it and let love breathe. Then shut the lid firmly, box it up and put it away. She'd done that, hadn't she? She'd loved her child and she'd put that love away. Lilli was no longer sure she could see the dancing girl. Torn net and laddered stockings, boots and black leather were her familiars. Seeing things for what they were. It was safer like that. That way no disappointments lay ahead.

Outcomes were unpredictable. Who could know what was in the other's mind? Who could understand what was said? It was all a matter of self-interest when it came down to it, loving, when all was said and done. There were small acts of kindness but mostly there was self-interest, plain selfishness and knowing that, understanding it, was part of surviving. And Lilli survived, despite her insecurities. She was powerful enough on the right territory; when punishing Maurice in the office, when walking the old tracks. But she was fragile with those she loved or grew close to. She feared their leaving and to precipitate that which she feared was Lilli's way of keeping herself safe.

She envied Paolo in his comfortable skin, wearing his life like a favourite jumper, baggy and loose. She put her arm through his and drew herself close into his side as if to catch his easiness. She clung to him, like a child at his side, reaching for his hand.

Paolo put his hand over hers, pressing it into his arm. He liked her like this; needing him, dependent. It didn't happen often. He wasn't always sure how she felt. In the time he'd known her he'd found her near and distant at turns. She often withdrew. Those times after lunch, it was most noticeable, when she prepared to go back into the world of The Seaview. The hotel seemed to wrap itself around her like the tentacles of an octopus, dragging her down. It was hard to understand what kept her there. There were other jobs, seasonal work; she could have worked for him, but something drew her towards it and it seemed that whatever it was drew her away from him. 'It's just a job,' she would say. 'Then give it up,' he would counter. She didn't, made no move to, disappeared into its rooms and stairways, its linen closets and its cellars, so that he felt she inhabited another life in which he played no part. He liked to think it was her mother's illness but he knew it was more than that. He was only just beginning to know her and understanding was still a long way off.

'I wish you'd leave the hotel. Hauser is a shit, everyone says so. You shouldn't be working for a man like that. There's no need . . .'

'Don't talk about that now, not today, please, you'll spoil it,' she said quickly, squeezing his arm in supplication, then withdrawing hers. She wasn't sure she could trust him. He wanted to change her, sometimes he did, making her needy, lulling her into a cosy dependency that caught her off her guard. He sapped her strength. Life with Paolo: she allowed herself to imagine it from time to time but the only picture she could easily conjure was them together in some foreign place, not here. Here was where it felt real, in the dreaming, when she walked the tracks with the baby strapped to her, when she felt the deep connection with the land beneath her feet, when she knew her journey was not yet over.

'What shall we do now? Let's get out of this wind.'

'We'll go to Vittore's,' he said.

She hesitated. It meant meeting more of his family. How would she be received? She wanted to be with him, not a crowd. Couldn't he see that? Was he shaking her off? She smiled at him and nodded nervously in agreement. They climbed the steps to the front, shook the sand from their boots and turned along the front past the pier and into the shelter of the town.

The town wore its winter habit, somnolent and grey. A seaside town in winter where people walked in their sleep and slept in cold rooms overlooking the esplanade. Echoing arcades of spilling coins were empty, last year's cowboy hats sat faded in the windows. Everywhere she saw the ghosts of day-trippers and kiss-me-quick merchants, who came to buy candy breakfasts of pink sausage, egg and bacon on paper plates and giant stripped dummies. She heard the buzz of cafés, chip shops, rock shops now standing deserted. The town had a melancholy air – the air of one left behind, abandoned by those it loved. The space matched her mournful mood. It was in keeping. She felt comforted and warmed by it, not least because she found herself walking its streets with a man she was growing to love.

She didn't like to admit it but it was true. Lilli no longer involved herself with other men. There was only her relationship with Maurice still to relinquish. The darkness at her centre had lifted, had begun to float away; at times she felt as if she had stepped into a great void, and she found herself in unknown territory, weightless, as if defying gravity.

They turned into a side street and hurried down, past the printers and the adult bookshop with its dusty window display and token leather whip. Coming out further along the main street Paolo stepped ahead of her and pushed open the door of Vittore's. Once inside the café Lilli was aware of a growing hunger, of how she had eaten little or nothing whilst at her mother's bedside. To her right was a long, high, glass counter. Its shelves were filled with sandwiches and continental rolls, dripping ham, cheese and salami, ready for the lunchtime custom. Behind, Lilli saw a black coffee machine like the one in the parlour, and, ranged above, similar, gaudy depictions of ices and sundaes. On the left were booths of plastic banquettes and Formica-topped tables, set with glass ashtrays and sugar containers with silver spouts.

Paolo led her through to the back where he was greeted by his uncle, Vittore, in an outpouring of Italian and arms. Lilli felt awkward. She was not used to such violent demonstrations of affection and she did not speak Italian. She looked around her and smiled broadly, hoping it was enough. To her relief she was largely ignored, as Paolo was greeted by several others, including a woman she assumed to be his aunt. In the corner on a high shelf a television peered down like an eye. They'd been watching the racing, sat around a table with a white cloth bearing dark coffee stains and a smouldering ashtray.

Vittore was Angelo's brother. They'd set up in business at much the same time in similar ways so that they'd both provided well enough for their families. When their children had been younger they had spent time together, aunts and uncles, cousins, on special occasions. Now they met less often but there were still times when the family gathered, when they would fill a restaurant and dine all day.

Paolo introduced Lilli to his uncle, his aunt Catherine, his cousins Luigi and Guido and the waitress Marie. Luigi kissed her hand and went to make coffee. They were seated and presented with espresso and small glasses of amaretto. The amaretto burnt the back of her throat and warmed her stomach. Before long a feast appeared: continental meats and cheeses, fresh bread, pears and almond pastries.

Lilli began to relax, realising that while they conversed wildly in Italian interspersed with the occasional sentence of English – out of courtesy she imagined – she was required to do nothing but eat. She offered the occasional nod or smile and savoured the food which gradually filled the hollow at her centre. She began to thaw, comfortable in the midst of this small, genial, gathering of family. They were what she believed a family should be, working together, playing together, eating and drinking, no trays on laps, no angry silence but at the table sprawling and noisy. An Italian family like the lump of pasta dough she watched his aunt working;

pulled and pushed, slapped and stretched but still whole. She envied Paolo and longed to be a part of it all, part of the Italian landscape that adorned the walls, a mural, ill-conceived, poorly executed, over-bright but filled with blue skies, sun, mountains and pine. She wanted to go there, to belong. She wanted this vibrant world that surrounded her, wanted life, wanted Vera to live. If only she could give her the chance to live changed like this, breathing in sun, shaking off the legacies of guilt and failure. She would take her on a trip abroad. They'd never been on holiday together apart from a trip to Butlin's with Edith and Nell and Ted. Never to an entirely different world, to the Mediterranean say; well it was possible now and for a brief moment she saw Vera there lying in the hot sun while it warmed her bones, bringing her back to health and life.

She touched Paolo on the arm. 'I've got to get back,' she whispered.

'Not yet, surely.'

'But anything could have happened and I'm not there.'

'But Nell is, she said she'd stay all day. There's nothing to worry about; it's fine.'

'Don't you see I've only got days, maybe hours left and I'm not there. I should be with her. I have to . . .' Lilli's tone grew more urgent.

'All right,' he said, wanting to calm her, 'we'll go.' He pressed her hand in his. 'Just let me finish my drink, see the 2.30 at Goodwood, then we'll go.'

Could she wait that long? She wasn't sure but knew she would have to; it would be impossible, impossibly rude to get up and leave without polite preparation. She left it to him. He managed it well, so that it was not too long before they left but long enough to digest their food, say proper good-byes and for him to promise they would stay longer the next time they came.

As they walked back towards the car she said, 'I'm sorry to drag you away. I'm sorry, it really was so nice sitting there, but I couldn't help it. I suddenly felt desperate. I couldn't bear the thought of her needing me and me not being there.'

'It doesn't matter, we can go again, anytime.' He paused, then said, 'I want you to come to Italy with me before next winter. Will you? We'll have all the time we need then to sit talking and drinking wine. You can meet the rest of the family. I'll teach you Italian. Will you?'

'Yes,' she said feeling no doubt that this was what she wanted more than anything. 'I will, I'll come.'

The Knoll

It was the only rise in the land for miles around. Frog Island, her grandfather called it. He grew up beneath it, at its foot.

'Can we go round the knoll?' she asked. She was calmer now they were on their way home. Things would be fine. Suddenly she regretted her panic. She wanted to make more of the day before it was spent.

He turned off the main road and made for the old island encampment, a stubborn relic that refused to be scoured by the sea, a grassy hill in these parts hiding a tough core of lias and marl. It had been a Roman fort, a watchtower from which great tides bearing travellers and invaders alike were heralded. From its vantage point you could look downriver to open sea or up into the depths of the marshes. It demanded to be climbed and as children they had regarded it a great feat to toil upwards and reach the summit of so high a point in so flat a land. They had been drawn by its call, to conquer and to look.

The road in front of them was narrow and winding, edged with tall reeds. The knoll seemed to pull at them like a great magnet drawing them ever closer. Lilli put her hand in her pocket and felt for the pebble from the beach and the armlet . . .

She steps into the dugout laden with her skin bundles. The baby lies in the woven cradle near the prow. Beneath, in the shallows, lurk watercrowfoot and arrowhead. On the surface frogbit and dense patches of rush. She pushes off from the wooden jetty and sits with hands holding onto the boat sides waiting for it to steady, to reach a balance. She paddles out beyond the overhang of alder while a pelican watches from the edge dipping its beak into the water and scooping a tench from the reed bed. Before her lies open water and behind her the rising sun casting its colour across the surface so that she paddles gently, in a lake of yellow and rose ripples.

She will not reach the island until the sun is setting, a long day in which she may meet the wash from swirling tides the nearer she approaches. In which the ebb and flow of water will suck and pull and she will need strength to resist . . .

'We're here,' he said, switching off the engine, 'what do you want to do?'

'Climb it,' she said without hesitation. There was time. If they were quick it wouldn't matter, she reasoned, Vera always slept more towards late afternoon, was probably sleeping now. They would be back anyway earlier than intended and you couldn't come to the knoll and not climb it. It stood before her like a talisman; to climb it could only mean good fortune, to retrace the old tracks would keep her safe, like a child having to step on the paving stones, never on the cracks, for cracks were bad luck. She could not account for the consequences if she left without climbing to the top. It was necessary. She set off purposefully with Paolo following and they arrived at the top forty minutes later, breathless but warmed by their efforts. They stood in silence, regaining their breath. Looking west to the bay she watched the sun sinking in the sky.

'You mean it,' he said, 'you will come? I know you'll like it. I need a change, we both need a change, something new, different, together. And if we want we could think of setting up for a while in one of the houses in the square or further up in the valley.'

'Yes, I want to, for a while at least,' but as she said it she began to wonder if she could leave this land, this place which consumed her, into which she disappeared, where she could walk into a shimmering mirage and reappear at will . . .

She stops to feed the baby pulling alongside the raised bog, grounding the dugout. She rests in the full heat of the midday sun, leaning back and listening to the murmur of damselfly and the hum of gnats above her head. A beaver swims alongside, weaving about her, following throughout the afternoon as she grows tired, the first to arrive at the wooden pier. Ahead she sees the blue drift of smoke rising from the camp. As she pulls the canoe into the side, stepping out and dragging it onto the land, the smell of burning meat fat greets her, making her mouth water, catching at her empty stomach. She lifts the baby from its cradle, strapping him across her chest, and makes her way over the grass on the low pasture up towards the camp. She climbs to the first dip in the knoll to the encampment where a low fire burns and the men beckon her in. They have seen her approaching. They have watched her for some time drifting across the silver water turned red by the falling sun, her silhouette against the scudded pink and violet of the mackerel sky.

She eats hungrily, roast pig in scraps and charred fish. The baby suckles contentedly as she unfolds her bundles and lays before the watchmen the cloth and braids of her living.

A low moaning calls from the shelter above. Inside the hut a woman lies on a woven platform covered with skins, her knees up, legs wide, her elbows bent and head back. Two women attend her pushing a wedge of mashed herb into her mouth for her to bite on, as the purple and red head pushes through. Then a rush of blood, her throat prepares to let out a final cry, then closes as the green juice runs down from her open mouth onto her lifeless body.

They clean the baby with wet cloth, diluting the blood, smearing the cotton, then swaddle him. They turn to the mother's body and wash it with love as only women who know can, and cover it with fresh moss, reeds and skin. She sits with them late into the night keeping vigil, dozing and waking, their faces fluid in the light of the dripping candle pots.

In the morning she collects her beads of amber, her trade done, but returns to the hut again to lay a gift of braid at the baby's feet. She makes her way down the knoll to the bank through the veil of early morning mist. They follow, carrying the woman's body, laying it on the bank while they prepare the raft and the pyre of seasoned wood and straw. She casts off, dipping her oar into the millpond sea. As she paddles the mist begins to rise and clear. Behind her she hears the crackle of lit straw, smells the drift of wood smoke. Steadying the dugout she turns to look at the knoll and watch as the burning body is cast afloat in a sea of reflected flame . . .

She was relieved to arrive at her door. 'Thank you,' she said, meaning it, 'I've had a lovely day, I'm sorry I cut it short.'

'It doesn't matter,' he said, knowing she needed to be back and glad to break the long and distant silence of their journey home from the knoll. 'There'll be other times. Shall I come in?'

'No, no . . . you go.'

He did not disagree. 'I'll come tomorrow to see how things are.'

'Yes, come tomorrow,' she said, leaning over to kiss him. She put the palm of her hand to the side of his face, suddenly grateful for his concern, his kindness to her, the way he loved her and the way she was in love: the way he had put something between her and this impending death, something to carry her through.

As she entered the house the grey heron took off from the rhyne, lifting its heavy body, opening its great wings and trailing its legs across the sky. From her bedroom window she watched it fly across the Levels, towards the sea. She took the small amber pebble from her pocket and added it to the dusty collection on her dressing table; a token of the day.

Vera

Vera died at 7.52 in the morning. Lilli was prepared. She knew that her mother would not live beyond eight o'clock. It was the measure she set when she realised that death was drawing near. Eight o'clock and no later. It would be over by then. She told herself that she should get dressed, be prepared. She got up and dressed, then sat down again next to the bed. She did not draw the curtains, did not let in the daylight but preferred instead to sit in the softer light of the bedside lamp warming her mother's hand in hers.

'How will I know?' she'd asked the nurse who had sat with her late into the night.

'Things will change, you'll notice them. Her breathing will be shallower. The colour will begin to drain from the face and her nose will look pinched, pulled in. After a while she'll get cold, her hands and her feet and you will hear it in the throat – the rattle. I'll stay with you if you like. I don't think it will be long now and I can stay, if you want.'

'No, I'll be fine,' said Lilli, 'just as long as I know.'

Nell and Ted had been in through the night but Lilli had sent them away when it got late and sat alone dozing, wrapped in an old eiderdown. In the early hours she'd seen the change, felt the cold creep into her hands. Vera had lain motionless, apart from the rise of her chest, wrapped in a blanket of morphine. There was no need for suffering, they said, best to keep her peaceful, and she'd agreed. She'd been glad of it, to see her no longer restless, twisting in the bed, tearing at her nightdress and bedclothes. Sufficient morphine to lull her into a rhythmic sleep. But where had she gone? Where had Vera gone? It seemed to Lilli that her spirit had already flown. It was impossible for her to say where Vera was, what she was feeling, what she could sense. Could she hear? The nurse had told her that hearing was the last sense to go.

Throughout the night Lilli had bent over her to dab moistened cotton wool around the gaping hole that had become Vera's mouth. Her lips had disappeared and the sweet, fetid smell of death hung there. Now as she leaned over she smoothed her hair and whispered each time in her ear little things – 'I'm here, I'm here, Mum' – for what else was there left to say? It was too late to say the things that hadn't been said, the things that couldn't be said, besides there was no sign, not the smallest change, to suggest that Vera had any degree of consciousness. Consciousness had disappeared with the doctor's decision to make her *comfortable*.

When Vera's hands grew cold Lilli drew the bedclothes up, closer around her as one would a sleeping child and slipped her own hand beneath the blanket to hold hers. She sat unmoving, watching the hands of the luminous clock move past seven towards eight, feeling the passage of life leaving. When Vera's last breath came she was able to define it in time, for herself and others. It was strange, she reflected later, that she could remember so exactly the time of death, the hour and minute of an event which had been remarkable in its timelessness, in which time had been suspended, just as it had the day she had given birth.

When she was sure that Vera was dead and that there was no more breath to come, she bent over her for the last time, putting her head into her shoulder and letting her tears fall. She kept the curtains drawn and the light as it was. She left the room to go down to the kitchen to make tea. She wanted to be alone. There was no rush, the nurse had told her that – don't panic, she said, when it happens, her death will come soon, it is what we expect, it is not a crisis, no need to rush and tell, just in your own good time.

She wanted to be alone to feel the separation, to grow used

to it, knowing already that this was a separation and a loss that she could bear, for Vera had left life. She had not left her.

On a morning in spring, when the sky had fallen to the land and the horizon was a sheet of blotting paper awash with watery ink, Vera was buried in the far corner of the church-yard. It wasn't far from the house to the squat black church. The bells tolled in the tower as they made their way up the curved path to the door. Men had gathered in ill-fitting suits and women in their Sunday best. People who had known her all her life, friends and villagers, the postmaster, the publican and his wife, the WI, cousins from Brent, a few from the old estate and the family led by Edith, fetched early from The Lyndor by Ted. The familiar faces appeared as if through a mist where substance eluded definition, but Lilli was glad they'd come. They quieted her. Nell cried most of all, Edith not at all, holding her grief in a body which appeared to be growing smaller, instantly frailer and nearer to death.

Back at Nell and Ted's house the sewing room had been cleared and the cutting table spread with white tablecloths. Nell and the women round about had made sandwiches, sausage rolls, cakes and tea. There was sherry for the women, beer for the men. It was noisy inside, loud with relief. The sober ritual complete, people began to relax, eat and drink. It was permissible to smile, to chatter.

Lilli began to move around the room, talking to people who had come for Vera and for her. She stood before them smiling, chatting, not quite feeling her feet, seeming to float above the floor unable to ground herself. She felt she watched from another place, on the periphery, watched herself fulfil her obligations, courteously in homage to her mother, watched but wasn't there.

Paolo had come with his father, handsome in his dark suit. He'd kept his distance, mindful of intruding on family, only stepping towards her at the graveside to offer an arm when he saw her sway and feared she would not hold up. Lilli was happy they were there, pleased that they brought with them their tradition of family, of respect and ceremony, pleased when he touched her gently on the arm and asked was she all right, could he do anything?

Maud Hauser in a grey coat and hat stood talking with the postmaster. Behind her at the window sat Edith staring and immobile, a cup of tea balanced in her lap. Despite her frailty, her face wore its usual air of disapproval.

'Thank you for coming, both of you,' said Lilli, approaching Maud, standing with her back to Edith.

Maud immediately took her hand. 'I'm so sorry, my dear, you know how much I liked Vera and it doesn't seem fair at her age.'

'No,' agreed Lilli, and wanting to change the subject added, 'I'll be back at work tomorrow now that it's over.'

'Oh now, I wouldn't rush back, it seems far too soon to me, really,' Maud said, nevertheless experiencing a flutter of excitement and relief at the prospect of Lilli's return to the hotel.

'I need to get back.'

A watery sunlight fell through the bulging glass of the window onto the side of Maud's face. Lilli saw the remnants of a bruise, blue and yellowing, inflicted she'd no doubt by the hand or fist of her husband. It lay uncovered, like a knot of wood, a daub of watercolour on her face. What about the others? Those covered up, lurking beneath, wondered Lilli? How many bruises old and new did Maud Hauser possess? Unaware of Lilli's scrutiny Maud continued her conversation with the postmaster. She looked at Lilli in an attempt to include her. But Lilli was only half listening. She was distracted by the anger rising inside her as she considered the fate of women like Maud at the hands of men, and then by a voice which penetrated her consciousness. It was Edith's voice; Edith, who was seated behind her and who was complaining to Nell.

'It's terrible in there, you've no idea, no idea at all. I never thought it would happen to me, never. I mean you don't expect it when you've got family, stuck in there all day.' There was a strained silence. 'If Charlie had stayed it might have been different. He didn't turn up then? I thought he might have come for the funeral at least, pay his respects, see her . . .'

'Ssh, Mum,' said Nell.

'Well, he knows, doesn't he?'

'Yes,' said Nell.

'Well then, if he knows where is he?'

He knows . . . he knows . . . The words echoed in Lilli's head, gathering meaning with each repetition. He knows. How? Who told him? She asked herself incredulous, silent. Where was he?

Maud continued talking. Edith's voice drifted in and out of Lilli's ear.

'Such a mousy little woman, Maud, always wears grey, suits her I suppose. He knocks her about, you know.'

'Ssh, Mum, she'll hear. Have an egg sandwich.' Ted appeared with a plate of sandwiches and things on sticks, none of which Edith wanted. Another sherry was what she wanted, she held up her empty glass. Nell flashed Ted a warning. He went to fetch her third glass.

'Well, that's something to be grateful for. At least we kept her away from him. I don't know how your father didn't kill him that night. What a carry on. She shouldn't be working for him you know, have you told her . . .?' The voice faded as Ted returned with Edith's sherry. An old friend of Edith's joined them; Nancy Morris, wife of the town fishmonger. The smell always lingered. But she was lucky enough, as Edith was known to remark, to still be living in the bosom of her family.

The conversation drifted into condolences and banalities. Lilli continued talking to Maud, unaware of what she was saying or of her own responses and wishing they would all go home. Paolo and Angelo said goodbye. Others began to drift away so that Lilli finally felt she could leave the few remaining guests and return home.

Back in the house she could think. Think what to do, what to do about Charlie and what to do about Maurice. Maurice first. What was it Nell hadn't told her? Why shouldn't she be working for him? Regardless of the answers she was determined that he would pay for his bullying of Maud, for the blue and yellow bruise that sat on her cheek, for the misery he inflicted around him.

She grabbed her purse and shopping bag, put on her red coat, untied her hair and went out to the bus stop. It would take an hour or more to get there, an hour in which to sit and watch, looking out on the first white flowering in the hedgerows, the soft yellow of willow unfolding and the swans nesting in the pond by the knoll. In the pocket of her coat, resting beside an elastic band and a hairgrip, lay the armlet . . .

She wakes early as the dawn breaks over the grasslands to the east washing the sky with lemon and pink and painting the cotton grass. From the water an early morning mist invades the dugout, clutching at her ankles, chilling her. The wildfowl are moving to the moor and a wedge of great swans cry out as they fly overhead. She leaves the dugout now in search of the track. It will take her back to the camp. She places one foot carefully in front of the next so as not to slip. Her hide shoes are freshly lined with sphagnum to cushion her feet. The baby is swaddled close. In her bundle she carries the precious amber for which she has traded her cloth. In a sewn pouch hidden in the bundle is his parting gift, which she carries with her wherever she goes, the blue glass beads. She walks until late afternoon, growing hungry as she watches the gulls on swampy islets feed on fish. By dusk she is home safely bearing gifts.

The town was quiet and the tide was out. It wasn't far from the bus station to the adult bookshop and she was able to buy what she needed and return to the bus station within an hour. She waited ten minutes for her bus home. She drank a lukewarm coffee from a plastic cup, bought from a kiosk, and grew nauseous on the black petroleum-filled air. When she got home she removed the parcel from her bag and took it upstairs where she put it away in a drawer in the chest on the landing.

The Clark's Shoebox

There was no sign of life. The sewing room was in darkness. They must be in the kitchen. She made her way to the back door, where she heard Ted's voice. Ted shouting almost, as she had never heard him before, at least not at Nell. Ted reserved his anger for matters of politics, matters affecting work or the land but not for people. Now he was loud and insistent.

'For God's sake, Nell, you told him, you bloody told him. You still have to keep in touch, don't you? Can't leave him alone even now, after all these years. And what if he'd come eh? What then? Bloody fantastic, oh yes that would've been great, bloody spectre at the feast. What about Lilli, eh? Did you think about her or were you just thinking about yourself? Fancy seeing him again did you, for old times' sake? What if he'd brought *her*, you stupid, selfish bitch?'

Lilli stepped into the kitchen, into the shock waves of Ted's anger and Nell's silence. She said, 'You told him, Nell, how? How did you tell him? Christ, Nell, you know where he is, you know where Charlie is, don't you?'

Nell looked down.

'You do, you know, you've always known, haven't you? Is that why he went then? Went because of you. You and him behind Mum's back – your sister's husband, Nell – my father. It's your fault.' Nell remained silent. 'What happened then? Get caught did you? Ted catch you or was it Edith? Did Mum know?'

'No, she didn't, and it wasn't like that. It wasn't like that, Lilli,' Nell cried. 'He didn't go because of me. Ted knows that. It was nothing really, we never really, well it never amounted to much. It was just a . . . he was a hard man to resist, Lilli, you know, and he made it his business to be irresistible to women and Vera never knew. We kept it from her. She was happy. Looking after you in the house. Charlie made her happy. It wasn't difficult for him. He could have kept any number of women happy. He was always round me, always there, always asking . . . I'm sorry but he didn't leave because of me, not me. He ran off with Pauline – you know – Rebecca's mother. That's who Charlie left for. He'd been seeing her for years, long before he had anything to do with me, and in the end she was still the one. He left with her, Lilli.'

Terrence and Pauline, Charlie and Vera on a hillside, hair flying in the wind, the photo in the Clark's shoebox. Pauline and Vera singing in the kitchen. He ran away with Pauline, Rebecca's mother. With Pauline.

'Did Rebecca know?' asked Lilli, close to tears, fighting the mixture of anger and sorrow that boiled inside her.

'I don't know,' said Nell.

'No wonder we moved away, no wonder I never saw her . . . no wonder she always hurried me by.'

The room became calm. The rage in the air dissipated. Ted and Nell watched and waited.

'Rebecca, Rebecca . . .' whispered Lilli. 'Where did they go?'

'They went to live in Ross-on-Wye and Charlie kept in touch. Because of you – he wanted to know how you were, that's all,' she said, looking directly at Lilli and then at Ted. 'And I thought you might want to see him now that Vera's gone. I thought it might help.'

Lilli resisted the temptation to forgive Nell, to put herself in her place and feel sorry for her hurt, to put her arms round her and say never mind. After a long silence she said coldly, 'There's something else I need to know. I want you to tell me what happened with Maurice Hauser.'

Lilli leaves the dark entry and slips into the back kitchen. The door is ajar and the house silent. The remains of Sunday dinner, scraps, plates, pans, lie on the draining board. A solitary fly buzzes over a roasting tin lined with congealed beef fat. There are no raised voices, no muffled sobs to be heard. She is glad. She will not have to cover their anger with the noise of the television. She will not have to block her ears or bury her head under the pillow. It will not be necessary to invoke the rituals she uses to cover cruel words or erase those which swim in her head like mantras, signposts to sorrow.

There is an uneasy silence, an absence of sound. She is used to this. The silences between her mother and father have become protracted. Sometimes they are only broken when they speak through her, especially at the table, at mealtimes. Passing their words and venom through her. Vera passing on her despair. Silence is easier but this silence is different, is not an illusion, there is no accidental interruption to fill the void, no half-heard foot on the stair, no dog barking in the distance. It is resonant with resolution. The house is devoid of life.

Lilli makes her way through the hallway, stepping as she always does between the squares on the patterned runner, past the dusty plastic roses (free with Daz washing powder), which sit in a cut-glass bowl on the hall table, and up the stairs. The door to her parents' bedroom is shut. She opens it. The drawn curtains filter the sunlight. Vera lies sprawled face down on the divan, an empty brown tablet bottle at her side.

She yells, screams, filling the void, 'Dad, Dad . . .' starts down the stairs, screaming, until they come running, neighbours running in, but no Charlie.

Red Nail Polish

Vera had the same photograph, the one Nell kept in the Clark's shoebox. The photograph of the four of them, Charlie and Vera, Pauline and Terrence, on the hillside that spring. Lilli found it among the others when she came to sorting things through – photographs of people and places, distant times in which she'd played a part in a life she barely recognised. Holidays on the south coast, Vera in her dark glasses perched on a deckchair. Vera and Charlie's wedding with deep red roses trailing and a veil whipped up by the December wind. Nell a shy bridesmaid, head to one side. The carnival and her bike festooned with crepe paper flowers alongside the fire engine.

It was painful this picking over of her mother, their life together. She wouldn't do it now. No, she didn't have to, there was plenty of time. It could wait. There would be a time when it needed doing, when she moved. It would be soon enough, she told herself as she pushed the albums back into the bottom drawer of the chest. She smiled as she caught sight of the brown-paper-bag parcel from the adult bookshop.

The albums could wait. It could all wait until her mother's scent, which permeated the house, lingering in the wardrobe, in her bed, amongst the linen in the airing cupboard, in the kitchen had faded. When she was ready to touch the few and tiny things Vera had kept about her, her treasures like the china poodle and the blue glass fish, gifts from Lilli, from her school trips; when they were ready to be packed away in tissue and newspaper, it could all wait until then.

She was glad he hadn't come. Charlie didn't belong there.

It would have been too much of a shock and he wouldn't have been welcome. She'd see him. She'd made up her mind about that, now she knew where to find him, have it out with him. All these years – he'd never bothered, why? She'd ask him that. Just, why?

She'd asked herself that question all through the years and she had invented many answers and many excuses for Charlie. What was it she wanted to hear? There were variations on a theme. The answers had become more sophisticated with the years but they all boiled down to the same thing. He'd wanted to keep in touch, of course he had, but it was the other woman.

Her. She wore red nail polish and tight black skirts. She was a glamorous figure, unlike her mother. A figure who menaced Lilli's imagination. She'd been hinted at often enough, but her identity had never been revealed. To Lilli she'd been a stranger, an evil enchantress, and a she-devil who had visited her black art upon her helpless father. Now she knew.

It wasn't how she remembered Pauline.

It was her fault. She'd stopped him. It hadn't been his fault. He'd thought of her every day – wasn't a day that went by . . . he'd bought cards, written letters but Pauline had torn them up . . . couldn't come back. Edith had made sure; he'd had his orders not to set foot. They'd been kept apart. It wasn't his fault. It wasn't what he wanted. That's what she wanted to hear. But the closer she came to finding him the less sure she was that it would suffice.

Was any excuse good enough? Could Charlie offer any explanation that would chase the nagging doubt, the suspicion of truth, which she kept locked away but which insisted on appearing unannounced? That he simply hadn't cared enough, that he was too selfish, that she was not good enough. Best it was out so she knew and she no longer wasted time in idle fantasies, which became more improbable each time they were aired. She would find out soon enough. She would ask Nell and she would see him here, not in Ross-on-Wye. Here, where he should have been all along.

Kingcups and Cottongrass

The lanes were laced with cow parsley and may, the white promise of summer. The rhynes were filled with green frogbit and duckweed. Kingcups clustered at their edges. As she cycled the short cut, along the old drove, the heron flew overhead, trailing its legs, sauntering seaward. The tidal flood of winter had receded, leaving low pockets of water drying as the fields grew lush with long grasses, pale lady's smock, buttercup and clover. The spring sun warmed Lilli's face and persuaded the first freckles across her nose.

She'd assured Maud of her early return to work. She would start back today. Maud would have a break soon, sooner than she imagined. But for now she would be pleased to see her back, Lilli thought. There were others expecting her, Edith for one, Paolo and Maurice of course.

Expecting what, she wondered, lifting her feet from the pedals, allowing the bicycle wheels to spin effortlessly downhill. It would be nice for once to be rid of the expectation of others. Nice to be free, to have no duty or responsibility, but only oneself to think of. She knew people, women even, who lived like that. Who'd been allowed to map their lives without consideration of those around them, who were not held by their history or imprisoned in their family. Why couldn't she be more like that?

An orange tip flickered past her nose. Now Vera was gone surely it was time for her to emerge, to break free, like a butterfly held captive, emerging from its cocoon, cracking the brittle shell, pushing out and shedding the brown papery husk. Floating out into a tracery of leaf and branch, settling and unfolding to show its painted wings.

She pulled up between the parlour and the hotel. She smelt the mud on the fresh summery air. A covey of white permed heads and bent backs spilled from a coach into Fiori's. They wore their macs, in case. Carried their rolled up clear plastic rainhoods (the ones whose strings grew soggy about the chin and dripped) in their pockets. They would keep Paolo busy, she thought. And Maria happy.

She glanced up towards the front, to a sky of floating islands in blue custard, before she entered the hotel. It was as if Maud never moved, as if she lived her life behind the curve of the reception desk, and the cover of a magazine.

'Lilli, my dear Lilli,' she cried, looking up from her copy of *Breakaway*. Lilli enjoyed her genuine delight, the animation that surfaced on Maud's upturned face. 'I'm so glad to see you. And how are you? Should you really be back so soon? I wouldn't want you to overdo it,' she said, all the while fearful that Lilli had made a mistake, that Lilli was not intending to work, that she was just paying a social visit, a courtesy.

'I'm fine, Maud. I'm glad to be back, back to normal.'

Maud hoped the relief did not show on her face. 'Well, you must take it easy now and say if you need time off for anything, anything at all I know what it's like. There's a lot to be done. It was like that when my mother died and only me to take care of it all, except Maurice. He took care of some of it, the money, it was left . . .' She stopped suddenly, she did not want to continue with that, not now. It was no use crying over spilt milk, he'd done what he wanted with it, all of it. She'd been foolish enough to let him and now she wished, oh, how she wished she had kept some of it, a little, enough for a holiday if nothing else, back for herself. 'Take yourself down to the kitchen, have some breakfast before you start. We're not busy and Maurice won't miss you, not when he doesn't know you're here. Go on.'

In the kitchen lunch was underway. Soup in great saucepans. Trays of sliced lamb. Vats of potato. Duncan was chopping mint. Its green juices ran into the veins of the wooden chopping board. Pearl sat in the far corner drinking a mug of coffee. She said, 'I was sorry to hear about your mother, Lilli, she was a lovely woman, she didn't deserve it. Are you all right, love? Here, sit down, I'll make you a cuppa.'

Lilli did as she was told, feeling suddenly frailer, near to tears as a result of Pearl's simple expression of regret. She stayed for a while in the kitchen's steamy warmth, safe in the underbelly of the hotel. When she'd regained her composure, when she was ready, she left and made her way up the stairs to the second-floor office.

Maurice was not expecting her. He found himself breathless, groping for words, ill prepared. Lilli sensed victory and a new shift in their relationship. He was weak and she powerful. It had always been so but there had been times when he had turned the tables, when she had suffered at his hands just like the others. That was to be no more. He was to suffer for what he'd done and they would begin today.

'Don't touch me,' she said as he went to put a hand on her breast. 'I don't want you to, not today. I've got work to do.' With that she turned and left. Outside his door she smiled to herself. 'I've got you,' she murmured, 'I've got you now.'

By the time she'd finished work the town had dispatched its visitors and the ice-cream parlour was relatively quiet.

'I thought you weren't going to start back until next week,' said Paolo from behind the counter, evidently delighted to see her.

'I want to get back to normal and I want to move.' She blurted it out, realising as she said it that she needed to be out of the house and away from the room in which her mother had died. It would also be easier, she thought, to be away from Nell and Ted for a bit, too. She was still angry with Nell. She'd never imagined Nell and Charlie – not Nell. She was too happy with Ted, and Ted was good and kind.

Lilli was angry with her. She'd betrayed them, keeping secrets, covering up. She was as bad as Edith.

'I'd like somewhere on the seafront,' she said with growing confidence, knowing what it was she wanted, what was best for her. 'On the seafront looking out over the estuary and the sea. It can't be that difficult. There must be plenty of places to let.'

Paolo liked the idea. It meant she would be closer to him. She clearly wasn't tied to the house or to Nell. They could spend their evenings together and their nights. They could make plans for the trip. He would tell his mother. 'A lot of places will be summer lets but I'm sure there'll be somewhere,' he said. 'I'll help you look.'

'I'd put the house up for sale tomorrow if I could; move as soon as I can. Have you got a *Gazette*?' Now that she'd decided, she wanted it to happen all at once, the next day. It couldn't happen soon enough. She could pack up and leave the house, it would stand. She'd make a new home, decide what to take and what to leave behind, what to give away. She'd take only what was hers, her treasures that lay gathering dust on her dressing table, the fragments of another life that called to her in another time, the life of woman; not so different from her own, a woman with a child.

The armlet was safe in her pocket. She felt for it as she left the parlour and wheeled her bicycle onto the front where she stood looking out to sea . . .

She'd been alone, just her and the baby, travelled alone, though never to the sea. The baby's father had not stayed long, she had sent him away preferring to be alone. It was what she'd grown used to. She was used to making her way in the world, after the wave. At first she had been afraid, but in time it had made her strong and she thought it for the best. Now she was not so sure. Now a longing rose up in her, now when she thought of him, of lying with him in the roundhouse, of

169

watching him go, and she wished he would return so that they might begin to make a new life. She wished that when she dreamed of the sea, the monster she had never seen with its hungry, gaping mouth, he would be there beside her to comfort her.

The Seafront

Edith sat compliant, in her usual chair, gazing out at the sea through the long window. The crocheted blanket covered her knees. First her son, then her husband, now her daughter. She asked herself, what was left? What point in her bingo-ridden, basket-weaving, bread and butter existence? She'd been put away. Rendered powerless, robbed of her dignity, she'd become an object of pity. People would be whispering about her, tut-tutting, she knew. She wished herself dead in Vera's place.

It was George's birthday and the staff were fussing about him opening his cards, bringing him morning coffee and bourbons, his favourite. Edith was glad to be left alone. She no longer regretted or resented the attention she did not get. As for coffee and biscuits, a drink maybe, but there seemed little point in eating. She was not intending to live much longer, not like this. She'd stopped wondering where their lives had all gone wrong, she lacked the will to pursue such entanglements and supposition.

Spring had moved into early summer. Edith neither denied nor acknowledged the change; spring, summer – they held no meaning for her. They were not seasons she could recognise, no longer places like the one she found herself in. Spring was a promise, summer, your salad days. Edith waited on no promise and cherished no hope. She would simply be; sit, exist for as long as it took. She would not acknowledge the sun splashing in. She would keep the crocheted blanket around her knees.

* * *

Visitors to the town paraded in the sunshine, along the sea front. A number of them had taken up residence at The Seaview. The hotel was airing itself. It had woken from its winter slumber. Windows were opened to chase the damp, musty air from the empty rooms. Beds were made up, guests welcomed.

Maud no longer enjoyed the luxury of a Monday off. Maurice had forbidden it, although now that Lilli was back she was ever hopeful. Maurice was not happy, she could tell. He was nervous, jittery, and Lilli did not appear to calm him as she had before. Still at least he'd kept out of Maud's way. The memory of their last brutal encounter was still fresh in her mind. It had been her failure to order the sausages that had precipitated the attack. They were short at breakfast and as a consequence Maurice had suffered a sausageless English breakfast. She had been rewarded by a fist in the face.

Maud was sat at reception, a cup of weak tea in her hand, lost in a *Baker's Tours Brochure*, which she kept hidden inside a copy of *The Hotelier*. She was prepared to forgo Torquay. A modest coach tour, something nearer home, a weekend, a day trip even. A day out on a Monday with Dorothy would be nice.

Above her in his office, on the second floor, Maurice was waiting.

Still Runs the Water

Lilli stared hard at her face in the mirror. She thought it different from the face she'd worn only a few weeks ago. It was more determined, stronger. The saxifrage blue of her eyes startled and summer freckles coloured her nose and cheeks. She applied her make-up with a deliberate care, slowing down each application, relishing the preparation, casting a spell in black and red. Eyes blacked with mascara, lips red, redder than usual, stretched and pursed, top lip over bottom accepting and spreading the Luscious Ruby. She teased her hair with a comb so that it was wild about her face.

She dressed with unusual care, putting on a black corset laced from pubic bone to breast, and attaching stockings to its taut suspenders. On her feet she wore her brown cycling boots. She pulled her nylon overall on top and put a pair of six-inch metal-tipped stilettos in her shopping bag, along with other items purchased from the adult bookshop and retrieved from their hiding place in the chest drawer. These included a dog chain, handcuffs, and leather straps. Maurice was in for a treat. She pictured him waiting in his office, pimply and pale like a turkey ready for trussing.

She replaced the photograph in the pocket of her overall; it was becoming creased and worn. When she was ready, she put on her coat and, picking up her bag, left the house.

The water gathered pace as it neared the weir. Lilli cycled alongside. Here it was calm still, masking the threat of torrent, the white and furious rage. *Still runs the water where the brook is deep* – for a long time she had puzzled on that proverb, one of the four, one for each side of the old biscuit tin in which Vera kept the buttons. She'd read them many times before she'd come to understand them, and this had taken the longest of all to fathom and so was always the one she recalled. It was only in her early adulthood that she had begun to appreciate its meaning.

Pondskaters drifted across the brown surface of the water. Flag irises cooled their feet at its edges, in the shade of the willows, where it lay like a liquid carpet, waiting to be unfurled; waiting for the ratchet and wheel turning and lifting, to release the flood. She heard the crash of water now as it fell through the iron cage and watched the slim green willow leaf tumble through the avalanche.

The Seaview was quiet. One of the chambermaids, Nancy, had taken over from Maud, who was attending to a complaint. She was filing her nails and reading the problem page of *Woman's Own*, wondering what she would do if her husband left her for a neighbour's wife. Move in with the neighbour, perhaps? Her neighbour was really quite presentable. He was younger and taller and fitter than her spouse and often looked her way and smiled when he was out washing his car. She'd seen him look at her. He was an attractive man. She wondered why she'd not thought of it before. She looked up and nodded as Lilli came through the entrance and passed the desk. Taking her coat off Lilli made straight for the faded blue stair.

The air in the hotel was fresher than usual; it had a salty outdoor tang. The curved mahogany of the handrail slipped beneath the palm of her right hand as she stepped deliberately up, her stockings sibilant between her thighs. In her left hand she carried her shopping bag, her presents for Maurice.

Maurice was waiting in a state of enervation peculiar to Mondays. But Mondays were different since her return. He was not sure what to expect. She was more of a tease than ever. She promised much but failed to deliver. Where once her reluctance had angered him, he found himself distressed at her heightened power. She'd become ruthless in her dealings with him. She'd taken control and this both excited and scared him. The green and silver Brut bottle stood empty on his desk next to his inhaler, which he felt he might need, particularly when he allowed himself to think of the new slim-line, anal dildo he had sent away for and which had arrived on Friday, leading to a weekend of feverish anticipation. He would use it this morning with Lilli, he thought. She could use it on him if she liked. He'd be careful, he promised himself, careful not to get over-excited like last week. He'd been a bit rough with her. She'd encouraged it, of course, provoked him, dared him. But he didn't want to spoil things just when they were getting started again. He didn't want to spoil things, not like he had with Vera.

He could have married her. She'd been keen enough in the six months they'd courted and he'd been a promising catch for a country girl in a seaside town. Vera had been impressed, surely she had; after all his father was an hotelier and a man of means. It was clear he would inherit. He had his father's business acumen and what he lacked in good looks he made up for in prospects.

Vera's mother Edith had approved the match, talked openly of a wedding, with everyone who was anyone there. He'd suspected that Nell felt differently and had tried his best to keep out of her way. He was right. Nell had despised him, finding him rank and chesty and altogether suspicious. Vera had been passive, submitting to his immature fumblings without protest or pleasure.

Her father had been uncertain, until the night his daughter arrived home with a streak of blood running from her hairline down the left side of her face, dripping onto her white blouse, while another, less obvious, ran slowly down the inside of her thigh to her ankle. Vera had been forbidden to see him again. She was sent away for a holiday to an aunt in Martock. Hauser was left to brood on his loss of control and

175

attempt to reconstitute the events of the evening in order to justify his sticky desire. Edith was left to mourn the cancelled nuptials and the reflected glory such a match would have bestowed.

Lilli did not knock. She pushed the door firmly open and stepped inside, then closed it behind her.

'You're early,' he said.

'Yes,' she said, bending to take off her boots. She reached inside her bag for the red stilettos and arched her feet into them. Maurice breathed in audibly. 'I've brought you something,' she said, 'a present for you.' She passed him the anonymous brown packet.

'Thank you.' He was surprised, not being at all used to small kindnesses, being more a man of small cruelties. 'Thank you,' he repeated with hesitancy, pulling a black rubber G-string from the packet.

'Put it on,' said Lilli. She walked over to the door and turned the key in the lock. Turning to face him she lifted the nylon overall over her head. It's static caught her hair, sending it into shock. 'Hurry up, I'm waiting.' She stood in her corset and stockings while he fiddled with the buttons on his trouser waist and fly. He stripped willingly, finally removing his underpants, knitted socks and polished shoes. He stepped into the G-string, over which his pale belly hung loose. It rubbed uncomfortably along his appendix scar but that was a small discomfort. It was easily ignored when he considered his growing if partial erection, pleasing so soon in the proceedings.

'On your knees. Get down.'

'Wait,' said Hauser as he bent to unlock the drawer of his desk to remove the dildo. 'A present for you, my dear,' he said breathlessly, emboldened by Lilli's mood. 'Use it on me if you like. I have some Vaseline.'

'These first,' she said, lifting the handcuffs from the partially open packet and snapping one onto his right wrist. 'Bend down, on all fours, there's a good dog, down.' She pressed on his flabby back until he was kneeling down. 'Good,' she said as she attached the other handcuff to the desk leg. He was going nowhere. She fastened the dog collar around his neck and pulled on the chain, jerking his head at right angles to his body. Keeping the collar taut she pushed the stiletto heel of her shoe into his left buttock. He gasped and grimaced; she ground it in, eliciting a sharp cry of pain. He tried to get up but the chain was tight and the handcuffs restricting. He was left on all fours. Lilli sat astride him, facing the thin string of plastic which separated his cheeks. She inserted the dildo into his anus, pushing it in hard, without a hint of lubrication or preparation. 'There,' she said, 'do you like that?'

Maurice could not reply.

'I said, do you like that, didn't I? Answer me,' she said, ramming the dildo home, so that Maurice cried out in a hoarse and strangled voice which barely escaped his throat.

'No, please, no.'

Getting up, standing over him, she saw the saliva dribble from his mouth. His face and neck were swelling and purple. She removed her final prop from the parcel, a small leather whip, and brought it down on his backside until she drew blood; more than once. Maurice was on the point of collapse when she took the camera from her shopping bag and inflicted the final humiliation.

Lying prone he tried feebly to reach for his inhaler. Lilli positioned it just out of reach. She took off her stilettos and pulled on her overall. She left him gasping for breath. Maud was back at the reception desk. Lilli approached her with a brown envelope in hand.

'For you,' she said, extending her hand. She waited while Maud opened it and revealed the two Polaroids, grainy but unmistakeable in content and subject. Maud found them shocking but not entirely unfamiliar. She understood and looked at Lilli with an expression of admiration and gratitude.

'I have others,' Lilli said, 'and I won't hesitate to use them. Tell him from me.'

A faint smile spread across Maud's face, then widened to a grin. 'Is he?'

'A bit tied up at the minute. Don't hurry. Goodbye, Maud,' said Lilli as she left the hotel.

Lilli made straight for the ice-cream parlour where she demolished a North Pole. 'I've left the hotel,' she told Paolo as he came to sit next to her in a seat by the window. 'I'm looking for a new job. You were right about Hauser. I don't know why I put up with him all this time, but there, it's all sorted out now. I won't be going back.' Paolo looked at her approvingly. 'I need to find that flat now – it can't wait.'

He nodded, sensing her excitement, not wishing to break the spell. It was what he'd hoped for, wanted, but had not dare express. Lilli was not a woman easily convinced or persuaded into action. She would decide. It was all falling into place. She would be nearer and they could begin to plan for the autumn. He'd already discussed it with his father, going to Italy. His mother not. She'd have some objection, he felt sure, chiefly on account of Lilli. It was nothing he couldn't overcome; he was prepared to forgo her approval if things were right with Lilli and things seemed to be moving in just the right direction.

'I can help you,' he said. 'We'll look straight away. Something for the summer would do, wouldn't it? That's if we leave in September. You won't need a long let.'

'I'm not sure,' she said, 'there are other things still, things I need to do.'

She was stalling, he could tell. Against his better judgement he pursued her. 'What things? There's plenty of time to sort everything out before we go surely?'

'Other things I haven't told you about.'

She took the photograph of the baby from her pocket. She felt a familiar ache. She looked at it, as she did every time, in a mixture of disbelief and wonderment. She passed it to him and he saw the baby cradled in unknown arms, a mite with eyes closed, nose wide and a mass of hair. He looked up from the photograph.

'She's mine,' she said, 'she was born when I was sixteen. She'll be ten now. I was sent away to London, to aunt Flo's. I had her there. They all came when she was born, Mum and Edith and Nell and Ted. I didn't know they'd taken the photo. It must be Nell holding her. Then she was adopted, it was all arranged. Everyone thought it was for the best. I didn't know what to think; anyway nobody asked me, well not that I remember. I don't know what I thought or felt. I was frightened but once she was there I didn't want to give her up. I wanted to keep her but I went along with it all. I thought that was what I had to do. Then when it was over we just came home and we never spoke about it, not once. We never spoke but I missed her, I cried myself to sleep missing her. I've always missed her. The crying may have stopped but it doesn't get any better. It just gets worse as time goes by. It's like an empty space left in my body where she grew. Once we were connected, growing together and then suddenly she was gone and nothing was left, just a hollow, hungry feeling. Now I wonder where she is and what she's like, what the colour of her hair is, what her voice sounds like. Does she look like me? Does she think about me? She must think about me, she must want to know who her mother is, if she knows that is. Don't you think? Why and what happened, where her family is.'

'Of course, if she knows.' It had taken him by surprise. He tried not to show it.

'I try not to think about it but sometimes I can't sleep and I lie there and I'm so angry that she's not with me, that we never had the chance, that I didn't keep her. And sometimes so desperate that I could have done it – let her go like I did. I can't believe it. Can't believe that they didn't even consider it, that they didn't even try. Couldn't they have tried? Other people have brought up their daughter's child or their granddaughter's child. I know, I've seen it so why didn't they? Didn't they care, hiding me away like that? What will she think? She'll hate me, won't she? I've got to let her know that I had no choice. I know she'll come looking one day. She'll come looking for me. You can now, you know. The law's changing, they told me. A woman explained it all.'

Marsha

It had been two days before the funeral, it was cut into her mind, like words chiselled on stone, an enduring inscription. She would remember it always . . .

Nell had asked her on the outing with Mrs Murdoch. It was a regular thing shopping for material. 'Why don't you come? There's nothing else you can do now. It'll be a break for you, from being here. You can go off while we look at material. Go and look around your old haunts, and we can meet up at lunchtime. We always have a good lunch and she pays. She can afford it, can't she?'

'All right,' said Lilli.

It was some time since she'd been to the city. She'd worked in a sandwich bar there once, for a while, living in the flat above with her friend Linda, drinking copious amounts of cheap wine at night and talking about men. She wondered if she would see Linda, then remembered she was away travelling now. Never mind if she did not see anyone she knew, that might be for the best, although it would have been nice to talk things over with Linda, tell her what had happened. She wished she knew where she was. She could have written to her. It was careless of her, the way she let people go sometimes, the way she pulled a shutter down somewhere in her mind and then moved on.

The city was small, easily encompassed, a city only by virtue of its cathedral. Mrs Murdoch preferred to shop there. She especially liked King's. It was old-fashioned. She approved of that, of a traditional material shop. They were becoming hard to find. Its dark wood interior smelled of linen. It was stacked with rolls of fabric: satin, silk, crepe de chine and chiffon, wool, brushed cottons and corduroy. They spilled from its shelves. Bolts of cloth were levered down and laid out on the wide counter. Unwound by expert hands they were drawn in yards between thumb and first finger and thrown up to float in the air before the customer in a shimmer of colour, like laundered sheets billowing on a line.

Mrs Murdoch liked King's and she liked to take Nell there with her. Nell could advise her on patterns. She generally preferred Vogue to all else; they were her favourites despite the fact that Nell found them a nightmare to cut. Mrs Murdoch was remarkably like a Vogue sketch, like the line drawing displayed on the pattern fronts, long and thin. Despite her age, her figure was elegant and she prided herself on dressing in the Parisian style. As the wife of a well-to-do businessman she felt it her duty to preserve her appearance. She required her clothes to be tailored to fit, handmade by Nell. She resisted the modern tendency to ready-made, considering it quite common and inferior. She'd welcomed Lilli on the day's outing, seeing her as something of a charitable cause, a woman in a predicament; her mother had just died, and added to that she was a woman without a man.

Nell and Mrs Murdoch made straight for King's. They would be there for several hours, Nell told Lilli. They arranged to meet for lunch at The Hole in the Wall at one o'clock. She left them at the double windows draped on one side with soft blues and greens, and on the other with a tangle of pinks and lime. She saw Nell glance back at her, then put her head down and push open the glass doorway, allowing the interior to swallow her up.

Lilli pulled her coat to her against the cold and made off in the direction of the Palace Green. As she fingered and smoothed the photograph buried in her coat pocket, she watched the mothers out with their prams, out with their small children, hands held tight. Mothers with their mothers. Out shopping. Out together. It might have been her, could be in the future. Paolo wanted children, he'd told her so, he wanted a family. It would be easy enough to arrange. They would have to marry of course, Maria would insist; a family wedding. Nell would make the dresses and she would carry a bouquet of old scented roses. She was beginning to think she would like that, now that Vera was gone and she was alone. He was a good man, solid and dependable. She envied the women with their prams. She felt like crying, but sensed that if she started to cry she would never stop. Her grief for Vera was still raw and fresh. Her other grief was covered, but nearing the surface every day and weeping like a wound which refused to heal.

She walked along the Green to Brown's Gate, then followed the road back along the north side of the Cathedral. She did not go in. She thought of it, going in, sitting for a while, lighting a candle, but it was too public. She might give way to tears. Instead she made for the back streets and found herself on unfamiliar territory. She passed beneath a small cobbled archway into a half hidden and narrow street. It was bordered both sides with Georgian terraces, two steps up to discreet front doors with brass plaques and window boxes. The brass plaque announced: St Andrew's Diocesan Adoption Agency. She stopped. Questions filled her head. Questions she wanted to ask, things she needed to know and a story she wanted to tell swam about her. They took hold of her and led her to the door.

It was opened by a woman with grey hair, plaited and wrapped like mufflers about her ears. She wore a neat white blouse, fastened at the neck with a small turquoise brooch, and a navy cardigan and skirt.

'Can I help you?'

'I'm not sure . . .' Lilli hesitated.

'Would you like to come in? Please come in,' said the woman. They stood in the hallway, alongside a blue jardinière and its trailing fern. The woman looked expectantly at Lilli.

'I was hoping I might be able to talk to someone. It's about adoption. You see, I had a baby adopted and . . .' She could not continue, pain flooded her. It was some time before she could speak. By then she was seated in a small room with two armchairs and a low coffee table, a box of tissues and a cup of tea.

'I'm Mrs Roberts,' said the grey-haired lady, 'there's just me and the secretary here now but I work for the agency. I'm an adoption worker, so perhaps I can help.'

Lilli spilled her story into the room. It fell from her like a rock falling from a cliff top, heavy and clattering, gaining speed as it crashed and splintered on the pebbled shore and scattered into the sea. Mrs Roberts listened. No one had ever done that before, not in that way. But then Lilli had never told anyone her story before, not someone else, only herself, over and over in her mind. Now it was out, washed up and away with the tide, far out to sea. She felt better by the time she'd finished and she held out the photograph for Mrs Roberts to see.

'It felt like I had no choice,' said Lilli. 'It was all decided for me and now I think about her more and more since my mother died. Marsha, that's what I call her. That's my name for her. It's a secret. We never talked about it once it was over, never talked about her. I've told people, one or two, but not how it felt, well not like I've told you.'

Mrs Roberts nodded. Lilli was aware that she had said almost nothing, that she just nodded in agreement. She understood.

'She's beautiful,' said Mrs Roberts, admiring the baby in the photograph. Then she said, 'I think there is something you should know, Lilli, it may help. There's a new adoption act, and now young people of eighteen or over will be able to see their birth records. They'll have the right to know who their natural parents are and which adoption agency holds their records. They'll have the choice. Marsha will have the choice of knowing who you are. You are her mother, you've never stopped being her mother, and one day, Lilli, she may come looking for you.'

Afterwards Lilli went to sit on a bench in the gardens by the moat. She sat there until one o'clock, not feeling the cold, unaware of her surroundings, only looking up from time to time to register a passer-by and the high defensive walls that marked the boundary between the moat and the Bishop's Palace.

She needed to absorb it all. It changed everything. Marsha was no longer her lost daughter; no more substantial than a fading photograph or the seed of a dandelion floating on the wind, blown away in childish games, disappearing into the blue. Marsha was suddenly flesh and bones. She'd grown, taken shape. She was material and tangible. For a moment she glimpsed her and it changed everything. It was possible that Marsha could find her and that she would come looking. Now there were ways that bound them, tracks she could follow, which they could follow, a way back to each other. A vista opened before her and a black curtain was lifted.

A swan gliding on the black ripples of the moat pulled at the rope attached to the small bell by the wall of the gatehouse. It was a century-long tradition which signalled time for food. Lilli looked up. She was hungry. It was time to meet Nell. She would keep her secret, she decided. She was not yet ready to share this new and precious gift. She would hug it to her and let nothing spoil it.

Over dinner at The Hole in the Wall she was content to listen, to catch Nell's eye and stifle a giggle when Mrs Murdoch returned the fresh peaches and asked for them to be peeled. She and Nell were not used to such assumption. But they ate with relish the skinned and dripping fruit, pasted with thick spoonfuls of clotted cream and Lilli thought about a daughter with buttery skin and fleshy limbs cuddled into her, sat at her side.

'So who were they, who were Marsha's parents?' Paolo asked. 'You and who else, Lilli, what about her father?'

'I don't know,' she said, looking down at the photograph. 'It could have been any one of them. I went with a number, on the riverbank, in the old railway carriages, the churchyard. Don't ask me why. I don't know who the father is. It's better that way. That way there's just me.'

'What about if she finds you? She'll want to know. What will you say? Have you thought of that?'

'I don't know. I just hope she'll understand. I was sixteen. I was sixteen and I slept with . . . I'll tell her I was a whore, shall I, I'll tell her that?'

'I didn't mean to say that, just that it won't be easy and she might be disappointed or angry.'

'I know but I've got plenty of time to prepare. I'll think of what to say.'

'Italy is a good place to think. There will be plenty of time there.'

'Aren't you angry, don't you mind?'

'Why should I? I only mind that you mind. I want us to be together no matter what. I want you to come away with me.'

Lilli closed her eyes and saw them sat together beneath a ragged vine, dappled by sun, in the village square outside his grandfather's house. She put the photograph back in her pocket.

'I'm coming,' she said, wanting to believe it.

Stranded Seaweed

'I want his address,' she said to Nell who looked up at her from the hem she was unpicking with the points of her scissors.

'I'm sorry, Lilli, I'm sorry,' she said putting her scissors down and laying the dress on her lap. 'I didn't mean it. They weren't deliberate. The secrets. I should have told you before about Charlie and Pauline but it didn't seem right as long as Vera was alive. I've seen them a couple of times, been to their house but they've never been here, although he wanted to. Charlie wanted to come to see you.'

'Does he know about me, about what happened?'

'The baby?' asked Nell. Lilli nodded. 'No he doesn't. It's quite ordinary, you know, where they live, just a terrace of houses. The last time I saw them she was working in the factory and he was driving a taxi. I think he regretted it. It wears off, the shine, the excitement, the whole desperate thing wears off and down into the same mundane life we all lead. It doesn't last. You can't make your happiness on the back of others' misery, he told me that. No one can and no one can keep it going forever, that first flush. They'd be worn out if they tried. The glamour went pretty soon, I think, not much glamour in leaving your children behind. She had two, don't forget, Rebecca and Joe. It spoils everything. That's why I couldn't; swore never to have a child, Lilli. I can't see where the happiness lies in all of it. I can't remember being happy as a child, not really, no fun, and then watching you. Seeing how much you missed him, everything washed up and wrecked and Vera too. I couldn't, can't. I couldn't be sure that I wouldn't go, that out of love, you know I wouldn't get up and leave. I did for Ted. I might have for Charlie. I never wanted that, better to be safe.'

Tears filled Nell's eyes so that she saw only the blur of a hem as they dropped onto the woollen skirt laid across her lap. She wiped them away with the sleeve of her printed blouse. She got up and went over to the sideboard where she found a pen and paper to write the address.

Lilli could not bear to see her like this. She loved Nell and didn't want her to suffer. She didn't deserve to – good, kind, honest Nell, despite the secrets. Lilli understood that both of them were trapped by their experience and both were struggling to put things right. 'I don't want it. Forget it. If I see him it will be here, nowhere else,' and saying this she crossed the room to Nell and put her arms around her and pulled her close. 'I'm sorry,' she whispered.

Lilli returned to the house. She would be packing up soon, moving with the summer to her new home. She had yet to find it but she saw it like a great clam opening up to let her in, like a pearly shell coiling its spiral skin around her. She lifted a conch shell from among those in the basket by the fireplace. She put it to her ear, and heard the rush of the sea and the crackle of stranded seaweed. She sat in the armchair and laid the armlet in her lap . . .

Green-winged orchids sprout underfoot as ferns uncurl, opening like baby's fists. The winter floods have subsided and the land beneath her feet is sprung with new growth soft enough for the baby to crawl unharmed out of the door of the roundhouse into sunlight. The baby has grown strong and healthy. He has survived his first winter. This summer she will collect tansy and mallow for love. It will be hot and dry, the old women of the settlement foretell. Hotter even than the summers of their youth. They will hang seaweed in the roundhouse to keep it from fire and in the hope of bringing new friends to replace their lost loves. Perhaps he will return, perhaps the seaweed will bring him back to her.

The Wind Off the Sea

Lilli woke early to the soft song of summer, to the promise of blue sky and birdsong and a warm sun. It shone in at her window, it called her, compelling her to begin her search for a new home. She got out of bed quickly, pulled on her jeans and rummaged in her wardrobe until she found the white cotton smock she saved for days such as these. Days when the sea rippled like a satin cloth thrown onto a table and smoothed down. She set off on her bicycle, pedalling effortlessly along the lanes through fields of ripening corn to where Paolo was waiting.

Armed with the *Gazette* they walked along the edge of the incoming tide towards the end of the esplanade, to Catherine Terrace. Even Paolo was persuaded to take his shoes off and dip his feet in the tepid wash of the sea. Lilli kicked at the water, lifting a rainbow of spray into the air, laughing as it splashed his shirt and soaked the newspaper.

It had been at the top of the To Let column, the first she had read: furnished flat on the second floor overlooking the sea. As Lilli stood below it, looking up at the pale curved façade and tall windows, she was determined to have it. It was sparsely furnished. It held what was necessary, enough places to sit, a double bed to sleep in, cooker and fridge and in front of the window, looking out to sea and sky, a small square table with a white cloth of the type they'd embroidered at school. It smelt of mothballs and cats.

'No pets and a month's rent in advance,' said Mrs Gibson crisply. As the owner and landlady, she occupied the ground floor. She made the rules. 'Will you both be taking it?'

'Just me,' replied Lilli.

'She'll think about it,' said Paolo.

'I'll take it. I'll have the rent for you in the morning. I'll start moving my things tomorrow.'

'Very well,' said Mrs Gibson.

Lilli turned to Paolo and said quietly, 'It will be cold in the winter with the wind blowing off the sea but I don't mind.'

'You don't have to think of winter, we will be gone by then.'

Lilli already knew that she would not want to give up the flat. It was her new home, her own. She wanted to spend the winter there, close to the water, watching it come and go in the rhythm of the seasons, light and dark. She didn't argue. She was too eager to get home, to go back and start packing and begin the process of leaving the past behind.

Part Four

Becca

Lilac

The lilac was in bloom. Patrick had cut a swathe through the long grass with blunt shears. They sat in it now, in deckchairs around a small slatted table, drinking tea and wine and eating the chocolate cake Rosa had made for his birthday. The air was heavy and filled with the drowsy perfume of lilac.

Earlier that day they'd gathered to say goodbye to Mick and Joe, and Mick's fish tank sat bubbling quietly in Patrick's kitchen. It had been easier than she thought, saying goodbye to him, giving him her present: a book on French painters, which in the end she'd had to steal from a bookshop in the Charing Cross Road. She'd waved him off and he, grateful for the ease of their parting, had promised to write, to come back soon, pressing money into her hand and telling her to take care as he kissed her on the cheek. They'd embraced as any brother and sister. As he climbed into the van and she watched him go, her throat had constricted and her eyes had filled. Turning back to the house she'd hurried into the garden and waited for Rosa and Patrick to begin the birthday celebrations.

Now, after food and a few glasses of wine, she felt better. It hadn't been so bad. The anticipation had been far worse. Her fear of losing Joe and of being alone had made her sick. She'd felt sick every time she thought about Joe leaving. For days she'd barely eaten and had lived on chocolate and cigarettes, but now she was hungry. She still had Rosa and Patrick, she reasoned – almost a family. She still had her friends. Mags and Simone had called the day before. Nothing had been said about events above the butcher's but their forgiveness was implicit. They'd forgotten. There were plans

afoot to step up the campaign and for a big meeting sched-
uled at the Town Hall. She was back in the fold and summer
had arrived.

'I love lilac,' Becca said.

'Then you should take some home with you, bunches,
armfuls,' Patrick said expansively. She pictured it in a great
jug on the table by the window. 'And I love chocolate cake,'
he said, looking across at Rosa. Becca saw the faint flush on
her cheek and the widening of her eyes.

They sat until late afternoon. The company sustained her
so that she did not think of Joe other than to be glad she was
not sitting in a hot, fume-filled van on such a day. She left
Patrick's house laden with branches and hurried home to find
the white jug from her grandmother's house, the one that had
always stood on the marble washstand in the china bowl.
She found it in the cupboard beneath the sink. She filled it
to overflowing and stood it on the table by the window.

It had been hot and muggy, too hot to do anything, and
she'd taken to her bed, to books and old magazines, and her
dolls, not venturing out for several days, living from tins and
sour-milk cartons. That afternoon she'd been dragged from
her lethargy by a sudden impulse and a rush of energy.
Pulling sheets from her bed she had stripped and cleaned the
flat in a frenzy of scourer and cloth. Resting now, looking
from chair to window, she fixed on the still life of white jug
and flower which cut its form into a canvas of pewter beyond
the window. Her house was in order, standing sentinel
against the impending downpour.

The Red Bathroom

The sky glowed purple as the storm broke over the Creek. The room was drowned in a heady perfume as the lilac released its scent like soil soaked in summer rain. She watched the lightning split the sky and heard the thunder crack. Then felt the first startling pain like a fist tearing at her inside, leaving her bent double and holding onto the table's edge. She had not felt anything like this before. It was not a niggle, a low moan or cramp, not the bloated dragging of menstruation, but a knock you-sideways, take-your-breath-away pain. She made for the bathroom, shuffling her way. Once there her insides emptied, everything running out of her so that she wondered had her baby dissolved within her and become liquid? She was afraid she would be unable to get up. How would she stand? Where would she find feeling enough to make her legs work when she was overwhelmed by this interior blinding, stretching pain at her centre that left all else numb? She clutched the curled lip of cool enamel, pulling herself somehow from the toilet to the bath. She leaned across and turned the taps, drawing warm water into which she stepped. She lowered herself carefully until she was seated, knees up, head bent, in a pool of water streaked with her blood, in a bath of rose pink.

She threw her head back and gripped the sides of the bath as her body lifted and heaved with each contraction. Her hair matted to her forehead as sweat poured, mimicking the walls around her, red and dripping. Walls closing in on her, squashing her so that she couldn't breathe. Hammering at her like her childhood nightmares. Walls of blood-red gloss. Why had she painted the bathroom walls red? Why not primrose or pastel blue? Pain clawed at her, the pain of soft tender flesh in a vice, tightening, breaking the skin, crushing bone and sinew to a pulp. She was held in a womb of pain, contained and trapped in suspended time.

She had no way of knowing how long she had been there or how often she had released and drawn water to keep warm. When finally she felt the baby drop, felt its head hit her, she saw the first light of the dawn at the bathroom window and heard the rain falling still. With the primeval, grunting urge to push came an exquisite ripping and then a tiny form, mucous covered, slipped into the cloudy water. She lifted the baby to her leg and from there to her stomach where he began to cry.

She lay exhausted, the water around her growing cold and the baby's cries somewhere far away in the distance. She struggled out of the bath and to her feet, holding the baby to her, then cut the cord with her kitchen scissors and pulled at it, dragging the afterbirth from her. She wrapped the baby in a towel, held him as she cleaned up and put on her dressing gown. Then laid him on the high bed while she looked around for something warmer to wrap him in. She was frightened that he would get cold. That he would die of cold. She was cold and shivering. He was stirring. She went into the hall remembering the blue crocheted shawl draped over the arm of the mannequin. She pulled it off. It would do. She wrapped him in it and went to make herself tea.

She drank it black as there was no milk in the flat; she was hungry for toast with butter but there was no bread either. There was nothing to eat for her or for the baby. It didn't matter, she reasoned; she would get bread and milk and soon the baby would be gone. She sat smoking. She hoped the baby wouldn't start crying again. Best do it now before he did. She dressed awkwardly and slowly; it was painful to move. She found a pad to put between her legs to soak up the blood and cushion her torn flesh. Outside the rain was falling, unabated. It had rained all through the afternoon and night and now into the early morning. There was still time before the day broke.

Returning to the flat she took off her wet coat and hung it to dry in the bathroom. She towelled her hair and sank into the armchair, holding Marianne in her lap. Her gaze fixed on the lilac in the white jug.

Patrick hurried through the churchyard, beneath a black umbrella. The rain slid from his polished shoes and ran in runnels at his feet. His sodden pyjama bottoms flapped at his ankles. Woken intermittently by the deluge, he feared that, not for the first time, the rainwater would creep beyond the open porch and beneath the wooden door, swelling into an unwelcome lake over the black and white tiles of the nave. Throwing his raincoat on, he had ventured out into the downpour to stop the flood. On reaching the shelter of the porch he rummaged in his pocket for the door key. As he retrieved it from the damp mess of matchbox, receipts and tissues, he was startled by the sudden and unmistakable cry of a baby. He froze then turned, looking about him. Closing his umbrella and stepping further into the porch he saw a cardboard box, patchy with the wet sitting in the far corner and rising from it the curl of a baby's fist. He approached cautiously as the baby continued to cry and the newspaper scrunched around it rustled with every kick. Disbelieving, Patrick looked down into the makeshift crib. A baby, red-faced and black-haired, squash-nosed and open-mouthed, lay wrapped in a blue shawl with what looked like a bath towel beneath. It was surrounded by headlines and newsprint from the *Mirror* and *Woman's Own*. He bent and lifted it from the box; hungry, he thought, and cold possibly. He wrapped the shawl more closely around the tiny body and, as best he could, put it under his coat. Leaving his umbrella he held fast to the bundle and scuttled back through the rain.

Patrick was used to babies. He had been born into a big

family where care of the latest baby had been part of growing up. He could make bottles and had changed nappies – albeit some time ago. He knew enough to know that this was a baby just born and in need of food and warmth. He knew also that somewhere out there was another in need of care, perhaps despairing. An impossible hidden pregnancy, a woman in need of hospital, of looking after, of help.

The kitchen was warm. Patrick found a dry box which had once held twenty-four tins of cat food. He lined it with a flannelette sheet folded thickly over the flattest pillow he could find. He constructed a nappy from a terry tea towel and pins, and swaddled the baby in a dry towel and more flannelette. He lay it down in the box. The baby screamed, howled for food. It was several hours before he could hope to feed it. Eight, the chemist would open at eight. He would wait until then. He would call on Rosa, who would come with him to buy what they needed to feed this starving scrap. Just an hour or two. An hour of rocking, of pacing back and forth until eventually, in a harmony of exhaustion, the baby stopped crying and together they dropped in and out of sleep, the baby balanced on his chest, breathing to its rise and fall, until just before eight o'clock.

'I'm coming, I'm coming. Wait.' Rosa's voice was hoarse still, not adjusted to the day. The urgent pounding at the back door had jolted her awake; her eyes were gritty with broken sleep. 'Who is it?' she called, opening the door to find him in the yard carrying something. What? 'Patrick?' She stepped out into the steamy aftermath of the storm. The slabs were warm and moist beneath her bare feet. The city and its fabric were breathing, delivering its breath up into a clearing sky and a yellow sun. 'What is it?'

'Last night in the storm' – the words tumbled from him – 'it was raining so hard I went to see if the rain was getting in, you know, under the west door like it does and I found this.'

He held the bundle up, leaning towards her. 'It was wrapped in a blue shawl in a box, a cardboard box,' he said, as if he was still not convinced. A baby in a box, left there in the porch – it had shocked him like a bad dream coming out of the blue and defying interpretation. Rosa took the baby.

'Was there a note? Was there anything in the box?'

'No, just the baby. It's a boy.' He took the baby back. He wanted it back. 'It's starving,' he said with urgency, 'I've had nothing to give him. I must get some food and bottles and . . . will you come?'

'Yes, two minutes.'

She dressed quickly and was back. Sergio was still sleeping and she had been careful not to wake him. There was no need for him to know where she was. She bothered less about such things now and he appeared not to bother at all.

In the chemist Rosa bought all they needed: bottles and milk, teats, nappies, pins. Later she would see a friend or two. She knew where she would be able to find clothes; the women round about collected them, helped out the poor in the parish, the single mothers who relied on the church. Patrick remained outside in what was now a bright morning in which he attracted a degree of attention from those out early or those on their way to work. There were a number of 'Morning Fathers', odd glances, turning heads. It was not usual to see your priest with babe in arms unless at a baptism, a family gathering, a wake even, but not on the corner of the street early in the morning. He was enjoying it and he was past caring what they thought of him. He knew it was impossible that Rosa's visits had gone unnoticed. He knew they were already talking about him. What difference would this make? The baby was crying again. He wished Rosa would hurry up. Here she was.

'Have you got everything?'

'Yes, for now anyway.'

They returned to the house and when the baby lay milky and full, its face no longer an angry purple, they began to speculate on whose baby this could be. Why was he left here, in the porch? Was it deliberate? Was it someone who knew Patrick, relied on him to take a baby in? Or had they expected one of the women to find it, coming in the morning to sweep the porch and clean the church? Was it deliberate or was it chance? It was a mystery he felt they were unlikely to solve. They would have to take action, hand him over, inform the police, but first let the baby sleep.

Patrick busied himself tidying the kitchen, finding the right places for things. The kitchen appeared instantly changed, decorated with tins of baby milk, bottles, nappies. Homely, he thought, thinking of home. Disturbing. His discovery had disturbed him. It was as if he had unearthed more than a baby from the box in the porch. For with the baby had come the return of his denial, of self-denial; there would be no children for him, no such intimacy or dependence. He wanted to keep this baby. After all, he'd found it; it was his to keep – finders keepers. An abandoned child not wanted left in his path. Already he could see how it might be with Rosa and a baby. The spilling over of the burgeoning love he felt for her. He had love he did not want to waste.

'We'll have to call the police,' Rosa said. 'They'll need to look for his mother. She must be out there somewhere, maybe not far away, she'll need help, poor thing . . .' Her voice trailed from word to thought, as she imagined a young girl sick, alone, in distress.

'I don't know,' Patrick said defensively, 'she could have caught a bus or a train, she could be miles away, she could be anywhere, anyone, they may never find her, never know . . .' But as he said it, hoped it, the realisation came that in the early hours he had spent alone with the baby, trying to console him, to stave off his hunger, he had been reminded of her. Something in the small helpless infant, something in his cry, had reminded him of Becca.

'Maybe you're right,' he said, 'maybe she's nearby.' He pictured her not well, this woman, alone, with no family to help, vulnerable. She would be desperate. In the brief silence that followed they both hesitated over her name.

Rosa said, 'She was sick such a lot, do you remember? Joe said she was always being sick. She looked pale, ill. But perhaps you don't remember. Did she seem ill when you first met her? What did you think?'

'Yes, thin and frail like a bird but with this extraordinary voice, smoking all those cigarettes.'

Rosa shuddered. 'It's her shawl, the crocheted shawl. I recognise it from the dummy in the hall. It was draped over her arm with a handbag, the blue shawl. We won't get the police yet, no?'

'No, not yet, no need. The baby's fine with me.'

Becca's Dream

The Creek had been washed by the storm. The river was full and the muddy banks were drying in the heat. Warmed by the sun's rays through glass, the lilac wilted in the vase, arching its heavy blooms. Becca slept fitfully in the armchair. Her sleep was peopled with ghosts.

Pearl came riding by on her old black bicycle along South Parade. As she approached she swung one leg elegantly across the frame to join the other and pulled herself to a halt at the gate. 'Where's Pauline?' she called to Becca, who stood small and squinting in the doorway. 'Where's Lilli? Where are they?' Becca opened her mouth to reply but could make no sound. Her voice was lost in the pink and purple lupins that threatened to overwhelm the small square of front garden with their hot, peppery scent.

Turning her back on Pearl she went back into the house where the acid stench of cat piss made her gag. The house was crammed with cats. They spilled from every room, jumping, reclining, crawling over every chair and tabletop, on every cushion in every cupboard. Cats in the house, cat piss and tom spray – Pauline hated them. Pauline would be angry with her for letting them in, leaving the window open. She looked around her. Where was Lilli? She needed her help but she was nowhere to be seen.

She began to lift and push, carry them out, closing widows, bolting doors. But to no avail for no sooner had she rid one room of them, no sooner was her back turned, than they came back to prowl and torment.

Becca woke sweating. She looked about her. It was a relief to find no soft creature brushing at her ankle, purring in her lap. For a brief moment she wondered if she had dreamt it all, baby as well as cats, but the dull aching in the lower half of her body told her no. The throbbing and the fear were too real, and the sudden waking realisation of what she had done clutched at her. Where's Pauline? Gone, Becca wanted to cry, gone. Gone and left us.

Pauline had abandoned them without a word, not a hint. Now she had done likewise; abandoned, dumped, ditched, left helpless and crying. She knew how that felt and now she had repeated her mother's mistake. But when you thought about it, maybe it was for the best. What did she have to give a child a new life, just starting out, in need? There were all the things she couldn't provide; no pram or cot, no father and no family, just herself, her struggling self. She could barely manage existence for one let alone take on another needy, dependant being, one in need of love. What did she know about maternal love? How could she think of keeping a child not just hers but hers and Joe's – her brother's child? Try telling that to a baby, better still a teenager, try that one for size. Oh, by the way I forgot to tell you, your uncle's your father, not that it makes any difference. No, she'd not repeated Pauline's mistake, she'd done something far worse and it was something that could not be put right. She could not see how it could be resolved.

Whatever future she imagined with her child was imperfect, stained, tainted, blackened by his origins and her guilt. It would be there for him and for all to see, her own dark secrets revealed, washed up and stranded like bleached and twisted driftwood, stark and glaring at the retreat of the sea.

No, she'd done the best thing. After all, there were others out there, more able than she to provide for him, without secrets and lies. Pub singers did not make good mothers, she was sure of that. He would be found and cared for. He'd already been found, hadn't he? She pushed the question away. It was too hard to think of him still lying there, unfound and unfed. Patrick would be unlocking the doors for morning confession by now. Patrick would find him.

She hoped it hadn't taken that long. She wanted her baby safe and warm. Suddenly she longed for him. Surely she could have kept him warm and safe, fed him. She could have tried to re-make, change things into something better. The feeling gnawed at her. She'd preserved him all this time. She had not had him sucked out, no bloody buckets of fleshy waste, no needles, or anaesthetic blur. So why stop now, why not carry on? So he was Joe's. Did Joe have to know, did anyone? She could stand apart from it all; she was strong enough; she could, fuck it, she could. But she wasn't thinking straight, was she? She was confused. And then there was the responsibility, it would all be too much.

She oscillated from dark to light, talking to herself in what she considered a voice of reason, countering it with the 'fuck it' voice of unreason and rebellion. She could no longer trust her thoughts or feelings. How could she put her faith in ideas which would not stand up and stay, which were knocked back in a mind that jump-started then slowed, which made up and then backed down? The process exhausted her. She longed for a cigarette. Instead she reached for her teddy and buried her face in its tired fur.

'Shall I go?' Rosa asked. Morning confession was over and they were back in the kitchen. Rosa had left the café offering Sergio no explanation; the ease with which she had done so had left her feeling light-headed. She was drugged with her own daring.

'What do you think?' said Patrick.

'What do you mean?'

'Well, who should go, what are we going to say?'

'We have to be sure first, I mean sure it's her. I'll know if I see her, I think I'll know.'

'Yes, you go then. A woman will be better, you'll know best what to do.'

'But she left him outside the church, she must have known it was you who'd find him. She wanted you to find him.'

'I suppose so.'

'You go, go to the flat. If she's still there it will be all right, she won't argue with you. She'll do as you say, she likes you, and she listens to you.'

'I'll take the cigarettes,' he said, feeling at a loss, not knowing what to expect or what he would say. Usually he was better prepared; his script was written or his role cast as the passive listener in a poor parish, soaking up its troubles and hardships, its injustices and grief, softening all with the song of absolution.

'Bring her back if it is, if you can. She'll need the doctor or the hospital. Tell her the baby's fine . . . no, don't tell her.'

'I'll see when I get there, see what's best.'

'You'll know,' said Rosa, standing up with him and moving around the table to where he stood. She put her arms around his neck, looked up and kissed him. He smiled and left her thinking not of Becca and the baby but of herself.

Becca moved slowly from the chair to the door. Her thighs were stuck with a viscid liquid. Hot jets of pain crackled in her lower abdomen, shooting into her legs. She should have stayed where she was; she would be found out, collected, processed and charged. One thing was for sure, she would pay for what she'd done, she deserved to pay. Opening the door she stood without speaking, taking in Patrick's bulk. He stepped into the hallway, easing himself past the mannequin as he followed her into the room. She sunk heavily into her chair, a surreal figure in the scattered museum of her life, her face like a mask, expressionless, her eyes unblinking.

'Becca,' he tried to begin, leaning forward from the bed where he perched, hoping for a glimmer of recognition, surprised when her mask crumpled at the sound of her name, when she began to howl. Tears flooded from her and she made no attempt to stop as they fell around her, wetting her front, streaming from her nose and mouth. He waited. He did not say 'don't cry' or 'dry your tears'; he waited and she was grateful for his patience and the way he did not grope for insubstantial and meaningless words. He made no attempt to stifle or deny her feelings. When her sobbing subsided he lit a cigarette and passed it to her. It felt damp in her mouth and she watched its white papery skin turn patchy and wet as the last of her tears fell. They smoked in silence, each drawing deeply, filling their lungs until she said, 'Is he safe?'

'Yes, he's safe, at home, in my house, with Rosa.'

'Is he . . . ?'

'He's warm and fed and sleeping. He's fine, Becca.'

'I had no choice, I couldn't say, I couldn't tell anyone, I know I should have but I . . .'

'Never mind, that doesn't come into it now. You need help, we want to help. You can't stay here like this. I want you to come back with me. Put some clothes on, Becca, a coat or something, and come home with me.'

Becca did not disagree. She did not have the strength. It was easier to do as she was told than bear the effort any longer of her tortured and confused thinking. He helped her pull her coat over her pyjamas. He felt the heat from her and saw the high spots of fever on her cheeks. She was weak, could she walk?

'Can you walk?'

'Yes I think so, I'm just hot, a bit dizzy but I can walk.'

'You can lean on me, on my arm. We'll take it slowly.'

'Not the high street,' she said.

'No, the back way, past the arches, we'll be out of the way and we can stop as often as you need. We can rest along the way.'

Eyes and Hearts

In the weeks that followed, Becca recovered. She sat for long periods in Patrick's garden where the weeds had grown tall and the Oriental poppies had opened their blind green eyes to reveal papery red cups and black sooty hearts. Sometimes she sang but only when she knew that no one was there to listen.

The baby thrived in Rosa and Patrick's care. Rosa stayed at night, sharing the broken sleep and the floor walking. At home Sergio asked nothing, fearing an answer. What he failed to understand he would have to endure. He allowed her to come and go without question. What he suspected he pushed firmly to the back of his mind, and his worry and his anger surfaced only when the Gaggia refused his ministrations and called out for her deft touch.

As for others about, as for the parish, tongues which might have wagged and doubts about the goings-on in Father Patrick's house were stifled by the baby's cries. It was a charitable act this taking in of mother and child. It was hard work. They saw their priest tired and worn, forgetful, his washing line hung with nappies. What they did not see, although many suspected, was their priest in bed, curtains wide to the open window, lying with Rosa, making love. Becca knew they shared a bed. She understood that it was not just the baby for whom Rosa stayed.

Becca slept alone; the baby slept in the carrycot in Patrick's room but Becca did not feel alone. She was strangely comforted by the three close by and by Rosa's evident happiness. Rosa was happy, very happy, and it was no more than she deserved. It seemed to Becca that Rosa had had a lifetime of fulfilling her responsibilities, putting other people's needs before hers, a lifetime spent looking after, a lifetime of forgiving. But still she retained her beauty and held no bitterness. Patrick paid her homage, bringing her the love she deserved.

And what harm was there in it? When Becca thought about it, it made her own sin less extraordinary. If a priest could, did fuck another man's wife without a crisis of faith, without guilt and self-flagellation surely she . . . Patrick was happy, he looked tired but happy. He was not carrying any great load and she began to feel that neither was she. A hole had worn in her bag of conscience and grief, and the sharp and angry rocks which had filled it were dropping one by one.

She helped in the house, cleaning, washing, cooking. She'd been out once or twice to the high street to shop but always alone; she did not take the baby with her. She did not feed or change him or pick him up. She did nothing for him. And although Patrick had registered him, as far as she was concerned he had no name.

The Washing-Up Bowl

'Can I help?' asked Becca, putting her head through the open kitchen window.

'No, I don't think so, it's nearly ready now. You can lay the table if you like.'

It was Sunday and Rosa was cooking. She'd taken to cooking early on Sunday evenings after mass, a special meal.

Becca came in from the garden where she'd been weeding; fetching out the tangles of bindweed and roots of dandelions from the hard earth. Joe's first postcard had arrived the day before. She'd been thinking of him out in the country, in the heat of the Massif Central on his way south, heading for Arles. She'd been thinking of Lilli, of the way Lilli said that picking dandelions made you wet the bed and oh how she'd believed her. Joe was fine. Everything's fine, he said. He'd printed his Poste Restante at the bottom.

In the kitchen the smell of garlic wafted from the hot pans. Becca was hungry despite the heat. She went over to the sink where she washed the dandelion juice from her hands and stood admiring her handiwork in the garden. It looked a little less overgrown. She let the tap run cold and drank a long glass of water. Then she set about laying the table.

Patrick arrived home hot and tired. He slumped into a chair and rested his elbows on the table, his head in his hands.

'Food won't be long. Do you want wine?' asked Rosa, turning from her sauce.

'You look tired,' said Becca. The baby, who had lain happily awake in the carrycot, began to fret; a niggle quickly built to a full-grown bawl. Patrick sighed and Becca saw him momentarily close his eyes and purse his mouth in reluctance as he lifted himself from the chair. Rosa's hands were full and she glanced anxiously over at the carrycot. It wouldn't hurt, reasoned Becca, not this once, to pick him up. She owed it to them for never once suggesting it, for never leaving him in her care. They'd placed no expectation on her, carrying the full burden themselves. It was the least she could do, she thought, as she walked over to the carrycot and leant into it, picking him up and out onto her shoulder. She patted his back as she'd seen Rosa do, rocking gently from one foot to another, rubbing, talking softly at his cheek so that she smelled his smell, so that he could hear and smell her. He quietened and she sat at the table with him in her arms.

They ate pasta with fresh tomato sauce and warm bread, chicken with mozzarella cheese and green salad. Becca ate with one hand, dripping tomato sauce down her chin. Patrick served her food and cut her chicken. They drank red wine. Their mood was sunny, jaunty. Patrick, transfused with good food and wine, was revived. He amused them with tales of choirboys at mass passing dirty magazines back and forth along the rows but singing with gusto. Becca laughed out loud.

'Ssh, you'll wake him,' Rosa said, nodding at the peaceful baby in Becca's arms.

'Not to worry, I'll feed him if he wakes up,' Becca said matter of factly, as if there was nothing unusual in this, as if she were part of the routine of care, and she began to sing softly in a voice barely audible to the baby in her arms.

'Good,' said Patrick, 'fine – more wine?'

They drank wine and ate rice pudding, leaning back in their chairs, full and content. In the garden Becca heard a blackbird call and another answer. She heard it like a bell echoing out across the fields of her childhood.

'He doesn't have a name,' said Patrick, 'don't you think it's time you gave him a name?' He held his breath. He and Rosa had registered the baby, giving his name as John. It had been the first to come to mind.

'But I don't know what to call him. I haven't thought of a name, not for a boy anyhow.'

'It doesn't have to be now,' said Rosa. 'He's gone this long without one, I don't think a day or two longer will matter, no?'

'What do you think,' she said to them both, 'for a name, I mean?'

'It depends,' said Rosa, 'on what kind of names you like.'

'Plain, I like plain names, not fancy, and nothing complicated or weird or after a pop star, like Dylan or Jules. Just something ordinary like . . .' But she couldn't come up with anything.

'What about a family name,' suggested Patrick, 'one that's been in the family for a long time?'

'I don't know.'

'Or a name of someone you like or admire, a friend, a hero maybe?' said Rosa.

'There's my uncle Percy, but that's no name for a baby. There's my grandfather,' said Becca, 'his name was Thomas. That's a family name. Thomas, Tom. I like that.'

'I like it,' said Patrick, 'it's a good old-fashioned name.'

'Then he should be christened,' said Rosa, 'don't you think?'

'There's plenty of time for that,' said Patrick, worried that they might be moving too fast for Becca. 'Don't think of that now, get used to his name first. Let's open another bottle of wine and drink a toast to Thomas.'

'No, Rosa's right, he should be christened. Let's christen him now, here in the kitchen. You do it, Patrick, christen him Thomas, please.' Becca's voice was urgent, her eyes took on the blue of a deep sea.

They cleared the table of all but their wine glasses and a freshly opened bottle. Rosa filled the blue plastic washing up bowl with warm water and placed it in front of Patrick. Handing the baby to Rosa, Becca went out into the garden and picked a child's posy of daisies and buttercups, which she stood in a cup in the centre of the table. Patrick blessed the washing-up bowl, took Thomas in his arms and, sprinkling warm water on his forehead and looking at Becca and Rosa, intoned: 'Parents and Godparents, you have come here today to have your child baptized in the Faith of the Church which we all professed with you . . .'

Then dipping his fingers in the washing-up bowl, he said, 'I now make the sign of the cross on the child's forehead and I invite you to do the same.'

Letter to Joe

Dear Joe,

I am sitting in Patrick's garden as I have been staying here with Patrick and Rosa for a while.

I am writing to let you know that something has happened which will be a shock for you. On June 13, I had a baby, a son. I have been here ever since and Patrick and Rosa are helping me, looking after me and the baby. I've called him Thomas, after Granddad. I was on my own in the flat when I had him. I'm sorry I didn't tell you before, when I was pregnant, but I couldn't. I couldn't tell anyone. Half the time I didn't believe it myself.

I haven't told Dad yet but I will soon. He is a lovely baby with lots of dark hair; everyone says he looks like me. Please don't ask me who the father is because I'm not sure and I want to forget about that and concentrate on looking after Thomas.

I am thinking of going to see Dad soon, once I've told him, and I am still thinking of trying to find Mum, despite what you say.

I know I can't stay here forever. I'm not sure what I will do. I don't want to bring a baby up here although I still have the flat, but I'll have to wait and see. What do you think?

I hope you're still planning on coming home before Christmas, then you can see him.

I know this will be a big shock, Joe, but don't worry as everything has turned out OK. He's a great baby. (I'll try and send you a photo next time.)

Everyone sends their love. Stay safe, have a good time.

Write back soon,

Love, Becca

P.S. The fish are fine.

Water and Broken Glass

Becca pushed Thomas through the churchyard and down into the high street towards the post office. The pram was black, a small Silver Cross, which could be lifted from its wheels and used as a carrycot. Patrick had acquired it along with an assortment of baby clothes. His parish had been generous.

Rosa was away on the south coast spending a few days with her daughter and helping with the grandchildren. Becca sensed that Rosa needed to get away, especially from Patrick. There had been a change in their relationship, a new mood. She'd heard them talking late into the night in the garden. Their voices had drifted up through the open window of the room she now shared with Thomas. There were discordant notes, strains of anxiety, a new tension. They disagreed more. There were arguments followed by periods of silence and then passionate reconciliation and frantic lovemaking. They were worried, and so was she.

From a selfish point of view Becca found herself to be happy in this family. She did not want it to disappear. She did not want happiness to give way to misery and distress. She feared finding herself once again with a desperate man and a needy child. She'd always promised herself, never again. That was how she had got through those times. 'I'll do this once,' she would say, staring at her face in the bathroom mirror. 'I'll look after them, I'll keep going, I'll pretend I'm OK, but I'll never do it again. I'll kill myself if it comes to it.' That's what she would say – to herself. That was her promise.

She posted the letter to Joe – Poste Restante, Arles. She bought mince in the butcher's and potatoes and veg from the market. She would make a pie, like her grandmother's, a shepherd's pie, brown and crusty on top with its juices bubbling through the mash. When she put her mind to it she wasn't a bad cook. She'd watched her grandmother often enough, chopping parsley and onions for faggots, spooning blackcurrants into their pastry shell, mixing Christmas puddings, cooking Welsh Cakes on the hot griddle. Maybe it was time to resurrect those skills, bring them back into use. Making pies went with having babies, she felt. There were aspects of her new domesticity that she enjoyed. She found she could take pleasure even in the symmetry and movement of a line of white well-pegged nappies floating in the garden, until she came to her senses, that was, and thought, fucking hell, what was she on about? How much of this was about hormones or chemicals rushing around her brain? She some-times wondered if she was loosing it altogether. Why was it that she no longer had to stop herself from feeling angry, what was that all about? She wasn't sure but she was sure of the growing connection between her and Thomas. He needed her. It was simple. She saw it in his eyes when he looked at her, when their eyes connected. It was like starting out again on a whole new life. She was no longer centre stage; he was. He would love her no matter what. She could see the inevitability of that. The responsibility frightened her if she thought about it too much. So she tried not to think too hard; she put it away somewhere in a box in her head; she was good at doing that. It had been another part of her surviving.

Becca had finished in the high street. She was walking back from the estate, where she had been checking up on her flat and Joe's, when she saw Simone and Mags alongside the waste ground by the path that led down to the Creek. Her instinct was to avoid them, to put her head down and pretend that she hadn't seen. Maybe they would disappear along the path towards the river; she wasn't sure she had anything to say to them. She'd felt different before, at the meetings. She knew they meant well but she hadn't seen them since Thomas had been born, since she had become a mother, with a son. Now she had no idea where she would stand.

But they'd seen her. They called to her, crossed the road and waved as they approached. They walked beside her, looking into the pram, remarking on Thomas, how he'd grown since they had first seen him. They reminded her of the occasion when they had called at the house and she had been in bed recovering still, sleeping, but Rosa had proudly showed him off. She thanked them for the baby clothes.

'It's so hot,' said Simone, 'too hot to do anything, too hot to sleep even.'

'We've been sleeping outside on the grass, between the flats. We're going down to Brighton at the weekend, it might be cooler there, by the sea,' said Mags. 'Why don't you come?'

'Thanks, but I'm thinking of catching the coach home. I'd like to see my dad for a few weeks, get some sea air.'

'That'll be good for the baby,' said Simone.

'Yes,' said Becca, smiling in at the pram.

'What about when you get back? What are you going to do? It won't be easy, on your own with a baby,' said Mags. 'You should join the One o'Clock Club. It's a really good place to meet other mothers. It's up in the Neighbourhood Centre, at the top of the hill, near the adventure playground. You're going to need help with childcare, Becca, if you don't want to be tied down. If you want to get a job that is.'

Becca nodded.

They'd reached the back entrance to the churchyard. Becca did not want to take them into the house. It was Patrick's. She didn't want Mags to *roll up* or take over, as she sometimes did, without thought for others.

'Shall we sit here?' said Becca, slowing at the bench beneath the apple tree. They stopped. Becca sat on the bench and rocked the pram up and down. The movement would keep him asleep and she didn't want him to wake up. Something in her found it difficult, the thought of being a mother in front of them, playing this unfamiliar role under close scrutiny. She was liking it more, that was true, but she wasn't at all sure that she was good at it. She wasn't confident at all. She still worried that Thomas would come to harm, that she would not be able to keep him safe.

Mags and Simone sat on the grass in the patchy shade under the sour green fruits. Mags began to roll a joint, resting her papers on a copy of *Spare Rib*, which she retrieved from her shoulder bag. Becca found herself looking forward to inhaling its rasping smoke. It had been some time. Simone looked around, making sure there was no one to see them. Mags appeared oblivious. 'You can't let a child stop you going out to work,' she said, looking down at the thin white tube that was taking shape in her coaxing fingers.

'I wasn't working before. Besides I'm not handing him over to some stranger, but maybe a club. I'll see,' she said, unconvinced. She was never one to enjoy enforced sociability and regular commitment. For her they constituted far more of a tie than a baby. An invisible tie, granted, but one that gagged and choked nonetheless. She knew all about the Working Women's Charter, she'd seen the posters in the high street. In her eyes it demeaned the role of mothers.

She was the last to romanticise but the first to understand how different life would have been with a mother. Good and bad, mothers were both: mothers loved their daughters, mothers despised them. Mothers were jealous; favoured their sons. Mothers were cutting with their tongues and grudging with their praise. They were wise and knowing, the soothers of fever, the warm and fleshy makers of food, selfless, self-centred, bitter with life, angry with men, clawing and sticking, demanding, guilt inducing, loving. Mothers were fierce champions, proud owners. Mothers were all these things. And Becca knew that any of these were better than no mother at all.

Herself as a mother, that was unknowable. She was only just beginning, but now she'd begun she knew she would not easily give up. She would not be leaving without a word, no matter how hard. She did not want a job. Other women could work if that was what they wanted. She was going to look after Thomas.

They smoked the joint quickly for fear of discovery; a churchyard was hardly the place. Their conversation slowed. Becca tried to gather her thoughts about women and work and motherhood, ready to articulate them, but found they were fractured like broken glass, pieces flying everywhere. Like her dream, her haunting dream.

It had come again only a few nights ago. The dream in which she watched a baby fall from a high cupboard and land in a bowl filled with water and broken glass; in which, no matter how hard she tried, how desperately, she could not save it from falling, nor could she pick the shards from its flesh. Becca shuddered – the dream, the dope in her lungs. The dream had unnerved her, made her think too much. She didn't want to think too much, especially about Joe and all of that. She needed to keep a lid on things. She needed to believe it would work out and that what she had done was no worse than what many others did in their lives. She hadn't meant to hurt anybody. But then how many people could say that? Most, she felt. Most, probably Pauline included, hoped they would not hurt, did not set out with that intention but . . . her thoughts were interrupted by Simone standing up and brushing the brown grass from her legs. Mags joined her.

'We've got to get a move on, got these posters to take down to the printers. See you when we get back from Brighton. Are you sure you don't want to come?'

'No thanks,' said Becca, 'but have a good time. See you when you get back.' She watched them walk away, through the side entrance that stood next to the wrought-iron gates and into the high street. It hadn't been so bad. They hadn't been overly interested in Thomas, which made things easier in a way. They'd said nothing about sons, about raising boys. There'd been no lecture on the dilemmas of feminist mothers raising men. She was thankful. It would have been hard to swallow. What did they know? Had they lived with men? Had they struggled to mother a boy whilst mourning the loss of their childhood?

Postcards

Becca put Thomas in the garden, covering the pram with a cat net and went in to make the tea. She would talk to Patrick that night, she decided, find out what was going on between him and Rosa. Were they thinking of ending it? Of course, it wasn't easy, a Catholic priest, an older woman. But they were happy together and it was right, and besides it was nothing to do with anyone else? People were gossiping but so what? People always did. Fuck them.

She'd talk to him about what she should do too. After all she couldn't stay forever, so what next? She trusted his judgement. He'd always been honest with her. He'd never judged her or others, come to that.

The piecrust tended towards black rather than golden. It had stuck around the rim, it would be a bugger to clean, she thought. Patrick didn't seem to mind. He was hungry and not unaccustomed to over-cooked food. 'Are you missing her?' asked Becca. Patrick wore an air of quiet distraction. He ate as if not tasting. 'She'll be back in a day or two, won't she? What's going to happen then?'

'What do you mean?' He looked up from his plate.

'Then, when she gets back, between you two, I mean.'

'I don't know. Nothing. Why?'

'Well it can't be easy, a priest and a married woman. I mean priests aren't supposed to . . .'

'Fornicate, fuck other men's wives, is that what you mean?'

'No, well, yes, I suppose I do, but I meant more than that, like have a woman, live with someone, in all senses of the word.'

'I know, bloody great isn't it?'

'Are you frightened?' she asked.

'What of?'

'Of what the church says, of hell or purgatory or wherever it is you'll go?'

'No, I'm frightened of losing her. I'm thinking of leaving the church.'

'Oh.'

'I always said I'd never let it chain me. It's madness, nonsense half of it, well most of it. I think I've always known I couldn't make it.'

'What does Rosa say?'

'Rosa says no. It's too much for her, you see, the responsibility. Me leaving the priesthood for her, not that that's how I see it. It isn't just about her but I can't convince her of that.'

'I suppose it's about her leaving her family too?'

'I know, wrong, it's all wrong,' he said, pushing away his plate and putting his head in his hands.

Becca cleared the plates and put them in the sink. She sat back down. 'Well I bet you're not the first, you know you're not.'

'I'm not but it doesn't really help. Most of them, the others, I know some myself, they keep it quiet, something on the side, a discreet thing, although sometimes not that discreet, but tolerated as long as it's not acknowledged. They go on like that for years and I'm not criticising. They're happy with that. I wouldn't be. It's not what I want and that's why it's about more than just Rosa.'

'What does Rosa want, do you think?'

'I'm not sure. I'm not sure she knows but we can't go on like we have been lately, like this.'

'Why not, you're not really hurting anyone that much. Fuck it, it's not fair. It's ridiculous,' she said.

'Then there's the difference in our ages. That bothers Rosa. She says it will tell when we're older, in ten years' time and that she'll have no peace.'

'She might be right.'

'She might be, but I just can't see it, I couldn't care less. I'll accept that it's a risk but there are always risks. Life without them, well can you imagine it? It's unlikely and this is a risk I'm prepared to take.'

She hesitated, then said, 'But I think it might be different for her. I think it's probably different when you've got a family like Rosa has and grandchildren. Leaving is a big thing and maybe it's too big a thing for her, it's too hard.'

'She's not happy.'

'No.'

'And I'm not.'

'And you could be happy together?'

'I think so. I think there's a good chance.'

'It could be hard building happiness when you think about what's left behind, the people I mean, the lives.'

'Oh, don't you start,' he said, shaking his head but relieving the tension with a smile. 'Let's have a beer, there's some in the fridge.'

They drank beer and smoked cigarettes.

'Look,' she said, 'there's nothing I'd like more than to see you two together, happy and us all here, staying here like we have been, how we are now this summer. But I know it can't be like that forever. It isn't realistic.'

'You can stay for as long as you like, you know that.'

'I know but . . .'

'Have you thought about what you want? About your future with Thomas? There's no reason for you to go,' he added, aware selfishly that as long as she stayed and that as long as the baby was here in his house Rosa would stay too.

'I've written to Joe. I told him I might go home for a bit and see Dad, you know, tell him the good news.'

'You should, he'll want to know.'

'I'm not sure about that.'

'He will, believe me.'

'I want to, very much,' said Becca. 'I've been thinking about trying to find my mother, of seeing her too. She left when I was eight and I haven't seen her since. I had a postcard once. He maybe knows where she is. If I can find out where she lives, then I could go one day. I've thought about it loads, just turning up at the door, her opening it and there I am. I've imagined it every way, good and bad, happy to see me, horrified. I play it over and over in my head. I think it might be easier going now, now that I've got Thomas. I'm not sure.'

'Well, it will be a shock if you do. You should be careful, maybe you should write to her first, that might be best.'

'Maybe,' said Becca, thinking no, no writing first. Why should she give her that choice? She'd had no choice, Pauline had gone without consulting her. You could say it was different, after all she was a child, but it felt the same to her. Anyway if she wrote, Pauline could say no, reject her, run away again. She would be the one to decide. It was her turn and she would see what it brought. Either way it would put an end to her fantasies of reconciliation and there would be a resolution. She could see that to others it would seem like a dangerous strategy but she'd been over it many times and she knew it was her only option. And she was less scared of it now. Less bothered about the outcome, now that she had Thomas and her life had settled into a routine and a rhythm like those of the people around her – ordinary people.

'I know why you say I should write first,' she said. 'It's a risk but you were the one talking about a life without risk.'

'You're right, I was, but I suppose I was thinking about you being on your own as well, with nothing to fall back on, nobody around.'

'But I won't be on my own because there's Thomas. That's what makes it all so different. That's why it's possible.'

'It's not as if you need to decide now anyway, there's plenty of time. We can talk about it again when Rosa gets back,' said Patrick, stalling.

'Yes.'

Later that night Becca wrote a card to her father telling him of Thomas's arrival. She posted it the next day.

Mattresses in the Garden

Thomas lay in his carrycot next to her bed. The moonlight cast its green shadows on the crumpled cotton sheet, which lay discarded on the floor. It was impossible to sleep. All over the city people were flaying in their beds, hot and restless, lying exposed, without covers, without air; not even the lightest covering could be tolerated. A heatwave had descended, trapping the city's inhabitants between close walls of brick, in acres of glass and diesel-filled streets. Those with gardens were considered fortunate. People had taken to dragging their mattresses downstairs and out onto grass courtyards and lawns. They lay in the night under hidden stars in the hope of finding air to breathe or the hint of a cool breeze.

Perhaps that was what they should do, thought Becca. She would suggest it tomorrow, put the mattresses and carrycot in the garden. Then again perhaps that was too public for Patrick and Rosa, perhaps they wouldn't want that.

Rosa had returned from the south coast. She'd hardly been able to bear the distance between her self and her new life, with Patrick and Becca and the baby. As soon as the coach had pulled out she'd wanted to be back and felt that it would be nothing to consign all of it, husband, daughters and grandchildren, to the past. Leaving Patrick would be far more difficult for it would be a betrayal of what she had become. It would be like leaving herself behind and embracing a future through which she could only walk as a shade, where she would have no substance or pulse.

They were overjoyed at seeing each other. Becca saw that and left them to it, to their tears and kisses in private. With

Rosa's return the house instantly became alive. They celebrated with wine and egg salad before Rosa left reluctantly for home and Sergio. Patrick busied himself in the kitchen, whistling as he washed up and then upstairs in the bedroom. Was he expecting her back? Surely not. Surely she would not return on her first night back? Sergio would insist, would want her there with him and it was too hot for argument or fuss.

Should they carry the mattresses into the garden? She'd ask Patrick later. Becca put Miles Davis on the turntable she'd set up in the kitchen and settled at the table, smoking a cigarette and watching the fish. Rosa appeared in the doorway, suitcase in hand. Patrick came down the stairs and lifted her case, taking it away. He'd been expecting her, Becca realised. They'd planned it, decided that she would leave tonight but had said nothing. He hadn't dared, she thought, in case Rosa had gone home and been persuaded otherwise. She might have changed her mind, faltered, ebbed like the tide leaving the shore, retreating from the sand it had marked. Patrick had been tortured, Becca had no doubt, enduring that long hour before her return.

Rosa sat at the table. She pushed her hair from her face with both hands and looked down at the tablecloth. Then she lifted her head and looked at Becca. 'God forgive me,' she said, 'he wasn't there, I left a note above the fireplace. He'll see it when he gets in. God forgive me, but you know I don't feel so bad. I'll go back tomorrow to explain, if he'll listen. I don't know how I can do it, Becca. Why don't I feel so bad?' Patrick was back in the kitchen, stood behind her chair, leaning over her, putting his arms around her. 'What will they all say?' she added.

'Who? What will who say and anyway who cares?' said Patrick.

'Everyone,' she said, 'they won't allow it and they won't let us go on living here once they know. It won't last.'

'Don't you believe it. There's many a priest living with a woman, in a cosy nest with their housekeepers . . .'

'But I don't want it to be like that, everyone talking and knowing but pretending not.'

'It won't be. We'll think about it, about what to do but there's no rush to decide.'

Becca was thankful. Patrick had said there was no rush. Nothing had to change, not immediately, no one had to go anywhere. She was happy for herself and Thomas and for them, but she agreed with Rosa, it wouldn't last and she knew it was time for her to decide what next.

The next day, with considerable effort, they hauled the mattresses into the garden and covered them with cotton sheets. Rosa was subdued. Sergio had refused to see her, ranting at her from an upstairs window. He'd closed the café. She expected that at any time her daughters would be summoned and come banging on the door, demanding her return to sanity and propriety. But no one came knocking. Rosa tried not to think about it, but it tumbled around in her head like washing inside a drum. Were hers the actions of a sane woman? Could she stay sane and make any other choice. The washing spun into a blur. She tried hard to resist the hypnotic circle.

They went into the garden after eight. It was no cooler than the house, warmer if anything but with more air. Patrick was out visiting parishioners. Rosa made iced coffee in tall glasses and they sat on the mattresses, drinking, picking at brown strands of grass. Becca smoked idly, toying with her ciga-rette. Softly, under her breath, she hummed 'Summertime'. They sat without talking while the sky became dark; the city dark of orange and mauve. The air around them was heavy and filled with the fragrance of night-scented stock.

The garden grew illusory. Wilting shrubs hung bleached of their colour, like spectres. Silken moths shivered across the sky like white moons. They landed close by on pale leaves and the lacy netting of the carrycot, reminding Becca of the summer days she and Lilli had spent trying to catch cabbage whites with their fishing nets.

Becca's thoughts turned to Joe. She'd heard nothing from him. It would be too early to expect a reply to her letter. But a letter had arrived from her father. It was brief but he was clearly happy to receive the news. Why didn't she bring the baby to see him? It would be difficult in the house as he had taken in a lodger but he knew someone who could rent her a room for a week or two and he would help with money. The room was in the town, on the seafront, and sea air was good for babies.

Sea air is good for babies, Becca said over to herself. It would be good for her too, to breathe in the pungent ozone and iodine, to fill her lungs. That was it then, she decided, she would go home. She would take her son Thomas home to the place of her birth, just for a week or two, no more. It would give Patrick and Rosa time alone with each other. She would go home. She felt a familiar twist in her stomach at the words, at the prospect of embarking on such a journey. Coming and going had never been easy and she understood when people talked of homesickness, because she was always left feeling sick whether she was coming or going, whether there or away. Now that she had Thomas it might be different. In him she'd found a reason, a routine and a love she'd never experienced before; with Thomas there would be no coming or going. But that wasn't all; it wasn't just that easy. She was new to it, this being a mother and there was still her apprehension; the sheer weight of responsibility and the inclination, which lingered, which had always dogged Becca, to deny her duties, to cast them off like a free spirit. She'd had enough of responsibility and duty too soon, too early. Her life had been weighed down with it. She didn't want that to repeat itself. She wouldn't fall into that trap again. But Thomas didn't feel like a trap. Since Thomas she'd felt more like a bird flown from its cage than a rabbit caught in a snare

She lay on her back. 'I'm going home for a bit,' she said, her words slipping up into the dusky shadow of overhanging trees. 'Dad wants to see Thomas and he knows where I can rent a room for a week or two. He'll help he says. It'll be good for the baby in this heat, sea air is good for babies.'

'Are you sure?' asked Rosa, somewhat alarmed. 'You'll be on your own. It's a lot looking after a baby on your own.'

'I'm sure. I want to go back and it feels like the right thing if I'm going to decide on what to do, going back to the beginning, starting again. Besides, Dad will be there, I won't be on my own,' she said to placate Rosa, knowing that Terrence was incapable of looking after anyone, not least himself. 'It won't be for long.'

'OK,' said Rosa, whose head was full of other things.

'Are you staying?' asked Becca.

'Yes. I've done it. I've left. I didn't think I would. I still can't believe it and I still don't know if I've done the right thing, but it's done.'

'Why did you?'

'I want to live, Becca, not drown in some kind of half-life, and I love him. I love how I feel and I haven't got much more time. I can't waste any more time. It's not as if they're children anymore, they don't need me, not in the same way. They'll get used to it and so will he. He has his friends and his dominoes, what does he care? Of course it's a risk but then if it doesn't work out I'll just have to think again. I'll go back to Italy maybe, I don't know,' she said, marvelling at the way the words fell, calm, detached, when inside she was in turmoil. 'I thought about it all the time while I was away, I worked it out. It's more important to make the choice, better than allowing fate to do what he likes with you, having your decision taken away. No? It doesn't matter whether it's right or wrong, I may never find out and everyone can argue about it and say what they like or tell what they would have done but in the end whatever happens I decide and that's right.'

'It's right,' said Becca, 'I can tell.'

Fishponds

Stepping down, Becca felt the tar sticky beneath her feet. She breathed in the sea air. It had been unbearably hot in the crusty velvet interior of the coach, rough on the backs of her legs and with a burning sun magnified and beating on her arm and the side of her face. It had been difficult keeping Thomas cool. Lucky that the pale young man had looked up from his book long enough to offer her his seat on the shady side.

Rosa had packed squash. She'd insisted on Becca pushing the large plastic bottle into her bag along with the other bottles, pins, nappies and the like, also a pack of cheese and lettuce sandwiches. Not long into the journey Becca had thanked God for Rosa and orange squash and doughy sandwiches. She'd tried to give a sandwich to the young man to show her gratitude but he had been too shy to acknowledge her offer or her thanks.

Terrence was waiting. It was a surprise; she was not expecting him, having decided that the local cider house and the company of friends would prevail. But there he was, standing a little distant but smiling, moving shyly towards her and Thomas. They embraced loosely. He lifted Thomas from her arms like a sportsman holding up a trophy. Becca collected the pram. He was pleased to see his grandson, Becca thought: proud.

'I expect you could do with a cup,' he said, 'and a sit down somewhere cool.' Becca nodded. Terrence handed Thomas back and lifted her case. They set off at his suggestion in the direction of The Bluebird Tearooms but ended up in The Ring O'Bells where Terrence showed off his grandson and downed a couple of quick pints of the emulsified liquid, which always reminded Becca of cloudy urine. Terrence beamed as they walked along the front to the boarding house.

Amberleigh was four storeys high with attic rooms. It stood out of the way at the far end of the seafront in a small terrace, apart from the smarter guesthouses and hotels. Its exterior was grey. The paint peeled from the sills and frames. It was like a great snake shedding its skin, inside and out, peeling off layers of grey to cream, of white to brown, revealing its other skins. She pushed the pram wheels over the resisting gravel that led up to the steps and the door, then took Thomas from the pram while Terrence put down the case and bumped it backwards up the steps, knocking on the door while he balanced the pram on two wheels on the top step. He disappeared inside as the door opened and Becca followed him in.

'This is my daughter, Rebecca, and my grandson, Thomas.' He looked at Becca. 'This is Janet.'

Becca was introduced to her landlady, all red hair and red lipstick as far as she could make out. Tarty, you might say.

'Janet Priddy,' said Terrence with a hint of admiration and affection in his tone.

Becca took an instant dislike to the woman but smiled all the same. Terrence handed her money and made small talk. The hall was gloomy, lit with a bare light bulb hanging from a twisted brown cord, its filaments like a viper's tongue. Its tiled floor was ingrained with dirt, pressed in with blown sand and gravel dust. It needed a good clean, thought Becca, with a bucket of soapy water and a scourer or brush. A mop or cloth would not suffice, it was a down-on-your-knees job, hard work, scrubbing away until it would reveal it's brick-red and black diamond patterned face.

Thomas began to grizzle. 'He doesn't cry all night, does he, my dear? Because if he does he'll keep the whole place up and that won't do, you know. I can't have my guests incon-venienced.' She looked at Terrence.

'Oh no, hardly ever cries, does he?' said Terrence quickly.
'No,' said Becca, 'he doesn't cry much at all.'

She saw a succession of sleepless nights ahead, rocking, pacing and singing. All babies cried, didn't she know that? Stupid woman. 'He'll be no trouble,' she added.

'Well you can leave the pram wheels here in the hall as long as they don't get in the way. Can't have my residents or my visitors tripping up now, can I?' She smiled seductively at Terrence. 'It's right at the top, but that's all I've got left. You're lucky really to get anything high season and with a baby as well . . .' They climbed the stairs behind her.

The place should be condemned, thought Becca, the whole place, she was certain of it. Nothing as full of movement as these stairs, banisters, floorboards, all shifting and creaking, could surely expect to remain standing. Her room was one of two in the attic. It had a single window which looked out onto black iron fire escapes snaking down to a shabby back alley where dustbins and black plastic bags spilled their contents to be gnawed by scavengers – rats, dogs on the loose, feral cats and sea gulls. To the left, over the rooftops, she could discern the trees of the churchyard and the Fishponds. The room contained a double divan, a Baby Belling with two rings and a kettle, a sink, a small table with two chairs and a wardrobe. It boasted wallpaper printed with orange rectangles and brown shaded circles and a dirty purple rug. It would do. Becca opened the window to let in the air.

Terrence came most days, as he had promised. Usually it was late afternoon, after work, on the bus, and he was mostly sober. He didn't stay long unless he was joining Janet for a drink in the evening, but his visits gave shape to her day, to days that were otherwise long and empty. He brought her a second-hand record player. She foraged in junk shops for old albums to play.

The heatwave helped. She was out early in the morning and back late, sometimes meeting Terrence at the bandstand and not going home at all until Thomas was sleeping soundly. She and the baby began to take on a coastal complexion, replacing their urban pallor with healthy cheeks and tanned arms.

She would make breakfast first: toast and jam, rusks, which more often than not she'd finish, then bottles for Thomas and sandwiches and chocolate. The day's supplies were packed into a bag and left to rattle on the pram tray as she pushed it along the seafront, down into the town and sometimes as far as the first fields on the estuary's edge where she and Lilli had played. Across the bay she saw the gallows of the power station, indistinct in the haze.

Some faces were familiar, the confectioner, the librarian, the cashier in the post office; they had always been there, all her life. Others, friends of her father's, less so, but still they stopped her to coo into the pram and remark on family likenesses. They asked after Joe. The one face she hoped to see, Lilli's, eluded her. She'd no doubt moved away. She told herself that it was hardly surprising, that even if she were here she could not expect to find her in a busy seaside town so full of summer visitors and after so long.

In the main her existence was solitary and she spent a good deal of time alone with Thomas watching the patchy orange and black fish twisting in their pools. She sat on the lawns of the Fishponds writing postcards to Rosa and brushing off the ladybirds that crawled about her.

Part Five

Lilli and Becca

Ladybirds

The town was besieged, swollen red. It swarmed vermilion like eyes pressed tight against a bright sun. Ladybirds crawled feverishly over every surface, colonising the front, covering plastic buckets and long-handled spades. Straw hats, inflated dinghies, racks of postcards and nets of beach balls were removed to the safety of their huts. The ice-cream parlour had been closed against the invasion, the sashes of The Seaview locked down. The spotted insects with their split backs and Kirby-grip legs outnumbered the day-trippers and locals, who fled along blood-red pavements to the safety of their guesthouses and homes. Ladybirds out on the town while their children were left alone, their houses on fire. Lady clocks and Lady cows. Freckled and luminous they accompanied the drought, going out in a blaze of glory before their second winter. Ladybird, Ladybug, Lady Day, rhymes and songs filled Lilli's head along with her grandmother's voice. 'Now my lady,' Edith would say when displeased with her, when she was in disgrace; 'ladylike' when she knew how to behave: 'Thinks she's a proper little lady, la-di-da, high and mighty that one, mark my words.'

It was the hottest summer for a quarter of a century. Drought bled the land. The strawberry season was over, ended prematurely by the sucking heat. In their narrow belt of red brick loam the fruit had withered. There were no Strawberry Fairs and no luscious bounty of dimpled hearts. Drought orders had been posted and farmers charged with pumping from the rhynes. Everywhere water was siphoned off and leaching. Unseen, in the basin below, the first cracks appeared.

Lilli was working in The Silver Lining. It sold pie and chips. There was little call for salad despite the soaring temperatures.

Maurice was in hospital recuperating. Maud had taken him an electric fan to alleviate his sweating. Word had got about. There were a few who had disapproved, many who had secretly applauded, and one or two who had been open in their congratulations of Lilli. The Rotarians were reconsidering his membership. Bob Ham had so far failed to visit him in hospital.

The house was for sale. Lilli was packing it up, selling it off, selling the memories. It was a sad place without Vera. She missed her, missed the way they had made their journey through the world together; Vera quietly dependent on her, waiting for her returning home to share the everyday, the chewing over of the unimportant, the minutiae of others' lives. She was glad to be away from it now, happy in her flat, on the seafront, sharing it with the stray kitten she and Paolo had found mewing by the dustbins. Paolo had warned against taking it in, worried that she would be found out, but so far she had managed to keep the tiny creature hidden. She was relieved to be starting anew, getting away from the clutches of the village, moving out from the shadow of the tower, which had eclipsed her life. It hadn't been difficult finding another job. The Silver Lining was a friendly enough place owned by Rene and Marco who were rarely there, leaving Lilli to run things along with Bobby the chef, who mostly stayed in the kitchen.

Lilli sat alone now in the empty café, watching the last stragglers from the swarm, waving the insects from about their heads. She drank in the stillness and silence, preparing herself for what lay ahead. They would be there by now, at Marsh, waiting in the front room, Charlie and Pauline, Nell and Ted. Lilli wiped the beads of perspiration from her brow; the heat was unrelenting. She put her head in her hands and tried not to picture them there, waiting. Instead she thought of her child, of Marsha. She tried to imagine her; how she looked, where she lived, how far away. What did she like? Was she happy? Did she live near the sea? Most days Lilli pushed thoughts of Marsha away, as quickly as she could, and locked them into a compartment somewhere at the back of her mind, but now they had begun to surface more and more and they refused to be put away.

Lilli lifted her head from her hands and looked up at the clock. It was time to go. They would be waiting. She got up and turned the faded sign on the door from open to closed. She slid the bolt across, walked back through the café and out into the back yard where her bike stood. She brushed the ladybirds from the seat and set out in the infested air, under a sky darkened by the swarm. She cycled hard along the old drove, willing her tiredness away, defying the cracking heat, until she arrived breathless, picking at the insects which had lodged in her clothes and hair now damp with sweat. Her head swam with possibilities. Her heart jumped and banged in her chest, like a caged animal demanding release, anticipating an end to years of imprisonment.

She slipped in by the back door and saw Charlie, who stood with his back to the window, in the penumbra of the tower; she knew instantly it was him. Nell was at his side. The room was dark and thick with the scent of lavender and stale cigarettes.

'Lilli,' he said, hearing her enter, turning and moving a step towards her.

'Don't,' she put her hand out to stop him and looked around at the others in warning; at Ted, at Nell and at the slight, mousy figure of Pauline sat in a low chair in the corner.

'So you came then,' she said, 'left it a bit late didn't you, waiting until she was dead?' Her accusation hung in the space between them. He didn't answer. He looked down at the floor. 'All the years when you could have come and you stayed away. Now she's dead and you're here. Well it's too late, too late . . .'

'Now wait a minute. I thought you wanted to see me. That's why I came. That's why me and Pauline came, for your sake.'

'For my sake? Well what about when you left, was that for my sake? You didn't think about me then did you? Didn't think about us, did you, about me and Rebecca and Joe?' she said. She turned to Pauline. 'Selfish. Both of you. Only thinking about yourselves.' Pauline said nothing.

Lilli looked at them in turn, Pauline pale and insignificant, Charlie old and worn. She felt her anger begin to slip away. She felt numb, felt nothing – no pain, no longing, none of the feelings she had anticipated, least of all love. Lilli realised that the love she had sustained for Charlie in her imagination was entirely gone. Her breath had not caught as she thought it might, as it had all those years ago when she heard his footstep in the entry, signalling his return from work, when they swayed through dark country lanes to the bright fair on his old green motorcycle, when he danced in the kitchen. No, her breath had not caught. Her heart had stayed still before the stranger.

Out of the shadow Lilli saw his face distorted in the gold-fish bowl that was the room, leering like a figure in the Hall of Mirrors, loose and waving like a ghoul. She watched him shift nervously, saw the purple veins that threaded across his nose and cheeks, the swelling of age about him. There were spots of congealed food on his shirtfront and arcs of sweat beneath his armpits.

'Selfish,' she hissed, 'pathetic . . .'

'It was a long time ago, Lilli, things were different and we didn't mean to hurt anyone, just . . .'

'Just couldn't help yourselves, just had to go and leave us. She was happy until then, happy in her own world, looking after you and me. She didn't deserve it, neither of us did. None of us,' she paused, 'but then I don't suppose you cared about that . . .'

'Don't be stupid, of course I cared. I cared about you both. I can't help that she's dead, Lilli.'

'Oh can't you? Well I'm sorry I suggested it, any of it. All these years, all this time when I waited, wanting you to come back, hoping you would come back and fetch me, write to me, anything. Anything, to say that it had all been a mistake, that you didn't mean it, anything.' Tears ran down her face.

'Don't,' said Nell, moving to her side, 'don't cry, Lilli, please; it's not worth it.'

'He's not worth it,' said Ted quietly.

'Well I'm beginning to wonder why we bloody bothered coming at all then,' said Charlie, feeling persecuted, growing agitated. 'We thought we were doing the right thing, didn't we, Pauline?' She nodded. 'Just trying to do the right bloody thing, you know, that's all. It hasn't been easy for us, you know, all these years without family, cut off like that, starting out again, has it, Pauline?'

'No,' she said.

'Don't you think I wanted to see you, Lilli? How could I? What would it have done to her? I wanted to, didn't I?' He pleaded, turning to Pauline.

'Yes,' she said.

The room reverberated in silence. Lilli's tears subsided and her focus sharpened. They were a million miles apart. He understood nothing of what she felt. She saw him close up, no longer the loved, lost father of a girl's imaginings, a man of substance and pride. She saw him plainly for what he was, for what he and Pauline had been, weak and feckless, succumbing to long-forgotten dreams and charms – longings of adolescent proportion. A fast boat moving through water, skimming waves, cutting across, dragging others in their wake, pulling at limbs, leaving them waving and drowning in the undertow. Saw him as a man who had seduced his daughter with his easy charm and beery breath, who had coaxed her adoration, who had left without her. She had nothing to say to him, could think of no words adequate or worthwhile. Forgiveness, reconciliation, mending, remaking, all her anticipated possibilities had vanished, evaporated into the air, like her body, dissolving into space, expanding like the surface of blown glass, like galaxies moving away, flying apart.

She was insubstantial, trailing like a painted figure by Chagall, rising above, floating. She lodged near the ceiling rose and looked down on the scene below. She saw her own figure, her hand resting on the chair back, opposite her shrunken father, Ted tall beside Nell, the top of Pauline's head, her thinning hair. She saw them through a convex lens, a tableau of players connected but separate, falling from the room, marooned in their separateness and in the motive and justification of self.

She hovered above the blue lino that cracked and curled at the room's corners. Her eyes roved along the twining leaves of the carpet's pink roses, across the tops of the dark wood table and the chairs that held down the floor like great polished paperweights. A pile of downy beans lay heaped in the colander on the table, their discarded pods scattered on the outspread newspaper. The heads of cornflowers burst like stars from the cloisonné vase. The shadow of the tower darkened the window blocking out the sun.

She was back down to see him go and watch Nell take them to the door. They were gone. She was thankful. Her head ached, her palms perspired, and her hair lay wet and sticky at the back of her neck. She left by the back door, out into a white heat. The ladybirds had gone. She made straight for the weir where she knew there was still water to be found.

Lilli lay back on the scorched riverbank. Brittle stalks scratched her back but the coursing of the river was soothing, carrying away its flotsam, taking with it the wreckage of lost cargo, the scraps, the lumber, the discarded matter. It was over. The long wait was over. She'd got what she wanted. Charlie had returned at her behest and she'd felt nothing, neither love nor hate. Nothing but indifference and the real-isation that he was no longer important in her life; that what had distinguished him all along had been his leaving. She'd clung to that. She'd clung to his abandonment like the roots of the partly exposed willow clinging to the soil of the riverbank, waiting for each new slippage and erosion. If only she could cling long enough, if she were patient, good enough . . . now, at last, she could let go. She was released from the spell. The spell he had cast over all his victims. She no longer heard his voice whispering along with the others. She had listened to them all, she had known no better, listened about Charlie, about Marsha. She had gone along with it, a history masked with secrets and lies. What rebel-lion she had staged had been mostly at her own expense. Now she was rid of him and the weight of family lifted from her shoulders. She was free to choose for herself, to accept; she was no longer compelled to wait, to resist. Never again would she be persuaded to give up what was hers. Now she had seen the past, the future beckoned, and in it Marsha. Her and Marsha walking together across the land.

When she thought of them all, when she thought of her child, she saw that everything must change. She reached inside her pocket and held the armlet tightly in her hand and closed her eyes to rest . . .

The baby is in her arms, brown from the sun, smiling up at her, pulling at her hair. He wants to play. She holds him to her hip while she prepares the pot, setting it over a low fire, boiling the water until the madder begins to release its dye. Other pots are bubbling, staining the clay. She stirs and prods with her blackened dyeing stick. It is hot work; the baby fidgets and grows restless. The fires will burn until late after-noon when the dyes will cool and be ready for dipping.

She walks to the jetty where the others are gathered, legs dangling in the low water, children splashing and shouting.

She wades in holding him at her waist, dipping his feet in first, submerging him gently into the water up to his chest so that he can hit the surface with his hands and send sprays of water around them.

She sees him through the damp haze of scattered water droplets, in the lemon light, across from her, his hair yellow with the sun, standing among the reeds and the bullrushes. He lifts the hessian pack from his back and throws it up onto the grassy bank. He is wading knee deep now across the cool water, moving towards her, smiling.

Picnic on the Sands

Lilli unlocked the café. She wedged the door open, stopping as she did so to watch the woman with the pram on the other side of the street, beneath the awning of The Galleon giftshop. She'd seen her once before, noticed her slight frame and wiry hair, seen her pushing a pram. She'd been reminded of Rebecca, pushing the old doll's pram around the Rec. She'd thought no more of it but here she was again, across the street. The memory re-surfaced. Rebecca. It was Rebecca, suddenly she was sure of it. She called out. She called to her across the near deserted street, 'Rebecca, Rebecca.'

Becca looked up. She was surprised to hear her name, that name. She looked around, narrowing her eyes against the bright sun. In the doorway across the street she saw a woman of her own age, wayward hair like hers, only red, smiling, leaning on the door jamb. Was it the face she had been looking for? Was it Lilli?

She steered the pram to the kerb, bumped it quickly down and then across to the other side . . .

'Bloody hell,' she said, 'it is. It's Lilli, Lilli Porter. God, Lilli, it's you! I can't believe it, I've waited so long . . .'

'I know,' said Lilli, laughing, 'me too.'

'I didn't know if you'd still be here, if you were still living in the town. I heard you'd moved away. I've still got your doll. You know, Marianne. I've looked after her for you, all this time.' Becca fought back the tears. The fields of her childhood stretched before her, their sad parting, their loss. They embraced, then stepped back, each unsure of what to say next.

Lilli bent to look in the pram. 'Lovely,' she said, 'she's lovely.'

'It's a he, Thomas.'

'Sorry. Have you been back long? Are you living here? Where have you been?' Questions tumbled back and forth, there on the street, acquainting them with the bones of each other's lives, until Lilli said, 'Why don't you come in and sit down? There's no one about, you can bring the pram in.' They manoeuvred the pram through the door and into a space at the back of the café. 'What do you want? Tea or coffee, or a cold can from the fridge? Do you want something to eat?' Rebecca looked pale, she thought, and thin.

'No, tea's fine,' said Becca, seating herself at a table in the far corner and pulling the pram alongside.

Lilli went behind the counter and put tea bags and boiling water in two cups. She stirred the bags with a plastic spoon and put some biscuits on a plate. She wondered if Becca was alone.

'Is Joe with you, then?' She pressed the tea bags against the sides of the cups.

'No, he's in France. He went with some friends in a van, should be grape picking by now, at least that was the plan. Is this your café then?'

'No, I just work here. The owners are off today. I'm minding it with Bobby. He lives here. He's out the back, probably asleep somewhere. He does the cooking.' She added milk to the cups and came round from the counter, placing a cup in front of Becca and the plate of biscuits. She sat across from her at the small table. Becca looked nervous, she thought, picking at the chips in the Formica at the corners of the table. Thomas began to cry. Becca lifted him from his pram.

'Shall I hold him while you have your tea?'

'OK, thanks,' said Becca, who drank her tea and smoked, ignoring the biscuits. Lilli rocked Thomas until his eyes closed and he drifted back into sleep.

After a while Lilli said, 'I saw them.'

'Who?'

Had she known? She must have, thought Lilli. But then she

herself hadn't, it had been kept from her. Her family had seen to that, they were good at secrets. Had Rebecca endured such a conspiracy? Well if she had, then best she knew.

'My father and your mother. Charlie and Pauline.'

'Oh,' said Becca leaning back in her chair as if she had taken a blow to the chest. So Pauline had been here. She reached for the cigarette packet. 'Where? When?'

'They came back,' Lilli continued, 'out to Marsh where the house is, where my aunt Nell lives. Two days ago. They've gone now.'

'Did they? Where are they living, then?'

So she knew. 'In Ross-on-Wye,' said Lilli.

Becca drew hard on her cigarette, paused to exhale and said, 'I want to see her. It's one of the reasons I came back, to see her, I mean. I've been thinking about it for a while, about getting in touch and now that I've got the baby it seems, well, more important somehow. I was going to ask Dad. I thought he might know where she was but I haven't. I can't. I don't want to bring it up. I suppose – I don't want to hurt him and remind him of it all. I thought if I did find out where she was I would go, just turn up on her doorstep with Thomas and . . . well, I'm not sure really . . .'

The door to the café opened and a group of three young girls looking for coffee and the jukebox entered noisily, followed shortly by a couple with a toddler in a pushchair. Lilli returned behind the counter to serve. She took orders and frothed milk for coffee. She shouted through to Bobby, then wiped the tables down and fetched knives and forks.

'I'll have to go,' said Becca reluctantly, 'I'm meeting my father by the bandstand, he'll be waiting.' She stood up slowly.

'Wait. What are you doing tomorrow?'

'Nothing.'

'It's my day off. Do you want to meet? I could meet you and we could go for a picnic on the sands, like we used to.'

'What about the pram?'

'We can manage that, we can carry it down. I'll bring some sandwiches.'

'Great.' Becca smiled.

'Two o'clock at the sliding steps?'

'OK, see you there tomorrow, two o'clock.' Becca waved goodbye as she left the café and hurried off in the direction of the seafront and the bandstand. On her way through the town she hummed 'It's All Right With Me.'

Behind the counter, pouring milk into a jug until it over-flowed and needed mopping up, Lilli stood watching the retreating figure. She felt like pinching herself. She'd never imagined them finding each other like that, Rebecca appearing, just walking in off the street. Things were changing already, doors were unlocking. It was meant to be, Rebecca coming home like that. Well, one thing was for sure, she would not let her disappear a second time. She would make sure that didn't happen.

The Sliding Steps

'There's sand on my cereal spoon and in my shoes. There's sand everywhere in this place. It's a mess. Look at these boxes. I'll be glad when you move out, Lilli. It's in my socks now. I can feel it.'

So what, she thought. She said, 'You just have to shake things out before you put them on, that's all.'

Paolo crunched on his cornflakes, feeling the grit between his teeth. He would be glad to get back to the ice-cream parlour. There was no sand there, at least not in the flat. Maria would not have stood for it.

Lilli liked the sand. She liked the way it blurred the distinction between inside and out, bringing the sea with it. She liked the mess, the jumble, her books spread around her, the boxes still unpacked, her treasures, things she would never throw away, precious things; her beads and bones, her dried seaweed and her crumbling herbs and wildflowers, seashells, the armlet, all laid out on a new and different dressing table, all sat before a mirror in which Lilli could watch the rise and fall of the sea.

Ted had not objected when he'd visited and he'd brought cream with him for the stray. He'd said nothing about her baggage or her room. They'd talked instead of the sea. Of how a night tide was black, of how she lay in bed listening to the soft crash of waves on the sand as if it were on her doorstep. They spoke of the drought, of how the sun had burned the mud white. Of the heat and the smell. The smell. There had been nothing like it before, fishy, rotten, over-ripe, the smell of decay. Ted had been content to see her establishing her own life, relieved to see that Charlie was to play no part in it. He told her that he was thinking of trading in the Cortina for a newer model and asked her what colour he should get.

From the tall window overlooking the sea, she watched Paolo go, back to Maria and the parlour. She was different, he said, different since she'd seen Charlie. She was more distant, and this Rebecca thing. He'd warned her against it, trying to recapture old friendships. He didn't understand. She walked across to the dressing table and lifted the armlet from amongst a tangle of beads and bracelets. She held it in her hand as she looked out at the low tide and the brushwood tracks laid by the shrimpers across the mud . . .

He has brought a bracelet for the boy, for when he is older. He will teach him how to make glass, how to fashion the zigzags and the spirals. She thinks there may be other children, a daughter perhaps; she would like that. A daughter to make glass and to weave cloth. In the scented dusk they lie together and whisper so as not to wake the child. They will journey to the sea, he tells her, it will be the start of their new life together. There is no need to be afraid.

They set off when the sun is past its fiercest across the dry swamp. On his back is a cradle packed with food for their journey; wheat and beans, a pot of curdled milk, and salted meat wrapped in reed grass. They follow one of the old tracks, the one that makes its way to below the beech ridge. In time it was lost, sunk beneath the peat. Now it has risen up from the hot and shrunken land to guide them to their starting point, to their first camp on the ridge.

She saw Becca from the window, sat on the sea wall beside the sliding steps. It was two o'clock. Lilli hurried to the kitchen and made four rounds of cheese and tomato sandwiches, doing her best to keep the sand out. She let the tap run cold, then filled a bottle with orange squash. She pushed them in a basket with a half-open packet of chocolate teacakes, which would no doubt melt. She folded the piece of paper on which Nell had written the address, put it in her pocket and left the flat.

'It's too hot for the sands,' said Becca as Lilli approached. 'Thomas will be too hot down there, it's burning.'

'All right,' said Lilli, 'we could go to the Gardens instead. It'll be cooler there, there's plenty of shade.' They set off, crossing the road to the Fishponds and entering the gate at the top of the churchyard, making their way down the sloping pathway, past headstones and burnt grass. It was cooler in the Gardens. There were a number of shady spots, benches and arbours, but they settled for the umbrella of the mulberry tree, whose squashy fruits had first to be cleared from the grass before they could sit down.

Thomas was awake and hungry. Becca took a ready-made bottle from her bag, along with nappy, pins, flannel and zinc and castor oil cream. They lay a towel on the grass and Lilli changed him. Becca helped with the nappy folding and pins and then settled back to smoke while Lilli fed him.

Fed and changed, Thomas was put back in his pram complaining, and Lilli rocked it back and forth until he relented and fell into a hot sleep. They ate their sandwiches and Becca was hungrily licking chocolate from her fingers when Lilli said, 'I've brought you their address, if you want it, that is.'

Becca took the folded paper, covering it in chocolate fingerprints. She unfolded it, looked at the address, then refolded it. 'I'm going. I made up my mind yesterday after I met you.'

'Don't expect too much will you? They're very ordinary really. A bit of a disappointment . . .' Lilli's voice trailed away. 'Leave Thomas with me if you like.'

'I will, if you're sure.'

Lilli saw the day stretch out before her – just her and Thomas. She would walk along the seafront with the pram, pop into the café to show him off, maybe even into the parlour to shock Maria, then out as far as the estuary. She would look after him and he wouldn't cry once. There would be nothing to cry for.

Pauline

Moving towards the back of the coach, avoiding the seat over the wheel, Becca settled in by the window. Despite the early hour the heat was intense and Becca felt sick. A large woman with an equally large bag and a plastic carrier squashed in beside her as the coach filled up. Her plump arm pressed against Becca's, pushing her into the window. Before long the woman was asleep and Becca spent the journey fending her off, pressed against the window in the relentless and magnified sun. Her nausea was persistent. She tried to shake it off by staring hard at the fields, the countryside that rolled by her like film, the red earth and scorched grass, russets and umber, negatives replacing the green.

They stopped briefly, once. She was grateful to step out into the shade for the cold drink, but her nausea had prevented her from smoking. Back on the coach she took to biting her nails, then picking at the threads on the handle of her woven bag, unravelling them, then winding back, slowly dismantling. She thought about Joe, wondered where he was and if he would reply to her letter. Had Rosa checked the flat for mail as she said she would? Was Thomas OK with Lilli? Meeting Lilli had changed things. It was like before; when she was with Lilli things were simpler, less confused. Lilli was a good thing and Thomas liked her, she could tell. Lilli had taken to him as if he were her own. Babies sensed these things. Becca knew Thomas felt the same as her.

Becca was relieved when the coach finally pulled into the bus station, but stepping down she was rooted to the spot, feeling her apprehension grow until it threatened to overwhelm her. What could she do? She couldn't run away now, could she? She felt like the land around her, a tinder box, ready to ignite. She must find the house, she told herself, knock on the door. She must not turn back now she had come this far. But would Pauline be there? And if so what then? Would she recognise her? Would she know it was her? She didn't know which was worse, Pauline there, Pauline not there and no reply. She searched in her purse for her taxi fare and with an effort of will propelled herself forward on shaky legs through the bus station and out into the street to the taxi stand.

The street was shadowy and dark. The sun fell on its terraced back. She opened the wrought-iron gate set in the low red brick wall and approached the front door. It was blue. Two empty milk bottles stood to one side. The house was well kept but hidden behind net curtains. It gave no clues. She pressed the electric doorbell and felt her heart knocking in her chest, jumping up towards her mouth.

The door opened and Pauline stood in its frame. There was no mistake. How could she have forgotten what she looked like? Does a child forget its mother? Pauline wore a gingham overall and pink rubber gloves. She looked at Becca, put her hands up to her face, covering her open mouth, distorting her voice and cried, 'Rebecca.'

'Mum.' They stood transfixed. Paralysed with looking.

'Rebecca,' cried Pauline. As she did so she took her hands from her mouth and placed them, one on each of her daughter's arms. She clutched at her, pulling Becca towards her, hugging her, then letting her go she dropped her hands and stepped back. As they moved apart Becca saw Pauline gather herself with a deep inward breath. She saw the tears on her mother's face.

'Come in, come in,' Pauline pleaded.

Becca stepped inside and followed her mother down the passage and into the kitchen where the windows were open and the light flooded in. They stood either side of the kitchen table.

'I'm sorry, Rebecca, I'm so sorry, I'm so sorry,' Pauline said, as more tears began to fall.

'I'm sorry too,' said Becca.

Becca slumped into her seat, exhausted, stunned, like a castaway thrown up on a foreign shore. It was cooler now but her head was hot and full. It swirled with Pauline – her voice, her face, her sorrow. Her words, Pauline telling her that it was all a mistake, all of it, apart from her and Joe. That she'd left them for Charlie and that it had been a mistake. That, surely, everyone could see. A mistake and a long time in the regretting. That's what it had been. That she hadn't even had her records for company. That Charlie didn't like Billie Holliday and he hadn't wanted her playing those records in his house – Pauline, telling her . . . telling everything.

It was past eleven although not dark when Lilli saw her. The seafront was lit with a necklace of coloured lights, strung with luminous beads. Their reflection sparkled and waved on the black surface of the incoming tide. Becca moved with them, making her way towards the flat. She arrived breathless and pale. Lilli turned from the window to greet her and saw her hand shake as she reached into her pocket. Becca lifted a cigarette and put it to her lips. She lit it and gulped it back.

'What is it? What's happened?' said Lilli. Becca didn't answer. 'Did you see her? Did you find them? Did something go wrong? Have you seen Pauline?'

'Yes I've seen her.'

'Well, what then, what happened? Was he there?'

'No, he was at work. It was just Pauline.' She paused. 'I've got something to tell you, Lilli, something I didn't know . . . I've never thought . . .'

'What? What is it?'

'It's Charlie.'

'What about him?'

'Charlie,' Becca took an inward breath drawing up her courage, 'Charlie is my father, Lilli. He's my father too.'

Becca grabbed Thomas and fled. Back along the seafront to the Amberleigh, clattering the pram wheels in the hallway, not caring who she woke as she climbed the stairs to her attic room, desperate for its safety, longing to put herself in a place where she could not be seen. She closed the door to the room behind her. The interior was hot and airless with an over-powering accumulation of heat. She put Thomas down and went over to the window and released the catch, pushing its rotting frame upwards to let in the night air. There was a whisper of a breeze. She put her head out of the window and hung in the air gasping it in. After filling the aluminium kettle with enough water for tea she put it to boil. In the meantime she lifted a vodka bottle from the small cupboard beneath the sink and set it down next to a glass on the table.

She had not expected it, the discovery that Terrence was not her father. Did he know? Pauline had said not, definitely, he'd been away, she'd lied about the dates – Becca had been born early was what he knew. And Joe? Joe was definitely Terrence's.

So that's how it was. Charlie, romancer and stealer of wives and mothers was her father. She wasn't sure what to make of it. She was sorry for Terrence; he hadn't deserved it. As for Charlie, she suspected he was unworthy, that Pauline had squandered her life on him and that Terrence – reduced by her leaving, wrapping himself in a blanket of beer and cider until it was wet and heavy with his accumulated sorrow – had been cheated and diminished. But one thing she was sure of, none of it had been her fault. A stack of unplayed records, a wasted life. A life spent behind the veil of net curtains without your children, wondering and wanting. Wanting to turn the clock back. Becca knew that she would never make the same mistake. It simply would not happen to her, she was far stronger. She would not do that. She would never leave Thomas. She would make sure of it despite the difficulties. Problems might persist but solutions would be of her making, she saw that now. She saw what lay ahead – her and Thomas, their life together. That was where her responsibility lay. It was time that others took responsibility for themselves.

She would not tell Terrence. That was for Pauline. She would see Lilli and tell her she didn't want Terrence to know. She wished now that she had stayed to talk. But she hadn't known what to say or where to begin. She'd needed time to think it through, time to grow used to it herself.

Her sister, well, half-sister, she liked the idea. She found herself smiling at it. 'To sisters,' she said aloud raising her vodka glass in the air. There had always been a bond between them. When she thought about it, there were simi-larities in the way they looked – they had the same wild hair. She'd found a sister, her sister, her friend, a woman of a similar age, to care about what happened to her and her child, to share with, good and bad, someone who under-stood. She'd found her sister and her mother.

Now it seemed she was beginning to grow a family. But what of Joe? Joe was her half-brother. Did it change anything? Did it make it only half as bad? For some time she'd managed to put it from her mind but this brought it crashing back, the call of parentage and connection. It seemed to make little difference. Brother, half-brother, it was still incest. There, she'd said the word, not out loud but to herself at least. Incest, a word spoken quietly, gravely, a word adults muttered under their breath away from the sharp ears of children. It happened out there on the moors, where the winters were long and dark and families were few. Where they were all related to each other anyway. But it wasn't always like that, it could happen otherwise, as she knew.

She would not risk it. Brother, half-brother, no matter, he

didn't know and she wouldn't tell. He might ask her when he came back. She would say no, definitely not, she would lie about the dates like Pauline. She would tell no one, not even Lilli, and never Thomas. It would be her secret alone. The trouble with secrets was that they were always told. People told. Secrets were whispered from one ear to another with the warning or the plea – don't tell – and even the best kept, once shared, lay like the links of a heavy chain, left to rust and curl about itself. They became entangled and inseparable and could be used to no good purpose. Secrets should be invisible, Becca decided, concealed and put away forever. They should be held inside and never revealed, no matter what temptation, so that in time they would no longer exist, they would no longer be true. That is what she would do with this secret, the one that could do nothing but harm. She would not cast it aside lightly, to be washed up like a message in a bottle on some other shore. She would lock it instead in an iron chest and throw it into the deepest part of the ocean where it would be nosed by sea monsters and blind fish with gaping mouths, where in time it would grow a thick crust of barnacle until it disappeared.

She would never tell. She could do it. She had the strength. Her decision made her strong. She had put the past behind her. She drank to that. And Pauline was sorry for what she had done. It didn't make it any less painful, her going off with him, her leaving them, but it was a new place to begin. Without sorry, there could have been no starting over. And Pauline wanted to be a grandmother, she'd said so; it was more than she'd ever dared hope for – a second chance. She wanted to see her grandson. Pauline would not let Charlie stop her, she would not allow it, not this time. She'd sacrificed enough.

Thomas stirred in his carrycot. Becca put the kettle on again, took a bottle from the fridge and warmed it in a basin of hot water. She lifted him onto her lap and shook the bottle so that drops were released on to the back of her hand. It was warm. She put it to his mouth and he sucked greedily. She stared from the window at the night sky, watching the stars reveal themselves above the rooftops like a scattering of sparkling stones. She would see Lilli the next day, she decided. She would go to the café to find her. She must tell her all about Pauline, about everything, except for that one secret.

When Thomas was finished, when he lay lulled in a milky warmth, she put him down. She was suddenly exhausted from the journey, the heat, the day, the alcohol and without getting undressed she lay down on the bed, put her thumb in her mouth and fell asleep . . .

A great slab of brown water surges through the salmon butts and up river. She is swept along on the wave at its very crest, high above the banks and fields. There are others alongside her, Lilli, Terrence and Joe, riding the swell, all carried along until it breaks and they are left floating on the spill water of the flood, floating without an ark.

A large black sow swims past, an upturned table and a wardrobe drift by. Cider barrels, withy wads, a pair of pink rubber gloves, a sheep in a hedge, a chicken house, rotting vegetables, a record player, a cot, all come floating. She tries to put her feet down but the land beneath her turns to jelly and Terrence and Joe have disappeared. She begins to swim, swim out through the debris across the fields to the open sea.

Water opens before her like a wide lake, glassy and undisturbed. There are steps leading down and Pauline is there lowering herself gently into the water so as not to disturb, not wanting to break the surface with a single ripple. She swims to her. They swim together in an oyster sea, which changes its colour like an opal in dappled sunlight. Around them are scattered the remains of the floral clock from the Gardens. Its flower heads and petals bob on the surface. Its hands and numbers spread out and are carried far away.

The Island

Becca pushed the pram along the esplanade. The sun was intense but the incoming tide brought with it a perceptible breeze, moving the air and acting like a cooling fan in a hot room. The front was already busy with people making their way to the sands; towels rolled beneath their arms, baskets filled with picnics. Lilli was nowhere to be found.

Becca had been to the café, then to the flat. She had scanned the figures on the promenade, looked through the ice-cream parlour window but could not find her. It was mid afternoon when she finally gave up.

She sat on the warm stone sill of the fishpond under an overhang of lime. Thomas lay sleeping in the pram. Her head felt thick and heavy. It throbbed. The water was clotted and low. It had evaporated, leaving a dry scum on the brick sides of the pond. It smelt of fish. She poked about idly with a stick she had found, looking for goldfish beneath the lily pads, whose edges curled and crisped, offering an ever-diminishing shade. Everything was wearing down. She felt it. Everything revealing itself, naked under the hot sky, bone-hard like the land. It was a strange new country; a world baked hard and rid of its disguises.

Rosa had written telling of the Fascists who marched in the streets of the capital, telling her that she and Patrick were fine, that Patrick was leaving the church, but everything else was fine, just the same as always, and it was best for her to stay put. But even here, a step away from the shoreline, Becca found it hard not to feel that everything had changed, that the old rules had somehow gone.

She wondered if she should go back. She felt it might be

safer with Rosa and Patrick, despite their warnings, safer in the confines of the city, away from the wide vistas that opened up before you, revealing new landscapes and their old truths.

Lilli woke late after a night in which the sea had inhabited her dreams, in which she had moved from waking to sleeping, hearing the gentle crash of waves on the shore, whispering of sisters. For some time she stood at her window watching the island, rapidly disappearing on the incoming tide, the armlet in her hand . . .

The spring-fed ponds beyond the beech ridge sulk and idle in the heat. Damselflies and myriad grey winged insects swarm the shallow pools and the shrill, dry grasses. Others have travelled to the edge of the sea but she has not. She is afraid a wave might come and overwhelm her, take her and the child. Her father had been many times returning with salty, white-fleshed fish, not like the earthy brown fish of the rivers. He told her then of how the sand was pale like the wings of a moth at dusk and how it grew in great dunes sliding into the sea. He told her before the wave took him. Now they walk together she thinks less of the wave; she is thinking instead of the relief water will bring and of air that is no longer exhausted.

They sleep in the open with the child between them, rising early, travelling in the coolest parts of the day, resting at noon, following the river. On the third day the riverbank widens into sand bank and mud flats, laced with shallow channels where traces of water catch the sunlight. The bay spreads before them; she shields her eyes and looks across the glittering water onto a low shingle ridge, an island of gulls and lapwing, of plover and teal.

Lilli left the flat, crossed the seafront and hurried down the sliding steps onto the beach. The tide was coming in and with it a welcome breeze and a freshening of the stale air. She took off her shoes and ploughed through the soft sand which scorched her feet, then out onto the flats where the sand was firm and off in the direction of the four-legged lighthouse and the dunes. Walking would clear her head, help her think. It would help her make sense of it all and know what to do. It had been a shock, Becca returning like that, spilling the news about Charlie and declaring them sisters, and all before she'd had time to think or known what to say. Then the way she'd grabbed Thomas and taken off.

Such a day they'd had, her and Thomas, out along the estuary and back, a sit down in the parlour where Angelo had clucked over him and insisted on carrying him about, Thomas twisting his head back and forth, catching his reflection in the long mirror and chuckling. Maria had been out shopping, which had been a relief, and Paolo had looked on indulgently and with tenderness, she thought. A perfect day, turned upside down by Becca's return and the new revelation. Just when Lilli thought she had uncovered all the secrets, here was another, bigger than any of the others, jumping up at her, pushing her over, knocking her for six.

Shadows of moving clouds danced across the beach, urging her onwards as she approached the belt of dunes. She climbed the dunes into the scrub where the pale fleshy flowers of broomrape wilted beneath her feet. In the rough thickets of sea-buckthorn and in the elder and sallow, blackcaps and warblers hid from the sun. Lilli sank into the sand, hiding with them, hugging her knees, pushing her feet into the coarse grass, looking up at the sky.

She had been the only one, alone with Vera, trying to make amends, yet all the while there had been another. She had been condemned to a half-life, for they had taken her mother's spirit then denied her what was rightfully hers, taken her friend, her sister, her blood. How different might it have been if they had been together, her and Becca, there to comfort and console, to share? And what had Becca endured? How much might Becca have needed her? She hardly dared think. But Becca needed her now, Becca and Thomas, and they needed each other. She must go back and find her and put things right. They must be together. Paolo would under-stand. She would make him understand. Enough time had been wasted, enough love lost. But no more. Lilli would not waste any more time. She would find Paolo first and tell him. Then she would find Rebecca.

She sat up, brushed the sand from her skirt and set off across the scrub, over the dunes to the flat sand where she let the water lap at her ankles as she followed the ebb tide along the arc of the bay.

The Meadow

The meadow sang in the hot wind. Above clouds gathered, massing in the heat. They moved through the bleached grasses. Lilli twisted a sorrel stem in her fingers and let the rusty seeds fall on the shrunken ground. A heron stood on the edge of the cornfield with its eye and ear tuned to the rattle of dry leaf, watching for the brown streak of a small rodent. Beneath its feet great cracks had opened in the land.

'I'm not going,' she said, turning towards him.

'What do you mean?' Paolo said, alarmed.

'I'm not going to Italy. I can't.'

'But I thought that was what you wanted, we've been planning it for months.' He put out his hand to catch her arm, to stop her in mid stride but she pulled away.

'I know and I'm sorry, truly I am, but things are different now.'

'What things? What's different? Is it the child, all that business? Is it Marsha?'

'Yes, in a way, but it's not just her, it's more than that.'

'What then? You can't live your life for a child you lost, Lilli.'

'But she isn't lost. She may come back, come looking for me, when she's older and I've got to be here.'

'Well, I didn't think we were planning to go away forever – a few months was what we said, wasn't it? Six at the most. It's not long, Lilli. It's not as if she is going to come looking yet.'

'I know.' She pulled at her skirt, which had snagged on the spur of a thistle. From the edge of her vision she saw the heron, patient, immobile, waiting.

'So what else, why?'

'Because of Becca and the baby. They need me.'

'But that's ridiculous, she's got her own life to lead, Lilli. Just because you were friends when you were young, just because Charlie left with her mother. She's got nothing to do with you, nor has the baby.'

'You're wrong, you couldn't be more wrong. She has everything to do with me. She's my sister.' She enjoyed hearing herself say the word and the way it slipped from her tongue. She savoured the luxury of saying it and the owning of that connection. It was the one good thing that Charlie had done for her, given her. How she wished it had been earlier; a sister to share the sorrow, to play with, fight and argue with, kiss and make up. There was so much they had to talk about and so much time to catch up on. She would tell Becca about Marsha. They would share their secrets. Their conversations would stretch late into the night. Together they would look after Thomas, even visit Edith. She would take her to meet Nell and Ted.

'We have the same father and all these years we didn't know. I need to see her. I'm going to look for her now. I've got to talk to her. She shouldn't be living in that boarding house, it's a disgrace. It'll be all right, I know it will. I've got to help her. I need to stay and I need to get to know her again and to get to know Thomas. All these years I've been looking for her without knowing it – that's how it feels – as if I've found something I'd only glimpsed before, something to make sense of all the lies and half-truths. I can see it now, a pathway stretching out in front of us – Becca's life and my life joined together and I have to follow it. It's not an excuse, Paolo. I don't need an excuse. I'm not leaving. I'm staying, and one day Marsha will come looking and I'll be here with a life and a family for her to share. I'm sorry.'

He was silent, looking across the field to the sea. She was sorry, sad for him and for the dream that was no longer to be realised. Secretly she hoped that he would understand and that perhaps he would wait.

'Then in the future, maybe,' he said with an air of resignation, 'it doesn't have to be now. I can wait too. Maybe in the future I can be part of it all. I can be here when Marsha returns.'

'You should go now if it's what you want, you shouldn't wait for me.'

'I'll see,' he said, as they turned back across the field towards the riverbank.

They lay on the bank together, no longer talking, unsure of what was to come. He undid the buttons of her white cotton top, revealing her breasts, and put his head and mouth to them. He licked the small rivulet of sweat that trickled between them. His hand was beneath her skirt, his fingers inside her. He unzipped his trousers and was in her quickly, moving with a hitherto unfelt urgency, pushing and twisting. He felt her with his hands and made her come quickly, made her say his name over and over as she looked up into the sky.

Shifting her head, inclining it slowly to the right, Lilli watched the heron rise from his stalking spot and lift his grey wings into the heavy sky. She felt the armlet caught in her pocket pushing into her thigh . . .

A sea eagle flies above them, floating and drifting on the thermals, looking down on the water and across the black estuary to scorched fields and red earth. He prises limpets and razor clams and small cockles from the rocks. They settle in a low pit beneath the dunes and he searches for stones on which to make the fire. They cook the fish and make their beds in the sand.

The night is hot and airless. The sea creeps secretly in until they are woken by its gentle wash, the shush of a sea that barely breaks. They wake the child and together they go down to bathe and wash away the sweat and dust of the journey. In the sky above them a great bear dances.

In the morning when the tide recedes they walk along the

great arc of the bay, looking out across the mud flats to the island white with gulls. With brushwood, with time, it would be possible to reach the spit of land, build a track, he says, out across the mud. But the sea would wash it away, she says, and besides there is enough work to do back at the camp, enough building of new tracks. A day or two, no more, then it will be time to return and the journey will be over.

She has seen the place from where the great wave came, she has paid homage to those she lost, she is no longer afraid.

Lilli left Paolo at the ice-cream parlour and went in search of Becca.

Amberleigh was only five minutes away along the seafront but she doubted Becca would be there, indoors, in such oppressive heat. She was not likely to be on the sands either; they were too hot for Thomas. No, she would be in the shade. Probably in the gardens, maybe even sat under the mulberry tree sucking at its sour fruit. She would look there first.

She took a short cut through the town, skirting beneath the awnings and sun shades, looking in at the café windows, and arrived at the gardens. Becca was not there; she was not sat under the mulberry tree or in any other of the shady spots. Lilli walked back up to the seafront through the church-yard. She looked in at the Fishponds but there was only an elderly couple on a bench under the lime. By the time she reached the boarding house, only to find that it was deserted too, a mild panic rose in her chest. Where was Becca? Common sense told her that Becca was somewhere in the town, out for a walk maybe, or out seeing Terrence. But intuition said something different. Intuition told her that Becca was leaving, that she was going back, that she was running away. Without further thought or deliberation Lilli quickened her pace so that soon she was running along the seafront and then down past the parlour to the bus stop. As she rounded the corner, breathless and sweating, she saw her, standing at the bus stop in the shade of the Co-op doorway, Thomas in her arms and the pram collapsed at her feet next to a small suitcase.

'Becca,' she shouted across the street, 'Becca.' One or two people turned to look, then Becca stepped out of the doorway squinting and searching for the voice. Lilli crossed the road at the corner and repeated her cry, 'Becca.' Behind her she heard the bus approach. It overtook her and drew up outside the Co-op.

Becca took a step towards her, ignoring the bus. 'Lilli? What are you doing here? Bloody hell, Lilli, look at you, you're soaked through.'

'Well look at you, what do you think you're doing.'

'Going back.'

'I can see that. Going back after all this? You can forget that,' she said, fixing Becca with her eyes like cornflowers in the pale wheat. The queue of people getting on the bus had diminished. It was preparing to leave. 'You're not going anywhere. You're staying here with me.'

'But there's Rosa and Patrick, all my stuff, things to sort out and . . .' Becca turned her head to see the bus doors closing and the bus pulling out from the stop.

'I'll help you,' said Lilli, 'we'll do it together.' Thomas began to fret. 'Let's get the pram up; anyway you've missed the bus. He looks tired.' Lilli reassembled the pram then picked up the suitcase. 'Put him in, then,' she said to a now dumbfounded Becca. Becca did as she was told and followed Lilli through the town and back to Catherine Terrace.

They sneaked in, Becca with the carrycot, Lilli with the wheels. They did their best not to laugh as they tiptoed upstairs. They shushed Thomas and hoped nobody would know or tell.

It was fate, Lilli said, her getting there before the bus. They were sisters and they should be together.

'I was going to come back,' Becca said, 'I was just going to sort things out.'

'Well I couldn't risk it,' said Lilli, 'you might not of, then where would we be? It's better like this. We can sort it out together. Write to Rosa. We'll find somewhere to live. Then we'll get your stuff.'

'I don't need that stuff anymore,' said Becca, 'I don't need all those boxes and magazines and all those dolls. I don't need it. Just the records though, I'll get the records for Mum.'

A storm gathered over the sea. Rain clouds massed in the darkening sky and the sea turned black. Its white knuckled rollers clawed at the shore. The drought broke in a thunderous outpouring and the land sucked and steamed as it satisfied its thirst.

Lilli stood next to Becca at the tall window, trailing her fingers through the sand that had accumulated on its sill. Together they watched the incessant rain and the white lightning. Becca lit a cigarette and inhaled deeply.

'You shouldn't smoke so much, you know. It's not good for you,' said Lilli.

'Bloody hell,' said Becca 'don't think you can start nagging me now, Lilli, just because you're my sister!'

Lilli turned from watching the rain and smiled.

Poste Restante

Joe sat on the steps of the Poste Restante with Becca's two letters in his hand. The sun slid over his back and sent his shadow falling before him. He checked the postmarks and the dates and opened her first letter. He read it through twice. It took him time to take in her words, before they stopped dancing across the gauloise blue of the paper. He read it slowly until it began to fall into place; her sick neediness, the difference that he'd seen but not recognised. A baby, it was not so surprising, a hidden baby.

Could it be his? As quickly as the question surfaced he pushed it away, discarded it like film on a cutting-room floor. He reasoned it away, out of his mind; it had only been that once, and there'd been others, he was fairly sure. Becca would have said, she would have known. Best leave it to Becca. She would deal with it, like she always did. She knew best.

He got up and folded the tissue-like paper back into the envelope. He moved out of the sun into the shade of the narrow street opposite. He sat down at a bar on the corner and ordered cognac and café, downing the brandy in one, letting the heat grab at his throat. He opened the second letter, quickly, afraid of what he would find. There was no mention of babies or paternity but his relief was short-lived, for with Becca's revelation that she was his half-sister came the pain of betrayal, his mother's betrayal, which worsened, stabbing at his chest. Pauline's lies. His father's hurt. His own enduring sorrow and now this.

What was Becca thinking of? Why had she been to see Pauline? Couldn't she leave well alone? He was angry with her. Angry that she'd uncovered all of this. Angry that she was no longer his sister but only his half-sister. That the connections of family and blood between them were diluted.

He ordered another cognac. It was not until he was on his fifth that his thoughts were numbed sufficiently to begin to see things in a different way – to throw off the cloak of his childhood and look forward. Perhaps it was not such a bad thing. He had already started out on the road that led him away from Becca. That's why he was here. They had to move apart and forge their own lives. He knew that. Becca sounded fine, happy almost. She was getting on with her life, making new relationships, living with Lilli, laying down a new track, just like she did sometimes when she sang, making the song her own. Perhaps it was time for him to do the same.

He would stay on. There was work in the vineyards. He wasn't going back, not yet, not later. Mick was moving on but not him. He'd met a woman, Janine. She had a studio down by the docks. He could paint there, live there, she'd said. It smelled of fish but it was full of light. The bright light of the south.

The Willow

The leaves have dropped from the willow, blown and gone. They float yellow and lifeless in the rhynes. The cattle graze the withy beds clearing the land before the November harvest.

'Knit one, pearl one, slip one.' In the lounge of The Lyndor, Edith knits the last sleeve of a baby's jacket in soft, duck-egg blue.

'Is it nearly finished?' asks George Wyatt who sits beside her.

'Nearly.'

'You've made a good job of that, Edith.'

She glances sideways and smiles at him in acknowledgement. Soon, she thinks, when it's time, I'll fetch his morning coffee for him, from the trolley, and two of his favourite chocolate bourbons. After all, it's easier for me. I can get about much better. I'm slow, just one foot at a time, but I never shuffle, not like Mrs Dyer. The crepe soles on these new slippers, from Lilli and Becca, help a lot. Funny little thing, that Becca, not very pretty . . . but still, she's family now and that's what matters. It makes all the difference. And that baby, now he is pretty, pretty for a boy, just like my Martin. He'll suit blue. Martin did. I don't like his name very much; surely she could have chosen something better than Thomas? Still he's a perfect baby, so good.

Edith hears the trolley wheels squeaking on the lino. 'Coffee and bourbons for you, George?'

She lays her knitting down on the empty seat at her other side and with a hand on each chair arm pushes herself to her feet.

'No coffee for me this morning. I haven't got time. I've got to get this finished. That baby's going to need a warm jacket now that winter's coming.'

His hair sticks to his forehead in curls. He lies in a tangle of flannelette and blue wool blankets. Lilli looks down on him and remembers her, remembers Marsha. He is like her, the same nose, the same blue eyes and more hair than a baby should have. She runs her little finger back and forth over his curled fist and gently lifts the blankets to cover him. Now he is still, his breath even and slow. She whispers to him, a song, a mantra, a prayer lifting like a skylark in the meadow, 'Marsha, Marsha,' like an ancient echo across the land.

'Who's Marsha?' says Becca, appearing in the doorway, sleep still patterned on her face, her eyes like a winter sea.

'It's a long story,' says Lilli.

'I'll make some coffee, then,' says Becca.

In the kitchen of the house Nell and Ted have found them, they drink black coffee and Lilli tells Becca of her lost daughter, of the child she gave away, who did not grow up beside her in this place, the child of another landscape. Lilli thinks that now there are no secrets, the secrets have all been spilled.

They do not go back to sleep, instead they wait for Thomas to wake and go out to meet the dawn. It is Lilli who carries Thomas strapped close to her in his sling, her breath on his head, his face looking up at hers. The sun is rising across the fields and fallen leaves glitter in the first low rays. Their breath drifts across the air like the mist that lies at the meadow's edge, obscuring the horizon.

The land beneath them is shrunken, reduced by the long drought. Ridges protrude, hard edges in the soft cushion catch at the soles of their feet. They feel the rhythm, the lime wood, they feel the track beneath their feet. They look down and see it exposed, risen up from the peat. They look up as the mist rises and the landscape of their childhood stretches before them. They are walking, walking on the lime wood track from Shap. The fen is sucking at their grass-bound feet . . .

They lay the poles of lime wood over the peat and fix them down, hammering in the long pegs. He works with his back to the sun, sweat dripping from his forehead. She hands him a cloth, then bends to pick up the baby. The women bring water and fermented liquors of elderberry and hips. They put them down in earthenware pots beside the track, along with wheat and honey cakes, wrapped in dock, and shallow bowls of cobnuts.

They rest at the hottest part of the day moving over to seek shade from the alder. The women sit in small groups, talking and sharing food. Children chatter and play around them, throwing pebbles and bar-shaped dice, blowing reed pipes and picking at the straw of the cloth god dollies.

When the sun is no longer vertical they set to again, piling peat on the poles with great wooden shovels; men, women and children alike. Now that the sun is in the west she works with the baby strapped to her back.

When the peat is thickly layered to the depth of their fore-arms and the tops of the pegs are poking through, they move away, leaving the strongest to lift the planks and lay them on the narrow bank resting in the angles of the pegs.

A new track is taking shape, stretching west across the marsh to the sea. In the winter it will submerge beneath the flood. When the moor dries in spring it will reappear. In the spring they will begin again. In the spring the lost tracks and walkways will reappear . . .